*Welcome
Back*

Books by Lin Stepp

DOWN BY THE RIVER

"A Smoky Mountain Gift" in WHEN THE SNOW FALLS

MAKIN' MIRACLES

SAVING LAUREL SPRINGS

WELCOME BACK

Published by Kensington Publishing Corporation

Welcome Back

A SMOKY MOUNTAIN NOVEL #9

LIN STEPP

KENSINGTON BOOKS
www.kensingtonbooks.com

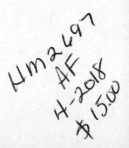

KENSINGTON BOOKS are published by

Kensington Publishing Corp.
119 West 40th Street
New York, NY 10018

All Kensington titles, imprints, and distributed lines are available at special quantity discounts for bulk purchases for sales promotion, premiums, fund-raising, and educational or institutional use.

Special book excerpts or customized printings can also be created to fit specific needs. For details, write or phone the office of the Kensington Sales Manager: Kensington Publishing Corp., 119 West 40th Street, New York, NY 10018. Attn. Sales Department. Phone: 1-800-221-2647.

Kensington and the K logo Reg. U.S. Pat. & TM Off.

eISBN-13: 978-1-61773-283-6
eISBN-10: 1-61773-283-4
First Kensington Electronic Edition: March 2016

ISBN-13: 978-1-61773-282-9
ISBN-10: 1-61773-282-6
First Kensington Trade Paperback Printing: March 2016

10 9 8 7 6 5 4 3 2

Printed in the United States of America

This book is dedicated to my church family and friends at St. Mark United Methodist Church, who have supported me, been excited with me, and encouraged me in my journey as a published author. Thanks especially to the St. Mark Book Club and the Rose Circle for their loving support . . . and to all in the church who came to my book launches, popped in at my signings, and shared my books with their friends far and wide. A special thank-you to former pastor Dave Graybeal and his wife, Tracey, and to current minister Kenny Faught and his wife, Chrissy—and to all on staff and in the congregation for always celebrating with me over each new book published.

ACKNOWLEDGMENTS

Others help me to be all I can be.

I have found such a wonderful publishing family at Kensington—and I am grateful to each one who works to prepare, produce, market, and promote my books. . . . Thanks to my great editor, Martin Biro, to production editor Paula Reedy, copy editor Christy Phillippe, publicist Jane Nutter, inventory manager Guy Chapman, and to all in marketing and sales who work so hard to take my books out to new readers. Special appreciation also to book cover art director Kristin Mills and artist and illustrator Judy York for the beautiful book covers on all my Smoky Mountain novels. They take my breath away. A special tribute, also, to Steven Zacharius, President and CEO at Kensington Publishing, New York, for heading this fine company with excellence and joy.

At the home office, in Tennessee, thanks to my husband and business partner, J. L., who shares my journey—helping me promote my books, keep up with financial aspects, and travel the road with me to signings and events. I couldn't be more blessed. Thanks also to my daughter, Kate, in North Carolina for sharing her graphics talents to help design my Web site and social media sites.

Finally, behind it all—and really first above all—thanks to the Lord for His ever-present help, guidance, and inspiration in all I do. . . . In the words of Erma Bombeck, "When I stand before God at the end of my life, I would hope that I would not have a single bit of talent left, and could say, I used everything You gave me."

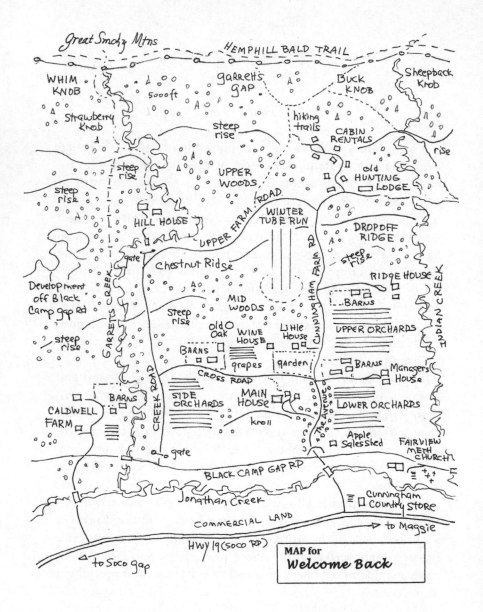

CHAPTER 1

With a scowl, J. T. stuffed a final sack of books into a corner of Lydia's trunk, amid the growing mound of boxes and suitcases. "Mom, I think these are the last bags to load and I doubt we can cram any more in."

Offering him a smile, Lydia reached out to pat his arm, but J. T. shifted away. He stalked off toward the house, the sullen expression he'd worn all morning still set on his face. He and his brothers had shown up en masse this morning to help her pack, not one in a good mood.

Tucking her laptop and printer-copier into the crowded backseat of her navy Mustang, Lydia turned to head back into the kitchen—only to find all three of her sons filling the small kitchen space, waiting for her and scowling. "What's all this?" she asked, crossing her arms.

"You don't have to go, Mom." Parker sent her a grief-stricken look. "We can unload all this stuff in a flash. You can still change your mind."

"We've talked this out several times, Parker." Lydia sat down at the kitchen table, motioning for the boys to join her. She probably should have expected a final, frontal ambush after watching them exchange glances and frowns all morning.

"But it still doesn't make sense to us." Parker's twin, Billy Dale—preferably called Will now—leaned toward her, popping his knuckles as he always did when feeling upset or anxious.

Lydia tried to think of what to say. "The new job back at

Western Carolina University is a move up for me to director of career services, in a school I like. It's the college where I got my undergrad and graduate degrees, held my first job as a student in career services, and where I first worked after graduation. I love Western—you know that. It's like going home to me."

J. T. frowned. "That's hardly the whole story, Mom. You're going home to the farm, too."

Lydia stalled for an answer, getting up to pour herself a glass of water from the Brita in the refrigerator. "I am *not* going home to the farm." She spoke each word slowly for emphasis as she sat back down. "I'm renting Hill House on the Upper Farm property."

"Same thing." J. T. scowled.

"It is not the same thing, J. T., and you know it." Lydia glared at him. "You also know why I'm renting Hill House at this particular time. Rebecca said your father might sell it, that they'd experienced a lot of bills since Estelle died. The house has sat empty for over a year, and a developer who wants to purchase the land tendered a good offer."

"And why is that *your* responsibility?" J. T. popped out yet another sarcastic remark.

She caught his eyes with hers. "Rebecca said Mary Beth was upset that the house and property might be sold. You know it would create a big gap in the property. She asked Rebecca to suggest I rent Hill House when she learned of my job offer at Western."

Lydia let her gaze sweep from one son to another. "Mary Beth is your sister. I have been here for the three of you all these years, but not there for her. She has never asked anything of me before this—not once since I left. I don't feel I can say no."

J. T. shook his head. "Mom, Mary Beth has hardly spoken to you since you left ten years ago. Or to us. Remember? She was angry at all of us for leaving."

"I know that." Lydia chewed on a nail. "I hope this might be my opportunity to mend fences with her. She is my only daughter."

"And we're your sons." Parker dropped his head into his hands, working hard to hold his emotions in check. "We love you, Mom. We don't want you to go. What will we do here without you?"

She reached over to tousle his hair. "You'll move on with your life and career, marry your sweet fiancée, and soon make more beautiful grandchildren for me like J. T. and his wife have."

Parker looked around the small, cozy kitchen of their house. "It won't be the same without you. I want you to stay. We all want you to stay."

"I know you do and I admit I feel torn—my boys here in Atlanta, but my girl, I've been estranged from all these years, and a new job opportunity back in North Carolina." She studied the anxious faces of her sons. "Can't you understand that I want some time to come to know Mary Beth now that she's grown, to get to know her twin boys—my grandsons? They're six years old and I've had no time with them."

Will scowled. "What you really mean is that it's safe to go back to Cunningham Farm now because 'Ding Dong! The Witch is dead.'"

"Billy Dale!" Lydia shook a finger at him. "That was a very crude and rude remark to make about your grandmother."

He slouched in his seat, unrepentant. "Why is that, Mom? Should we all pretend Grandmother Cunningham was a dear saint and a sweet person now that she's dead? We all know better. She ran the four of us off the farm, remember? It's why we're here in Atlanta now."

"There were other reasons why I came to Atlanta and why you boys came with me." Lydia straightened her shoulders. "Working at Georgia Tech on full-time staff paved the way for all three of you to get your educations tuition-free."

"Mom, we know that." J. T. reached across the table to take her hand. "We're grateful, too, for how you stood with us to help us have the opportunities and futures we wanted, rather than staying on the farm."

The twins added their hands over J. T.'s, bringing tears to Lydia's eyes at their unexpected show of affection. "We just worry that you'll be hurt again with Dad so nearby," Billy Dale said.

Lydia drew back her hand in surprise and crossed her arms

defensively. "You talk like your father is some sort of monster. You know that's not true. He deeply loved all of us. He was good to us."

"But not good enough." Parker frowned. "He wouldn't stand up for us against his mother."

"That would be a hard thing for any son to do." She studied her nail, avoiding her son's eyes. "Especially in your father's situation, when your grandfather had died and left your grandmother—and the farm—in your father's care."

J. T. made a fist. "He let her bully you and make you unhappy. Then when we grew old enough to want a life away from the farm, he let her go after us. She had a mean heart and a cutting tongue, Mom. You know it's true." He paused, trying to curb his anger. "She could make a victim bleed with her words and actions, and she enjoyed wielding her power doing it."

"Mary Beth was the only one she didn't bully all the time except for Dad. Probably why Mary Beth decided to stay," Parker added.

"Estelle *was* a difficult woman." Lydia could hardly deny it.

A small silence filled the kitchen—each of them swamped with their own rush of negative memories.

"Are you going to try to make up with Dad?" Parker asked, voicing the question none of the boys had asked before.

Lydia smiled. "It isn't as though your father and I had a specific quarrel, Parker, that needs 'making up.' I simply wanted different things than the farm could offer at the time."

"That's *not* an answer to Parker's question." J. T. ran a hand through his dark red hair, so much like her own.

Lydia tapped a nail on the table. "I'm not going back to the farm to resume a relationship with your father. We've been separated for ten years, J. T. A lot of time has gone by. We've both made different lives, grown apart, and become different people."

"But you haven't divorced," Billy Dale added. "And you've never dated much, if at all, in all the time you've been here."

"You know I've been busy raising you boys and working," she answered, watching them raise their eyebrows and pass looks back and forth as soon as she said the words.

Billy Dale grinned and shook his head. "Funny, we all managed to have our share of women over these years, some good ones, some real losers. We all worked, went to school, but still found time for a social life. We even managed to get married or engaged—J. T. married to Laura, me to Amelia, and Parker engaged to Marie."

"Yes, and I'm so pleased to have all three of you settled—"

J. T. interrupted. "So now you can go back and see if there's still something between you and Dad. That's really it, isn't it, Mom?"

Lydia waited a moment to answer, getting up to put her glass in the sink. "I loved your father with all my heart at one time. In many ways I will always love him. But I'm not returning to reestablish a relationship with him, and I'm sure he's not eager to renew a relationship with me."

"He's never pushed for a divorce in all these years. Perhaps he does want to get back with you. If so, what will you do?" J. T. leaned forward as he posed his question, making Lydia uncomfortable.

"I have no idea, and I think you boys are letting your imaginations get the best of you speculating in this way. Your father and I are two middle-aged people, after all."

Billy Dale laughed. "You're not even fifty, Mom. You're hardly dead and buried. People start whole new lives and enter passionate new relationships in their forties, fifties, and even afterward today."

Lydia blushed at her son's candor. "Well, thank you for that sage advice," she said, covering her embarrassment. "That certainly reassures me about my vitality and future opportunities."

"Just be careful, won't you?" Parker gave her an appealing look. "We really don't want to see you hurt again."

She looked at her sons in surprise. "You really think your father would intentionally hurt me?"

"He did before." J. T. spit out the words. "It's not something we can easily forget."

"Listen. I've grown and matured a great deal from that young woman of thirty-eight who left the farm ten years ago. I've lived on my own, made my own way, and managed my own problems and affairs." She pushed her thick hair behind her ear. "I think you can trust me to handle your father and anything else that life brings my way in North Carolina, don't you?"

Parker sighed. "No one is ever so wise that love can't catch them unawares and toss them for a loop."

Billy Dale laughed, punching his brother in the arm. "Spoken like a man who's just taken the big plunge and finally gotten engaged. There's no escaping now, boy. Marie's got you hooked and is reeling you in."

Good-natured teasing ensued then, lightening the moment, for which Lydia felt grateful. She stood up from the table, glancing at her watch. "I need to get on the road. I want to get to Maggie Valley by afternoon. It's about four hours with stops."

She started out the back door, the boys trailing behind her, continuing to ask questions and showing their concern. *Do you have your cell phone? Did you gas up yesterday so you won't have to stop along the way? Did you put maps of Georgia and North Carolina in the glove compartment?* As if she needed the latter to find her way along the familiar route.

"I have everything I need, and I'll be fine." She smiled at them, taking in the rangy good looks of her young men one last time—J. T. tall, long-faced, muscular from his workouts in the gym, his hair wavy like hers with red glints highlighted in the sun, the twins nearly as tall, sturdy, broad-shouldered, nearly identical in appearance, with the dark, sable-brown hair and handsome features of the Cunningham men.

She hugged them each before climbing into the car, knowing how much she would miss seeing them and being a vital part of their daily lives.

"Hey, wait." Billy Dale raised a hand as she put her key in the ignition. Sprinting to his truck, he reached in, retrieved a plastic bag, and brought it back to Lydia. "Here. Amelia finished this purse for you last night and told me to be sure and give it to you." He pushed it through the car window. "She put snacks and stuff in it, too, in case you didn't want to stop along the way."

Lydia glanced into the richly embroidered, velvet-brown purse to see pieces of fruit, snack bars, a package of almonds, and a bottle of water.

She studied her son's face a last time. "You tell Amelia thanks and that I absolutely love the purse she made. It's beautiful. She knows so well what I like."

"Yeah." He dropped his eyes. "She cried this morning when she gave it to me. She's real torn up about you leaving."

Lydia blinked back her tears. "Me too." She blew kisses and started the car, knowing if she didn't leave soon she'd break down and cry, only making the parting harder.

Waving a last good-bye, she backed out of the driveway of the little brick bungalow, giving a last look to the ivy creeping around the doorway and up the wall, finding it suddenly hard to say good-bye to the modest house she'd called home during her years in Atlanta. She drove through the quiet streets of Morningside, past Piedmont Park and the Atlanta Botanical Garden, and then onto the busy freeway rushing between the downtown suburban area to the west and Georgia Tech's vast campus on the east.

An hour outside of Atlanta traffic she let the tears out at last, knowing how much she'd miss seeing her boys every day, grieving that they felt upset with her over her decision to leave. However, as the miles slid by and the freeway began climbing into the mountains, Lydia began to look ahead with anticipation to her move. She'd cut off Interstate 85 onto Highway 441/23 earlier to journey over scenic rural roadways and stopped in colorful Sylva, North Carolina, at City Lights Café, for a quick lunch and to take a few minutes to run upstairs to check out the City Lights Bookstore. Now she turned off Highway 23 onto the Blue Ridge Parkway for the last lap of her journey.

Lydia's spirit finally grew peaceful on the quiet parkway. At Waterrock Knob she stopped her car to look out over the rolling Blue Ridge mountain ranges and felt a sudden clutch at her heart.

This is home, she thought with a sigh. *This beautiful part of the North Carolina mountains. I've never been a city girl at heart—I know that—and Atlanta, despite its cultural wonders and attractions, was only a stopover place for me. Here's where*

I belong, where the air is crisp and clear and where the sweep of green forested hillsides fills the senses.

Being in the mountains again helped Lydia feel more certain she'd made the right decision in coming back. She'd only be four hours from her boys in the city, after all. She could visit anytime she wanted.

The elevation dropped away as Lydia headed down from the Blue Ridge Parkway at Soco Gap into Maggie Valley, the highway now winding in a long ribbon between the high ridges of the Blue Ridge Mountains and the Great Smoky Mountains. She noticed a few changes as she drove downhill from the parkway and felt certain she'd see more in the commercial area of town later. Ten years was a long time and she hadn't come back, even for a short visit, before now.

As a first surprise change, she spotted a new country store by the familiar turn at the Farm Road. She slowed, reading the sign as she passed: Cunningham Country Store. *Well, well.* They had finally renovated that old, broken-down store building on the corner into a viable business.

It looked rustic, charming, and appealing, making Lydia smile and then feel a tug of pain at her heart. She'd proposed the idea of opening a store in that old building many times over the years, only to have Estelle ridicule her ideas and her enthusiasm time and again.

Shrugging away the old pains, she drove down the rural road, clattering over the low, wooden bridge across Jonathan Creek before coming to a battered stop sign and intersection. The arched sign for the Cunningham Farm, and the long avenue of trees to the main house and farm buildings, stood directly across the road, but Lydia wasn't ready to take the old familiar road yet.

She turned left instead and drove a mile down Black Camp Gap Road before turning right at the western end of the farm to reach Hill House via the old Creek Road. After opening and shutting the entrance gate, Lydia drove uphill through the farm property, past the Side Orchards and a few outskirting farm buildings on her right, with Garretts Creek twining along behind the trees to her left.

Cunningham Farm lay within a long rectangular property bordered by Garretts Creek to the west and Indian Creek to the east. The land rolled in undulating layers of rich, green farmland and gently wooded hillsides from the lower valley to the steeper, forested slopes above. At its northern end, the property stretched to meet the Great Smoky Mountains National Park boundary, the farm acreage covering over 3,800 acres in all.

Glad for the new car with its V-8 engine power, Lydia felt the vehicle shift gears and begin to climb smoothly up Chestnut Ridge toward the turn to Hill House. A smaller gate protected the driveway to the house, which lay on a ridge near the Upper Woods. Hill House, a small, double-gabled country home, sat on a high peninsula of land, almost surrounded by Garretts Creek as it wound its way downhill from Strawberry Knob and the mountains above. Not a broad stream, Garretts Creek never endangered the snug house on the hill above it, but Lydia had always loved listening to the merry sounds of the mountain creek and walking down to wade in the cool waters on a hot summer's day.

She sighed as her gaze took in the idyllic scene. *How could John even think of selling this property?* she thought as she wound up the driveway to the old house.

But Lydia knew the answer, in a sense. Development had spread its fingers deep into the mountain lands west of the house as tourism grew in the valley. Log mountain homes now sprawled across the hillsides on the adjacent property not far away. Rebecca said you could even see the house lights blinking through the trees sometimes in winter. It would take only a minimal investment to wind a road through the woods to the Hill House property.

Lydia well knew the lucrative offers of developers proved hard for a farmer to resist when facing a difficult financial year after reversals or hardship. Other Cunningham generations had, by necessity, sold off vast tracts of land along the highway and on the mountainside that had once belonged to the family.

She pulled her mind back to the present as she came to the

end of the driveway in front of Hill House with its gabled roofline. The old shade trees and shrubs formed a panorama of rich green around the old home place, and in the warmth of June, early summer flowers—yellow sedum, pink astilbe, white Shasta daisies, and orange lantana—crowded the flagstone pathway as it curled toward the front porch. It was as lovely as she remembered. Tall purple cornflowers and white hollyhocks grew against the side of the old garage, and pots of pink begonias stood invitingly by the front porch steps.

Lydia's heart caught in her chest as she drew nearer and saw a big banner draped over the front porch railing that read: "Welcome Back." As she got out of the car to walk closer, Lydia saw that the letters painted on the sign looked a little crooked and childish but the message felt very sweet.

Smiling, she headed toward the old screen door, knowing she'd find a spare key hidden under the fern on the wicker stand by the front door. But before she could get there, the door opened and there stood John.

Lydia stopped short, not prepared to see him this soon. Her breath caught in her throat. He stood tall and handsome, dressed casually in jeans and a lightweight flannel shirt rolled up to the elbows, his dark hair showing only a scattering of white around his temples since she last saw him.

"Uh . . . hello, John." She scrambled for something to say. "Did you make the sign?"

He grinned, his eyes twinkling with merriment before he laughed—a warm sound that tingled along Lydia's senses. "No, the boys made it, with Mary Beth's help." He walked closer to study the sign. "They cut up an old white shower curtain and painted the letters on with markers. It took them the better part of the day. They were hoping you'd like it."

"Well, tell them I do."

She swallowed, ill at ease, twisting the key in her hand and watching John scratch his neck, obviously uncomfortable, too. They stood awkwardly, shifting their feet, not sure what to say to each other next.

"What are you doing here, John?" Lydia asked finally, annoyed by the continuing silence. "I don't need your help in settling in to Hill House. It's been a rental for over fifteen years. I hope you haven't come to say you changed your mind about me leasing it."

She watched his smile fade and his face close up. He studied her then for several moments without an answer, making Lydia feel churlish for being so inhospitable.

Finally he spoke. "I thought I ought to come and explain the cat."

Lydia's eyebrows lifted. "What cat?"

He stepped back inside and returned in a moment with a fuzzy ball of a kitten, meowing and clinging to his shirt. "This cat."

She stepped up on the porch to take the kitten from his arms. A little smile touched her mouth as she examined it. "It's a calico kitten."

"Yeah." He grinned again. "Showed up yesterday in a box on the front porch with a note in it saying: *This here is for Miz Lydia.*"

Lydia couldn't help but laugh. "Oh, gracious heaven," she said, sitting down on a porch chair to cuddle the kitten. "Surely that old practice isn't going to be revived."

"I reckon it might. Folks haven't forgotten you like calico cats." John leaned against the doorway of the house, watching her with the kitten. It began to purr as she stroked it.

"I'd have kept the kitten down at Main House, except for Annabel," he explained. "She's getting cantankerous in her old age, and she was giving the kitten a hard time."

"You still have Annabel?" Lydia looked up in surprise. "That cat must be about fourteen years old now."

"Yep, and we still have Trucker and Junie, too. That's two more calicoes we got gifted with after you left. Notes with them suggested you might want to come back to look after them. Mary Beth and I didn't have the heart to carry them off to the pound."

Lydia shook her head in wonder. "People don't forget things easily around here, do they?"

"No, they don't." His tone grew soft, and Lydia looked up to see him watching her with tender eyes.

His look made her nervous. She wet her lips. "I remember when the first calico cat got dropped at the farm—"

"So do I," John interrupted. "We were newlyweds, and you told a number of folks around the valley how much you loved calico cats and how you'd always had one."

"They started showing up on doorsteps and in baskets and boxes for years after." She moved the conversation quickly forward. "Annabel got left on the porch of Main House in a wire chicken cage. Your mother found her and threw a hissy fit." Lydia's face fell at the memory.

John moved past the subject. "Somebody left Trucker in the front seat of my truck while I ate lunch at Pig's Bar-B-Q in Maggie. Junie showed up in early June a few weeks later. Those two bonded and left Annabel alone so she didn't bother them like she did this one."

"Poor thing." Lydia watched the kitten nod into sleep on her lap.

"Here." John reached for the cat. "I'll put it in its box in the house so you can start unloading your stuff. I know you're eager to settle in after the long drive."

She smiled up at John as he lifted the kitten. "I came across the parkway coming in. Stopped at Waterrock Knob. It was so beautiful. A cloud lay deep in the valley over the mountains, all misty and shroudy."

It seemed so easy to pick up, just like in the past, and to start sharing with him. It seemed like only yesterday they'd sat on this porch and talked.

He reached out a hand to smooth his fingers down her cheek. "It's a pretty place at Waterrock Knob, isn't it, Lydia?"

Feeling like she might suddenly cry, Lydia slid away from his touch, stood, and headed for the car. "I'll start unloading." She didn't turn to look at him. "I need to go into Waynesville to the grocery before dark falls."

"No need," he said behind her. "Mary Beth put in enough food to last a few days, and Ela Raintree made a casserole for your dinner and put it in the refrigerator for you."

She turned without meaning to. "Ela and Manny are still here?"

He nodded. "Not much has changed. Ozetta Sheppard sent you an apple pie, Doris, green beans, and Nevelyn, one of her loaves of homemade banana bread for your breakfast. She said she remembered you liked it."

The tears threatened again. "Tell them thanks and that I'll be over to visit tomorrow."

He took the cat into the house and then returned to lift a box out of her open trunk.

"I can do this, John." She lifted her chin. "You don't need to help."

He looked at her as though she'd said something foolish and then hefted yet another box onto the first and started toward the house.

Lydia sighed, following him toward the porch with her own load. She hadn't expected John to walk right back into her life in this way so quickly, and she wasn't sure she liked it.

They unloaded the car in silence, although Lydia's awareness of John, working closely alongside her, began to invade her senses. Once, as they passed in the doorway, they brushed against each other intimately, making Lydia's blood rush. She looked up to find John's eyes on her, watching her, looking for a response. Panicked, she dropped her gaze, pushing into the house with her armful of clothes.

Listening for the screen door to close, she knew he stood a moment in the doorway, watching after her. *What is he thinking?* she asked herself. And then she wondered whether she even wanted to know.

As they finished unloading a short time later, Lydia came out to find John closing the trunk of her car.

"New car?" he asked, obviously noticing the fresh smell that only new vehicles seemed to have.

"New to me," she answered. "A dealer's car, only a year old, but nicely cleaned." She laid her hand on it. "I needed a good car for getting around the mountains again. Left my small city car with Parker."

She saw a flash of pain cross his face. "How are the boys?"

"Good," she answered, not adding any more, and unsure whether she could even take on that subject after all the emotions of the day.

"Clyde will be glad you didn't buy one of those foreign cars." He sent her a grin, easy with himself again.

Lydia laughed. "I thought of that when I shopped. I knew he'd only fix my car for me if it was a Ford."

"Yeah, well, Clyde's funny that way."

"Is he doing all right?" Lydia knew Clyde Sheppard had some cognitive slowness that made life difficult for him.

"He's good." John nodded.

Their conversation felt stilted again, and Lydia found herself growing uncomfortable once more. "I need to settle in, John," she said at last, hoping he'd take the hint. "I'll look after the cat. I don't mind. It will be company."

He leaned toward her and his nearness made her catch her breath. "You're still a beautiful woman, Lydia Ruth Cunningham." He lifted a hand to touch her face, grazing the backs of his fingers softly down her cheek. "You take my breath away. You always have." He swept an arm around her and kissed her before she realized what he intended to do.

Looking up at him with wide eyes afterward, her heart hammering, Lydia whispered, "I don't know if I wanted you to do that."

He winked and kissed her forehead. "Well, too late."

He ran a hand down her back and beyond in an all-too-familiar way, and then the two stood staring into each other's eyes like a couple of starstruck teenagers, John's arms still wrapped around her back.

He smiled at last, when Lydia couldn't seem to find any words, and then he moved away to start down the driveway. "I'll see you later, Lydia. Call if you need anything."

Waving a hand, he strolled away down the road in that loose, loping walk of his, the picture so achingly familiar to Lydia.

"Oh Lord, what I have I done by coming back here?" Lydia wondered out loud as he disappeared from view. She didn't know whether she felt ready to resume a relationship with John—or if she even should. There was so much unresolved between them.

Shaking her head at her thoughts, she wandered back up the flagstone walk to settle in to Hill House.

$\mathscr{C}$HAPTER 2

Finding the cat on the front porch of Main House gave John the perfect excuse to go to Hill House and wait for Lydia to arrive. The day before, he, Mary Beth, and the boys drove over to hang the sign the boys had made for her, but he knew no legitimate reason to return to the house today. They'd lived separated for ten years, after all.

John tuned in to the conversation in the Main House kitchen.

"I can't believe folks would sneak right up on a body's porch and dump off a little kitten." Ela Raintree huffed around the kitchen as she complained, making warm milk for the small, frightened scrap of fur they'd found cowering in a cardboard box.

"Better than drowning it," her husband, Manu, added. He leaned against the kitchen counter watching her.

Ela stifled a gasp. "I'm surely glad you went out to trim the front shrubs early this morning and found the poor little thing on the porch. With Annabel pushing its box around and hissing the way she was—it probably scared that kitten half out of its mind."

"What do you think we ought to do about the cat?" Manu asked John. "Annabel is old and crotchety in her ways now, and even Trucker and Junie didn't act kindly toward this little mite. If I don't take it to the shelter, somebody will need to tend to it until it gets enough size on it to make its way around here."

Ela turned to glare at him. "Well, don't you be looking at me when you suggest that. There's three cats around this house already to take care of plus the two dogs—John's collie, and our Harley."

"I'll carry it up to Lydia's place," John put in. "She'll have some time before she starts at the college in August from what Rebecca said. Maybe she'd like to mother it. The note did say the kitten was for her, after all."

Manu grinned, pushing back the battered straw hat from his broad face. "So it did. Seems only right then, since the kitten got left for her."

"Hmmmph," Ela grumbled, setting the bowl of milk down into the kitten's box. "It's not much of a way to welcome our Lydia back, by dumping her with a kitten."

"Might be she'll like it." John leaned over the box to touch the kitten's nose down into the milk. His move did the trick and the kitten started to lap up the milk hungrily. "I'll take it up there this afternoon after my meeting at the extension office in Waynesville." He looked at Ela. "Will you keep it until then?"

"I suppose. I'll keep it here in the kitchen." She nodded at her husband. "Manu, you go dig around in the attic and find some of those cat things Miz Lydia packed away years back. There should be an old wicker cat bed, a litter box, that scratching post you built for her, and some cat toys. You can take those to Hill House when you go put the new bolts on the doors later."

She turned to John. "Do you want Manny to take the kitten to the house when he goes? He can shut it in the laundry room and leave some food. Then you can check on it in the afternoon before you head home."

"That would be good," John answered. "It will be okay there."

Ela turned her back to peek in the oven. "I'm making an extra casserole for Lydia so she won't have to cook tonight after her trip. Ozetta, Doris, and Nevelyn have sent food over, too. Manny, you'll need to take that up, as well."

He nodded. "Then I'd best be getting the shrubs trimmed and the rest of my yard work done."

"Thanks, Manny." John lifted a hand in a half wave as Manny let himself out the back door. He still praised the day he'd met Manu Raintree and his wife, Ela, and learned they were looking for work in the valley. They'd moved into the small house behind Cunningham's main house, simply called Little House, Manny doing grounds and maintenance work around the family home and farm and Ela settling in to run the kitchen and household with a steel hand, despite her diminutive size. She and Manu were Cherokee in lineage and pleased to find work and a new home in the area near Ela's parents, after living out West for several years.

After his Waynesville meeting, John came home, cleaned up, and decided to walk to Hill House rather than drive. He could stroll through the Side Orchards rows on his way to check for pests and disease among the trees. The spring fear of frost and freeze was past, but with the apples forming, the trees needed checking often for other threats.

He looked at his watch as he arrived at Hill House. Nearly four. She ought to be here any time. He could hang around to tell her about the cat.

John shook his head at his own rationalization. The bold truth was he couldn't wait to see Lydia again. Like a kid, he'd felt both thrilled and nervous for weeks since learning she planned to come home. He'd dreamed of this for all the years she'd been gone, hadn't he? Hoped it would happen somehow, even with all he'd failed to do to keep her here before.

When he heard her car pull up at last, he headed toward the door, not wanting to startle her by being inside when she let herself in.

She'd just leaned over to find the spare key under the old fern, when he opened the door. Her eyes widened in surprise as she stood up, dark hazel-green eyes rising to meet his—beautiful, expressive eyes he'd dreamed of in the night hours time and time again when he couldn't sleep.

John's gaze slid over her, seeing her form still tall and firm, if fuller in a few spots. Her hair, the same thick, rich auburn, shimmered with red glints in the afternoon sun. She wore neat brown slacks and a loose, delicately embroidered vest slipped over a flirty white shirt with small tucks across the front. A smile touched John's lips as he saw the strappy embroidered shoes on her feet, sparkling with decorative rhinestones. Lydia had always dressed with a distinctive flair and, even when dressed casually, found a way to look feminine in a way few other women did.

She spoke at last, stammering—obviously rattled to see him. After a moment, she glanced toward the sign over the porch railing, asking him about it.

He told her how the boys had made it, and then an awkward silence fell as they each wondered what to say after all this time. *What should I say?* John thought.

Finally, he saw her frown, annoyed, and then she snapped out some words telling him she didn't need his help, even asking if he'd changed his mind about her leasing the place. Her words pricked at him. Did she really think he'd tell his own wife she couldn't rent their house? Or go back on his word? It hurt to think she thought so little of him.

John bit down his anger and told her about the cat. He went in the house to bring out the kitten, meowing piteously and clawing at his shirtfront. John watched Lydia's face soften as she walked up the porch steps and pulled the kitten from his shirt to cuddle it in her arms.

The cat, and the story about it, eased the strain between them until the tension turned in a new direction. A sensual one. He knew Lydia sensed it, too, and he watched her fidget and grow nervous, wetting her lips like she'd always done when she grew aware of him in a physical way. His ego soared to know he still affected her. He'd wondered if he would after all this time.

They reminisced then, John savoring the sound of her voice and watching her stroke the little cat on her lap until it relaxed and fell asleep. He walked over to take the kitten from her to put it in the house. Leaning over her, he caught that familiar, heady gardenia scent of hers, making him catch his breath in memory. Lord, he loved her still and had missed her so.

John smiled to himself an hour or so later as he walked down the driveway from Hill House. He hadn't expected his first meeting with Lydia, after all this time, to turn out like it did. He never envisioned touching or kissing her. He'd thought it enough to see her here again, but brushing against her while he helped her unload the car and catching the floral scent of her kicked up that old awareness between them, addling his senses. As he glanced back at the bend in the road now, she still stood there by the porch, a hand to her heart, struggling with her unexpected emotions—a picture he'd hold in his memory for a long time.

As he walked on down the road, John ran into Sam Sheppard, the Cunningham Farm manager and his friend since boyhood.

"Did Lydia get in all right?" Sam asked. "Doris sent me over to check and see if she needed anything."

"She's fine, settling in. I helped her unpack. There's no need for you to go up to the house now unless you want to. She mentioned she'd probably make the rounds to see everyone tomorrow."

"Good. Then I'll head on back home," he replied. "Doris and Mama were working on dinner when I left, and Clyde was helping Papa out in the barn, trying to repair one of the farm tractors. They could probably use a hand." Sam fell into step with John as they started back down the road again.

As they ambled along, John's thoughts wandered back to his time with Lydia and he found himself smiling once more.

"Seems like you're in a real good mood," Sam said, slowing to let his eyes move to a couple of squirrels scampering up a tree by the road.

"Yep."

"Things must have gone well with Lydia."

"Better than I expected after ten years," John admitted.

Sam waited, walking on beside him, not probing, but John knew he had questions in his mind. Sam had watched him and Lydia court, stood up at their wedding, paced the hospital with him before J. T.'s, the twins', and Mary Beth's births. He'd known the kindness and wisdom of John's father, the trials they'd all endured with his mother, the problems with her after his father's death. He'd sat with John on an old bench in the orchard after Lydia walked out, knowing he needed a friend. John knew, too, that Sam was aware of how much he'd missed Lydia all these years, even though they'd never discussed it.

"She's still beautiful," he told Sam.

"I couldn't imagine her being anything else." Sam sent him a crooked grin.

"I didn't know how it would be after so long, how it would feel." He kicked at a rock on the side of the two-lane road. "But it was good. Maybe because we were at Hill House, where we first lived. We fell right back into talking after a few awkward moments, sort of like things had always been."

"It's like that with old friends, even when they haven't seen each other in years. They fall right back in step," Sam put in.

"Yeah, I saw that." John slowed as they came out of the wooded area of the road, stopping to look across the Side Orchards and the farm below.

Sam paused with him, pushing back the battered John Deere cap he always wore.

"More happened," John confessed then. "Those old feelings kicked up, and I acted on them without thinking."

Sam raised his eyebrows with undisguised interest.

"No, not that." John chuckled. "But enough to show me I have a chance with her. She still has feelings for me."

"She didn't scratch your eyes out or slap your face?" Sam winked at him.

"No, and considering all that's happened, that's a good sign, I'd say."

"Sounds promising," Sam agreed.

They walked on, turning left to follow the old Cross Road toward their homes. Sam veered off the road at one point to look at one of the trees in the Side Orchards, examining the early apples forming.

His eyes moved to John's as he walked back to the road where John waited. "She did come back, John," he said. "To me, that says something."

"There were other reasons why she came back," John answered. "But the fact that she did gives me hope."

"Well, good luck with it." Sam let the discussion go then as they followed the road past the barns and gardens behind Main

House. With a few words of good-bye, Sam walked on, heading toward his own place, while John lingered, leaning on a fence rail of the garden to think.

It had been a long time since he'd felt a rush of emotions like today. As he told Sam, Lydia hadn't been immune to them, either. He'd watched her grow gradually more nervous as he helped her unpack and settle in. It reminded him fondly of their early courting days and the careful dance around their building emotions they'd played then.

Caught off guard, Lydia had tried to keep busy and push her feelings away. John remembered that about her. She never seemed comfortable to simply linger in the moment when heavy emotions flared up or to savor them bit by bit as they evolved. But once words moved out of the way, Lydia hadn't fought him. That had always been the way between them. Words and communication sometimes proved awkward, but intimacy was always sweet.

He smiled again at the memory, wondering what she might be thinking now as she unpacked and settled in. Was she thinking of him as he was of her? The way ahead might not be easy, but John knew now he might hold a chance to win her back. Maybe. With Lydia nothing was ever simple or straightforward.

*C*HAPTER 3

After John walked out of sight, Lydia turned to walk back into the house and realized her knees felt shaky and weak. She sat down in a wicker chair on the porch, fanning herself with her hand.

"Good heavens. What just happened here?" she asked, trying to settle her emotions and collect her thoughts.

Over the last years, she'd imagined many scenarios of meeting John again, even of being alone with him. She'd often planned out what she might say to him, how she might act. She'd envisioned how she would handle the arguments that would be inevitable between them.

In all her imaginings, it never dawned on her that passion would flare again between the two of them or that he would kiss her at their first meeting—and not simply a chaste kiss of fondness, either. He'd taken her breath away, left her speechless. How had that happened? When he'd held her close against him, there'd been no doubt he desired her. Not that anything was wrong with that, or sinful, with them still legally married. It was just so unexpected.

Lydia heaved a huge sigh. When she and John parted ten years ago, that aspect of their relationship hadn't been in very good shape. They'd been almost celibate for years, their daily relationship more one of fond friendship. She couldn't recall the last time John looked at her as he did today, called her beautiful, or made her feel desirable as a woman.

She fanned herself again. In honesty, she couldn't recall since she was a young woman feeling so overwhelmed with emotions or feelings as intense as these. And the last time she'd felt like this was with John when they were both in college, so young and so much in love.

She twisted her hands, trying to make sense of it all. *I don't understand this. I really don't. I feel so unprepared—*

The mewing of the kitten in the house interrupted her thoughts. "Poor little thing." Lydia jumped up at the sound. "I forgot all about you."

She let herself in the screen door of the house, found the frightened kitten, and took it into the kitchen to find food for it. A knock sounded at the door after she had fed, cuddled, and settled the little cat into a blanket in the box in the kitchen.

"Hey! It's Rebecca. Can I just let myself in?"

Lydia rounded the corner of the kitchen as her best friend since college days, Rebecca Albright, came into the house.

Lydia crossed the room to give Rebecca a warm hug.

"When did you get here?" Rebecca asked.

Lydia checked her watch. "About an hour and a half ago."

"Sorry I didn't get here earlier to help you unload." She dropped her purse on the couch. "Is there anything left to get from the car?"

"No. John stopped by to help me."

Rebecca raised her eyebrows. "How did that go? Did you quarrel?"

"No." Lydia felt herself blush.

"What's that blush?" Rebecca pulled her down to sit on the sofa with her. "What happened? Are you upset? I don't want you running off on me back to Atlanta before you're even settled in."

Lydia wrinkled her nose, not wanting to talk about her encounter with John—even with Rebecca. "A little chemistry flashed around in the air, that's all. I don't know quite what to think of it yet."

Rebecca leaned back against the couch and crossed her arms. "You've never gotten over John Parker Cunningham, that's what it is. Nor he over you. I've been telling you that for years. He's never dated anyone or even showed an interest in another woman since you left."

Lydia frowned. "Well, he certainly didn't demonstrate any blatant interest in me before I went to Atlanta, so this all came as a surprise."

"It's a new day." Rebecca grinned and spread her arms across the sofa back. "I'm just glad to hear you're not quarreling."

Lydia glanced around. "Perhaps it's this place. John and I lived here when we first married and stayed here with our children until Grandpa Will died."

"I remember. If you, John, and the children could have stayed here instead of moving in with Estelle, all your problems might not have happened."

"No, the problems were already going on." Lydia shook her head. "They simply got worse when we moved to Main House and rented out this property for income."

"You started working then, too, right?"

"Yes, I went to work full-time in the career center at Western, thanks to Aunt Martha paving the way. John had also taken an extra part-time job on the side to help." She sighed. "But our move to Main House still proved necessary. So many hospital bills had piled up when Grandpa Will had his heart attack, those two surgeries, and then died. Then a bad freeze that spring practically blitzed the apple crop."

Rebecca put a hand over Lydia's. "That was such a difficult time for all of you."

"Yes. Especially for the boys, just starting their teen years. They had to work so hard on the farm, enjoyed so few pleasures."

Rebecca frowned. "And Estelle gave them the devil and the dickens practically every day."

Lydia closed her eyes. "She was unhappy after Will died, and she didn't really like sharing the house with us, despite how much room it had. She also didn't like the spartan economies we had to practice, disliked the strain it put on all of us."

Rebecca gave a disgusted snort. "She disliked not being the queen bee in the community like she'd always been, the big benefactress in every charitable effort. She missed hosting all her groups at the house without having children underfoot."

"That's true, I suppose," Lydia admitted.

"The truth is, Will Cunningham spoiled Estelle and catered to her and everyone knew it. He let himself run into heavy debt, trying to keep her happy, and then everything came due when he died."

A familiar wash of negative memories rolled over Lydia, making her feel heavy and leaden.

Rebecca got up to walk around the living room. "The house here still looks great, doesn't it?" she asked, shifting the subject. "I remember all the fun we had decorating our first homes together when we both got married. You had such a creative flair. I always envied that."

Lydia looked around. "It's surprised me to see how little the house has changed after being a rental for so long."

"It was built well and it has good bones." Rebecca walked over to look out the window. "John picked his renters carefully, too."

Lydia smiled. "You helped with that, Rebecca, handling it through your and Tolley's realty agency." She paused. "How is Tolley?"

"Good, and our kids, Rachel and Mark, and their spouses are great, too—as are our grandbabies." Her wide smile deepened, making her dimples flash in her full cheeks. She brushed her short blond bangs back from her forehead. "I wish they all lived closer, but Charlotte and Columbia aren't too far to go for a visit."

"All four of those grandbabies are as cute as pie."

Rebecca glanced at her watch then. "What can I help you do before I leave?"

"Not a thing." Lydia got up to see her out. "I won't start at Western until the end of summer when fall term begins. It's a huge vacation block for me, and the first I've had in years. I'll enjoy lots of time piddling around the house, working in the garden, and playing with my grandsons."

"Well, you deserve some happy times." Rebecca gave her another hug. "And I'm looking forward to some girl times when we can work it in."

"Me too." Lydia walked out on the porch to see her off. "You give Tolley a hug for me and tell him I'll see him soon."

Letting herself back in the house, Lydia walked through the downstairs rooms with pleasure, remembering the familiar layout of the old country house—living room on the right front, main bedroom and bath on the left, sunny kitchen and dining room in back. The laundry and pantry lay just off the kitchen, and a big, screened porch stretched the full width of the back of the house. Upstairs three small bedrooms and a second bath squatted under the eaves. She hugged herself recalling the good times she and John had shared here in their early married years.

The small house perched in an idyllic setting on the knoll of its green hill. Creamy white in color with long windows framed in black shutters, it had two gables on the upper story and a large, inviting front porch welcoming visitors as they walked up the curved flagstone walk. While Main House, the grand, brick historic Cunningham family home, stood imposing and impressive on a high dramatic hill overlooking the lower farm, Hill House sat cozy and charming, snuggled in its green woodland above the creek on the Upper Farm. Lydia loved Hill House—always had—and she'd agreed to rent it because of its attraction and appeal, as well as to help the family retain the property.

As she explored, Lydia found most of the original furniture and décor still in place. Here and there she discovered new furnishings and accessories, or worn pieces reupholstered, but she knew she could put her personal stamp back on the house easily with what was here. She'd brought no furniture from Atlanta, leaving it all with Parker.

She unpacked after her house tour, putting her clothes away in drawers or closets, arranging her personal things where she could enjoy them. She heated some of Ela's casserole and Doris's green beans for dinner, called the boys to let them know she'd arrived safely, played with the kitten she'd christened Trudi, and then at seven, took a hot bath and curled up on the sofa in a soft linen nightdress to read a book.

A knock at the door came as darkness fell. It startled her, and she got up quietly to pad over to the window to look out on the porch. It was John.

She opened the door. "John, whatever are you doing here so late? You scared me knocking on the door after dark."

He held out the covered basket she hadn't noticed in his hand before. "It's another cat."

She tried to hold back a grin. He looked so serious in offering it to her. "Another calico, I'm presuming."

"Mary Beth found it on the porch of the country store when she started locking up to go home. We have no idea who left it." He ran a hand through his hair. "She'd have brought it up to you herself, but she had to get the boys bathed and ready for bed."

"Well, bring it on inside." She opened the door.

John stalked in and put the basket down on the couch. "I'm sorry, Lydia. Maybe I shouldn't have brought another kitten, but I didn't know what else to do with her right now."

Lydia sat down on the couch, opened the basket, and scooped out another calico kitten, this one predominantly white with black and gold markings. "She looks about the same age and size as the other kitten, but with more white coloring and shorter hair."

"I'm really sorry about this," he apologized again. "It's not much of a welcome to get dumped with two kittens the first night you arrive. Manu can take them both to the shelter to-morrow if you don't want to keep them. Or Mary Beth said she might put them in a big box on the porch of the store with a "Free" sign on the box."

"Stop worrying, John. I don't mind having two kittens here in the country." A smile twitched at her lips. "But if any more show up, don't you *dare* haul them up here."

He grinned at her. "We're putting out the word tomorrow around town that you've been doubly welcomed with calico cats and not to drop more off." John rubbed a hand behind his neck. "Surely there can't be more than two in the valley, any-way. The coloring isn't that common."

"Let's see if they'll get acquainted." She stood up to look for

Trudi, who had scampered out of the room when John knocked on the door.

Retrieving the small cat from the kitchen, she brought it back to sniff the newcomer. After a little hissing and checking each other out, they began to play together, batting at the tassels on a throw pillow.

"Looks like they're going to accept each other with no trouble." She smiled, watching them tumble off the couch and chase across the floor. "I think I'll name our newcomer Ava. Trudi and Ava. How do you like those names, John?" She turned from watching the kittens to see his eyes sliding over her.

"My Lord, you need to put some clothes on, Lydia Ruth."

Lydia looked down at herself in surprise. "It's just a nightdress, and it hangs past my knees."

He swallowed. "Well, it's thin . . . and in the light, well . . ." He swallowed again, not finishing the thought.

"In the light what?" Lydia watched his discomfort with a small sense of wonder welling up inside her.

He hesitated, his eyes moving up and down her, making her shiver. "It's revealing," he said at last. "Especially with the light behind you."

She moved slightly out of the lamplight. "John, we've been married twenty-eight years and lived together for eighteen of them. You've certainly seen me in clothing much skimpier than this nightdress." She smiled. "In fact, often in much, much less. I can't remember you having a problem with it before."

He walked closer to her. "Then I was a danged fool."

He lifted his hands to touch her hair and then traced them gently down the sides of her arms and around to drift behind her back to draw her against him. "I had no idea what I had, Lydia, when you were in my life. I'm so sorry I let my affection for you slip away, that I didn't find a way to let you know every day how precious you were to me. How beautiful. To let you know you light up my days with your voice, your smile, your loving ways."

John pressed his face against her neck. "Even remembering the scent of you haunted my dreams these past years."

She put her hands against his chest, pushing him away from her as his hands began to explore more intimately. "This is too soon for me." She sucked in a shaky breath. "We've been apart for ten years. There are so many things we need to talk about, resolve, and work out between us before we can consider being a couple again."

"Why?" He let his fingertips skim down her arms. "Why let another hour, another minute go to waste when we don't have to? Who knows what might happen tomorrow and what we might regret in not savoring this minute right now?"

She sighed and leaned against him. "Oh, John. You always could be a sweet-tongued, romantic man when you wanted to be. I'd forgotten."

He found her lips then, kissing her, the passion rising between them. "Let me remind you of even more good things."

Lydia put a hand to his face, stepping back slightly in his embrace. "Of all the things I expected when I saw you again, this was not one of the things I thought would happen."

"What did you expect?" He kissed her nose.

"Arguments. Awkwardness. Quarreling. Angry looks. Stony silences. Recriminations. Maybe hurt." She bit her lip. "I was afraid of more hurt."

His eyes grew pained. "I'm sorry there was so much of that. So much hurt and disappointment. So many misunderstandings. So many problems with . . ." His voice dropped away.

"So many problems with your mother?" she finished for him.

"Yes." He didn't say more.

Her mouth tightened. "We need to talk about that some time. We need to talk about a lot of things."

"Or let it all be in the past." He buried his lips in her hair, moving them around to kiss her ear.

A shiver ran over her. "That was one of our problems, John— that you didn't ever want to talk things through. You always wanted to deal with problems tomorrow, some other time. Or pretend they weren't of any importance or weren't there at all."

He shifted away from her, glancing down. "Too much talking has a way of putting a damper on things."

She followed his glance. "It's just as well. I'm not ready for more between us yet."

He backed away. "Then put some more clothes on, would you?" His voice sounded cross now.

Lydia watched him. "Maybe it's time for you to go home." She walked over to the door. "You brought the cat and it's late. I need to get some rest."

He stalked toward the door and then stopped, turning back toward her. She heard him sigh deeply. "I meant the things I said earlier, Lydia."

She put a hand to his face. "I could feel that, and I'm touched and pleased," she admitted. "Thank you."

His eyes searched her face. "Have you thought of me over the years?"

"I think this may not be the best time to get into that, John." She crossed her arms over her breasts, feeling suddenly modest.

He followed her gesture. "Is there someone else?"

Lydia shook her head. "No. But that doesn't mean I'm ready to jump into a relationship with you, or with anyone, without giving it time and thought."

She watched him consider that. Then he turned to start out the door without giving another reply.

However, before walking down the steps of the porch, he turned. "Mary Beth and Ela hope you might come down to the house tomorrow. They'd like to make dinner for you if that would be all right."

A chill slipped up Lydia's spine at the thought of entering Main House again, of facing the ghosts of so many bad memories.

John glanced toward the sign on the porch rail. "The boys, Bucky and Billy Ray, are real excited about it."

He knew the trump card to throw in the pile, she thought. "Of course I'll come." She offered a careful smile.

"It will be all right, Lydia," he said, as if reading her thoughts. "That was then and this is now. Think of it like the scripture— 'Old things are passed away; behold, all things are new.' "

"Slightly out of context, but we'll see," she said, shutting the door. "We'll see."

CHAPTER 4

Every day moved at an active pace on a working farm. Today, as a favor to his friend Neal Caldwell, John walked around his orchards with a young farmer, Tom Kilgore, who planned to add apple trees to his property.

As the boy walked ahead of them to look at a row of trees beginning to fruit, Neal said, "I appreciate your time, John. Tom is a nice kid and trying hard to give his family farm a future. There are some old apple trees on the back property of his place but he'd like to plant more."

Neal, an agriculture and forestry agent for the Haywood County Extension Office, often advised and worked with young farmers. He also lived on the neighboring property and had grown up with John's sons.

The boy turned to John. "How many varieties do you have at Cunningham Farm?"

"We have thirty varieties now but focus on twenty-five main ones. Five are experimentals I'm working with to see how they'll produce. I like finding the old Appalachian varieties and cultivating them." He gestured to the rows ahead. "Here, you'll see some of our oldest trees on the farm. We call this area the Lower Orchards and above the flat barn and greenhouse you see on the slope above us are the Upper Orchards. To the west end of the property lie the Side Orchards. We have three orchards on this farm. I understand from Neal that you have some apple rows on your land already. Neal can help you determine where you might want to cultivate more in the future."

The men walked along between the rows of apple trees as they talked. "Apple trees can grow to thirty feet tall and fifteen feet wide with a growth of eight to twelve feet per year. They require rich soil, good drainage, and full sun." John stopped to pull down a leafy branch for Tom to examine. "This is a strong, healthy tree, trained to a productive shape as it grew, by cutting, trimming, and tying off, to bear the best fruit possible."

Neal jumped into the conversation. "Nearly all domestic fruit trees today are grafted trees. I can help you learn the methods for that when we examine your own trees more carefully. John does some of his grafting directly in the field and some in the greenhouse."

"How do you know the best area on your land for apples?" Tom asked John.

"Rolling hills and south slopes, like you see here, make an ideal location for apples." John gestured to the land rising upward with each row of trees. "You should never plant apple trees in a low-lying area that's a frost pocket. It can kill the blossoms or fruit as cold air settles around the trees. Choose a high site so cold air will flow away from and downhill from the trees. Good air drainage is critical."

Neal reached down to pick up a handful of soil from around one of the trees. "Apple trees will tolerate a wide range of soils as long as the pH is adequate and the nutrients are not too limited. You can add nutrients as needed by testing the soil."

John grinned. "Neal can do that for you as your county agent."

"I can," Neal agreed. "I can also recommend fertilizers. Established plants benefit from fertilization every few years. A soil test can show the nutrient levels in the soil, but it's smart to use leaf mulch or compost instead of store-bought fertilizers as much as you can—especially in the blooming season."

Tom looked up at the rolling hillsides of the farm. "How big is your place here?"

"About two miles across and three miles up to the park

boundary. Nearly thirty-eight hundred acres, but only the lower half of the farm sits at the right elevation for the orchards. The upper land is too mountainous and the air too cold."

"You have a hunting lodge and rental cabins up there, don't you?"

"Yes. We try to find ways to use all our land productively," John answered. "We even have a winter tube run on the Upper Farm Road. We grow pumpkins, vegetables, have some pecan trees, berry bushes, and grape rows. We even make a Cunningham wine in our wine house. Everything is an opportunity for income. I don't like my livelihood overly tied up in only one enterprise."

John sighed. "You can have some real disappointments farming, Son. I guess you already know that growing up on your family's land."

As the boy asked more questions of Neal, John glanced up the road to see Lydia walking across the avenue from the Manager's House. His heart kicked up a notch at the sight of her.

"Excuse me," he said, turning to Neal and Tom. "I have something I need to take care of."

"I can see that." Neal grinned and punched him on the arm. "I'll finish taking Tom around the farm. Thanks for your time, John."

Tom stuck out a hand. "Yes, thank you, sir."

John shook the boy's hand and then started up the road at a quick pace. He headed Lydia off as she stopped by the road to prop her arms on the fence beside the big vegetable garden.

She looked up and smiled at him as he drew closer. "I'd forgotten how wonderful a vegetable garden looks in early June when everything is leafing out."

John reached under the fence to pluck off a ripe strawberry to hand to her. "The strawberries are in. You can come down and pick all you like. I remember you like them."

She smiled, popping the plump berry into her mouth.

"We've got potatoes, zucchini, and summer squash coming in now. Pole beans and limas, too." He propped a booted foot on the fence. "The corn rows are looking good but won't be ready 'til July."

Lydia reached under the fence to pick a few more strawberries. "You can take a bucket and find blackberries on the upper property now, Lydia. You should remember where. Cherries are already ripe on those old trees near the lodge, too, and blueberries will be along later in the month. Help yourself anytime. There's always plenty."

John studied her while she enjoyed the strawberries, licking the juice off her fingers. She had her thick copper hair pinned up in some sort of clasp today but, as usual, it drifted around her face and down her neck with a will of its own. It made him itch to put his fingers in it. He could see some of her legs today, too, since she wore those cutoff slacks women favored now. She had on another T-shirt, too, but wore a sheer, sleeveless orange tunic over it in the color of ripe pumpkins. And she wore orange tennis shoes.

He snickered.

"What's so funny?" she asked.

"The shoes. You've always had more colorful shoes than any woman I've ever known."

She raised her chin defensively. "I got them at a seventy-five-percent-off clearance sale. They weren't an extravagance."

He winced. "I wasn't criticizing—just remembering with fondness."

"Oh." She shifted her eyes away from his, a slight blush touching her cheeks.

"Did you walk over?" he asked.

She laughed. "No, I drove. Had some visiting to do. But when I went to Manager's House to see the Sheppards, and to visit Ozetta and Doris, Clyde decided to examine my car." Lydia spread her hands expressively. "He said I needed new spark plugs. Soon he had the hood up, already working, so of course I had to leave the car with him."

"Of course." John laughed with her. "I'll bet Clyde got real excited about checking out that Mustang."

"He did." Lydia nodded. "I got to see Sam, too, for a few minutes before I went in to chat with Ozetta and Doris—and got to thank them for the pie and food they sent up." She paused.

"Sam hasn't changed a bit. I swear, I think that John Deere cap he had on was the same one he wore ten years ago."

"Naw. It's a new one." He grinned. "Sam just roughs them up quick."

"I was trying to remember how long the Sheppards have lived on Cunningham Farm."

"Since before my time." He reached over to pick up a stick, turning it in his hand as he answered her. "Sam and I grew up together, you know. He's managing the farm now with his son Charlie's help. Sam's dad, Eugene, managed the farm before Sam—still works on the farm even in his eighties—and Eugene's father managed the farm before that. I don't remember him. He worked for my great-grandparents."

"They're all wonderful people." She leaned against the fence rail. "I like all the Sheppards, and I was glad to learn you renovated Ridge House, the old farmhouse above the Upper Orchards, for Sam's son Charlie, his wife, and their family."

"Did you see Charlie and his wife, Nevelyn, yet?"

"Yes, and I visited with Ela and Manu. Met Harley." She paused, wrinkling her nose. "Where'd that yellow dog get the name Harley?"

"Manu found the mutt as a pup alongside the road during one of the annual Harley motorcycle festivals in the valley. Dog must have felt frightened by the cycles. Barks at every motorcycle that comes around."

"Thus the name." Lydia grinned, propping a foot on the fence beside John's. "That's a cute story."

John liked the look of their feet side by side on the fence again.

"Who were you talking to down at the Lower Orchards?" she asked.

"That was Neal Caldwell and a young farmer from over near Waynesville."

Lydia's eyes brightened. "That was Neal? I didn't know he'd come back to the valley. Last I remember, he'd moved to Columbia, South Carolina, and got married there."

"Neal's the new agriculture and forestry agent for the Haywood County Extension Office. He came back two years ago and is living with his dad right now—good company to Burgin, who's lived there all alone since his boy Dean married and moved out."

He paused. "Neal's marriage, I understand, proved short-lived. A girl in the military, stationed at Fort Jackson. She quickly regretted settling down, divorced him, and moved on before they'd been married two years."

"I'm sorry. I always loved Neal."

He leaned companionably against her. "He loved you, too. You practically raised him after his mother died when he turned seven."

"I remember that as a hard time for him—and for his brother and his father." She turned her eyes to look at John. "Has Burgin ever remarried?"

John shook his head. "No, he can't get past the memory of Nadine—even though a number of eligible woman have chased after him."

"Does he still own the hardware store?"

John grinned. "Yes. Caldwell's Hardware is an institution around here. Burgin's there every day and Dean works in the business now, too."

"I remember Neal always championed Mary Beth when all the boys teased her. Insisted she get to play their games many times when J. T., the twins, and Dean announced them a 'no girls' activity."

John laughed. "I'd forgotten that." He looked thoughtful. "I think those old protective feelings about Mary Beth may still be lingering around—along with a little more."

Lydia turned to him in surprise. "Mary Beth and Neal?"

A half smile played over his lips. "I'm not sure Mary Beth has noticed except around the edges. But Neal's a good man. It wouldn't trouble me to see the two of them get together. Mary Beth deserves some happiness."

Lydia released a deep breath. "Sonny Harper always seemed an impulsive, reckless boy," she said. "It troubled me when I heard Mary Beth ran off and married him."

"She was passing through an unruly time then," John explained. "Got caught up in the drama of Sonny and his band, the Flat Ridge Boys. She sang occasionally with the band. Went to performances. Felt important with all her peers."

John saw Lydia grip the fence rail while he talked, her face tense.

"I knew she'd grown enamored with the band," he continued, knowing she needed to understand, "but I had no idea she and Sonny had become that serious." He frowned. "They'd dated off and on a little, and then Sonny asked her to the senior prom."

John paused, looking back. "Mary Beth looked so pretty and grown-up on prom night in a long, fussy white dress, and Sonny wore a rented tux, his dark hair all slicked back nice and neat. Just two kids, excited about a dance. It never dawned on me they'd run off and get married that night."

He raked a hand through his hair. "She'd turned eighteen the week before. I couldn't annul what she'd done, Lydia, and she seemed purposed she'd done the right thing. All starry-eyed and in love with Sonny. She moved in with him into his parents' basement apartment in town, next door to Sonny's father's upholstery shop."

"What happened?" She put a hand on his, sensing his discomfort.

"I don't fully know." He threaded a hand through his hair again and sighed. "Boy started getting wild. Acting irresponsible. Took off on trips with the band. Stayed gone too much." John shifted restlessly. "Mary Beth got pregnant the first summer after they married despite the talks I had with her about that. Soon she couldn't travel with Sonny. Then she had twins on top of everything else."

Lydia squeezed his hand. "Poor child. I remember how hectic that time was when our twins came—and we had J. T., too."

He sat down on the old bench beside the garden fence, and Lydia sat down beside him.

"Mary Beth's been a good mother," he told her. "Had to grow up quick. Too quick and with too many sorrows for a young girl. Those babies weren't even two when Sonny took off on one of his road trips and never came back." He kicked at the dirt near his feet. "He finally called his parents after a few months to tell them he wasn't ever coming back, that he and the band had found some big opportunity out in California. Said it wasn't any place for a woman and children."

"He didn't even call Mary Beth himself?" Lydia's eyes widened.

"No." John felt his anger rise. "Just expected his parents to take care of her. He left Mary Beth in an embarrassing situation. As soon as I heard about it, I went to get her. Brought her and the babies, Billy Ray and Bucky, home."

"I'm proud of you for that." Lydia squinted in the sunshine to catch his eyes with hers. "It couldn't have been easy."

They both left unsaid between them the difficulties it must have caused with Estelle. A proud woman, she wasn't fond of being a part of failures or embarrassing situations.

John moved over the unspoken thoughts between them. "Mary Beth's doing all right, Lydia. A few years ago, she renovated the old building on the highway, on that piece of commercial land we own, and opened a country store. Did you see it driving in?"

"I did." She smiled. "It looked good."

"I remember you always wanted to open a store there. Insisted it would bring in extra money and could be successful. You pointed out how it would complement the farm, appeal to the tourists, being on the main highway, and draw in locals if the store carried some basic groceries." John looked down the avenue toward the direction of the store as he talked. "You claimed it would save folks a run into Waynesville to the market when they just needed milk, bread, or pickup items."

"And has it been successful?'

"Yes." He spoke the word with a tight nod. "We should have opened it years ago. It's actually giving the farm more of a reputation, drawing visitors to the tours and events we host at the orchard. You should go see it, Lydia. I think you'll be proud of what Mary Beth has done with it."

"I'll go down soon."

He threaded his fingers in a familiar gesture. "The store

quickly got too busy for Mary Beth to handle on her own, so she hired her friend Nancy Grace to help her with it."

"Nancy Grace Killian?" Lydia's face lit up. "Mary Beth's best friend when they were girls?"

"It's Nancy Grace Peterson now—and they're still the best of friends. She married a boy who teaches in the Fish and Wildlife Management Program over at Haywood Community College. Nice young man. Seems a good match."

Lydia sighed and stood up, brushing off her slacks. She turned to John and smiled. "I've enjoyed this talk, John. It's helped me catch up. Thank you." She looked across the Farm Road. "I need to go see if Clyde is finished with my car now so I can go back to Hill House and check on the kittens."

"How is that going?"

"They keep me busy." She laughed. "I'm actually glad now there are two of them. They play together, sleep together, and entertain each other." She laid a hand on his arm as he stood. "I hope we can talk more later. It's been good."

He wanted to respond that they had their whole lives ahead of them to talk all she wanted, but he decided not to press his luck. She needed time to reacclimate and settle in. To feel at home again.

Instead he asked, "Did you talk to Ela about coming down to the house for dinner tonight?"

She looked toward the imposing brick house on the hillside knob. "Yes. I said I'd come, but I asked if we could eat picnic-style on the back porch instead of in the dining room."

John nodded in understanding. He knew the formal dining room held some of the worst memories for Lydia. Estelle, seated royally at the head of the table, would inevitably wield her tongue in subtle criticisms and innuendos toward Lydia while she held her captive through family meals.

"I'll see you then." He looked at his watch. "I'd walk with you to get your car, but I need to meet with Neal again before he leaves the farm."

"I'll be fine." She sent him a sunny smile and turned to walk across the avenue and back down the side road to the Sheppards'.

CHAPTER 5

Gathering her courage, Lydia drove directly to the Cunningham Farm entry road to Main House for dinner that night. The Avenue rolled gently uphill into the family orchard, framed by neat, gray-weathered fencing that marked off the boundaries of the fields. Spreading oaks reached their leafy arms across the drive, lending to the ambience of the Avenue's charm. On a high knob, Cunningham's Main House stood in tall Georgian splendor, an imposing two-storied statement to the wealth the Cunningham family accrued in the early 1900s.

From family stories, Lydia knew the area in and around Asheville rose in prominence as a curative destination in the 1880s to 1930s, drawing tourists, health seekers, and wealth to its doors. In that early season of its booming economy, Asheville became known as the hub of North Carolina. Agriculturalists, with rich lands and products to sell in the city, prospered. John's grandparents, John and Mary Cunningham, built and expanded in this era, cashing in on the rising tourism and economic development.

She remembered feeling entranced the first time she drove up the road with John to meet his family and see his home. Lydia bit her lip. Now she felt anxious. Her stomach hurt and she was filled with dread.

Lydia pulled into the drive beside Main House, stopping as she got out of her car to admire the symmetrical, orderly shape of the large brick house, with its paired chimneys and long windows neatly aligned on both stories of the home. A tidy walkway led to the wide, decoratively crowned front door, sheltered beneath a pillared porch entry with its crisp, white balustrade railing over the roof.

The family had always been so proud of the house built by William and Elizabeth Cunningham, so proud of the farm and the land and the family's long heritage in the area. She crossed her arms against herself and thought, *It's not that they shouldn't be, it's just that . . .*

Her thoughts trailed off, and Lydia sighed. It was just that Estelle Cunningham took pride one step too far and turned it into prideful cruelty. She ruled like an autocratic queen. Her critical spirit always found ways to condemn, and she seldom offered a word of encouragement or praise. Lydia frowned. Estelle had a way of sucking all the joy and gladness out of any fine moment, of making you feel guilty to laugh, to love, or to enjoy life.

With resignation, Lydia turned her steps toward the winding walk that led around to the back of the house. Here a broad screened porch stretched under shady maples with a patio and a green lawn behind it.

Ela Raintree waved at Lydia from the porch, coming to open the screen door for her. "Come in. Come in." Her broad face, wreathed in smiles, helped Lydia to relax.

Mary Beth looked up from where she decorated a long table, draped with a colorful runner and set with festive stoneware. "What do you think?" she asked, smiling and trying to smooth over the awkwardness of the moment.

"It looks lovely," Lydia said, noticing all the special touches in the napkins and table decorations her daughter had added.

Lydia stood silent then, letting her eyes move with hungry delight over her only daughter, so grown-up now, so softly beautiful with her reddish-brown hair, much like Lydia's, brown eyes like her father's, a face round and gentle, her mouth lit with a tentative smile.

"I've changed a lot." Mary Beth ran a hand nervously down her yellow blouse, smoothing it.

"Yes. You've become a beautiful woman." Lydia walked over to give her daughter a hug, but the embrace felt stiff—the two of them so unused to hugging.

"Rebecca told me you'd rented Hill House to help us keep it in the family. Thank you for that." Mary Beth chewed a nail. "I know it will make more of a commute for you when you start your work at Western."

"It isn't that far, and I like Hill House," she replied, offering Mary Beth another smile.

Lydia hated that the two of them felt like strangers, working hard to make conversation. Once they'd been so close, lying in bed together to laugh and talk, sharing the happenings of their days.

John and Manu came in the back door, easing the tension. With them came a big collie, pricking his ears at the sound of a new voice.

Lydia squatted down to hold out a hand to him. "And who is this?"

"It's Cullie." John laid a fond hand on the dog's back. "Say hello to our guest, Cullie." The dog put up a paw appealingly for Lydia to shake.

"He looks like Shep," Lydia said, remembering the collie at the farm when she left.

"Probably kin somewhere down the line. We lost Shep two years before Mother died. Got Cullie then for the boys." He smiled. "It wouldn't be Cunningham Farms without collies and calicoes."

"Speaking of cats, how are those kittens doing?" Manu asked, heading for the kitchen to help Ela.

"Just fine," Lydia said. She'd insisted Manu and Ela join them for dinner, an unheard-of event in Estelle's time.

Estelle snorted in derision once when Lydia dared to suggest it in the past. "You don't eat with the help, Lydia. Surely even you know that."

Embarrassed, Lydia had to disinvite the Raintrees to John's birthday party, which proved no surprise to Ela. "I figured you didn't check with Mrs. Cunningham first," she said with a twinkle in her eye. Ela had always taken Estelle's ways in stride in a way Lydia seemed unable to do.

Bustling out from the kitchen now, Ela brought the last of several steaming dishes to the brick sideboard along the wall. John strolled over to examine the offerings. "Umm. Umm. Pork loin roast, fresh green beans with new potatoes, corn casserole, sugar-glazed carrots, fresh yeast rolls, and homemade coconut cake. This looks like a fine dinner."

Mary Beth blushed. "Daddy, you don't have to catalog everything like you're reading out a restaurant menu."

"And why not?" He grinned and reached over to buss her cheek. "We have the best restaurant in town with Ela doing the cooking."

Ela smiled with pleasure, but then looked around with annoyance. "It's time to eat. Where are those boys? Here we are ready to sit down to dinner and those rascals aren't home."

"Oh. They'll be along any time," John said, filching a stalk of celery from a relish dish. "I saw them playing near the old hunting lodge earlier."

Mary Beth looked out the screen door with irritation. "Well, they were supposed to be back by four to get a bath and clean up."

"Don't worry. Lydia's seen her share of grubby boys before." John sent a grin her way. "I don't think she'll mind if they're not spit-cleaned and polished."

"Not at all," Lydia agreed, washed in the sweep of old memories that John's words brought to mind.

Just as Ela started to shoo them toward the table to sit down, the boys came racing across the side yard, hollering and screaming as they ran.

"We saw the ghost! We saw the ghost!"

Lydia managed to catch their words as they banged through the screen door, letting it slam behind them.

"Whoa!" John reached out a hand to catch one and then the other of the six-year-old twins.

Both boys turned huge brown eyes to his. "No kidding, Daddy John, we really did," said one excited voice after the other.

Manu came in from the kitchen, carrying a pitcher of tea. "I saw those boys through the kitchen window running like the devil himself was chasing them down the hill. What's going on? They hurt?"

"We saw the ghost, Manny!" a young voice piped in to explain, as Manu set the tea on the sideboard. "Billy Ray and me both saw it—all creepy and white, slinking out of the woods."

Billy Ray interrupted. "It had blood on it and everything. It howled and waved its arms at Bucky and me." He moaned and demonstrated.

Bucky pulled on John's arm. "It said for us to go away and never come back, and it had a scary, dead voice like this." He parroted the words in a gravelly voice with more dramatic hand gestures.

This caught Mary Beth's attention. "Where were you?"

"Just playing around near the old hunting lodge." Bucky shrugged and then his eyes grew large again. "Do you think the ghost lives there?"

"I don't believe in ghosts." She shook a finger at them. "And neither should you."

"But we both saw it!" Bucky protested.

"Someone probably played a trick on you." She walked over to smooth down their brown hair and tuck in their polo shirts. "Now, both of you need to calm down and get ready for dinner." She nodded her head toward Lydia. "Your grandmother is here, and you haven't even said hello."

The boys turned dark chocolate eyes her way. "Are you Nana Lydia?" asked Billy Ray.

The sound of the name warmed Lydia's heart. "Yes, and thank you for the nice welcome sign you made me." She walked over to lay a hand on each of their cheeks one by one, not sure whether they'd like to be hugged by a grandmother they knew so little.

"Is the sign still hanging on your porch?" Billy Ray asked. Lydia studied him, trying to see a way to tell him from Bucky, clad in a similar dark green shirt.

"Yes. The sign is still there," she answered him, deciding his longer eyelashes and that faint brown birthmark near his ear would be her clues to tell him from his identical brother.

Billy Ray pulled on her hand. "Will you sit by me?"

"I'd love to." She let herself be led to a seat by two chattering boys and then over to the sideboard to fill her plate.

"Honest, Mom, we really did see a ghost." Billy Ray climbed into a ladder-back chair beside Lydia's at the table. "No foolin'. You can ask Davy Crowe."

"And what does Davy Crowe have to do with this?" Mary Beth asked.

"We were playing with him up near the lodge. Davy and his family don't live far away, just across Indian Creek below Sheep-back Knob."

Bucky butted in between bites. "Did you know Davy's grandparents, his grandfather's sister, his mom and dad, his older sister, Izabelle, *and* his brother, Nalin, all live together in that one little house?" He grinned, obviously pleased at his recitation. "Davy said sometimes Cherokee families do that—all live together."

Mary Beth leaned forward across the table. "And how do you suddenly know so much about how the Crowe and Youngblood families live? Were you and Billy Ray over there today? That's across the creek and you're supposed to get permission to leave our property or to visit anyone's house *before* you go."

He dropped his head. "I guess we forgot."

Billy Ray diverted the subject. "Davy's mother told us she saw the ghost one day, Mom. She thinks it's the spirit of that Indian named Red Hawk who got killed at Drop Off Ridge a long time ago."

"Pah. That old legend." Manu snorted. "No one even knows what ridge that really happened on."

"What's the story?" Lydia asked, curious.

He scowled. "In some Indian tribes a long time ago, one punishment for a bad crime was to be bound and pushed off a high cliff to one's death. Cherokee once lived in these hills. Many hid out in this area after the government started moving the people west. Legends say an execution happened in this actual area, but it's only speculation that it occurred at Drop Off Ridge or on our property. I've heard other places mentioned."

"But maybe it really did happen here!" Billy Ray waved his fork in excitement. "Maybe we saw that Indian's ghost, and maybe he doesn't like anybody to come around where his spirit lives."

John cleared his throat. "I played all over that ridge as a boy and so did my sons, and Mary Beth, and none of us ever saw a ghost there."

"We didn't make it up, Daddy John. Honest," Billy Ray said.

Ela passed around a basket of rolls. "To be fair, John, others have seen that ghost up there this last year. Billy Ray and Bucky aren't the first."

"She's right, and that does trouble me," Manu said. "Right now it's only pranks and scares, but it worries me it might go further."

"What's all this about ghosts?" a new voice asked as Neal Caldwell let himself in the screen door.

"Hello, Neal." John stood up to greet him.

"I didn't mean to interrupt dinner, but I wanted to drop these soil test results by on my way home. They just came in." He handed John a manila envelope.

"Have you eaten?" Ela asked.

Neal hesitated.

Lydia got up and walked over to give him an affectionate hug. "I'd love for you to stay if you can, Neal. It's such a pleasure to see you."

He smiled. "For you, I couldn't say anything but yes." They shared a few pleasantries, and then Neal encouraged everyone to sit back down while he went to fill his plate.

"Have you ever seen the ghost on Drop Off Ridge?" Billy Ray asked Neal as he sat down with a plate heaped full of Ela's good food.

"No, but I've heard a few tales about folks who have." Neal lifted his eyebrows in a conspiratorial way.

"Me too." Bucky squirmed in his seat with excitement. "I heard

Mrs. Green, down at the store, say she thought the ghost was probably Nance Dude's ghost come back to get more little children."

"Buckner Dean Cunningham!" Mary Beth exclaimed. "When did you hear that?"

He lifted his chin. "She was telling Mrs. Klemmer about Amy, the Plemmonses' little girl, seeing the ghost at Sheepback Knob. I wasn't eavesdropping or nothing. They were just talkin' near where you had me putting candy in the barrels."

"I heard her, too," Billy Ray claimed. "That's another reason me and Bucky ran away so fast. We're scared of Nance Dude."

Lydia wrinkled her nose. "Are those old stories about Nance Dude still circulating?"

Neal grinned. "Well, sure, and especially around Halloween. Those tales used to scare the dickens out of me—especially the one about her ghost coming out every Halloween to catch kids and bury them alive in her cave. It really creeped my brother, Dean, and me out."

"Well, you ought not to scare the boys with more of those old fables." Mary Beth crossed her arms in irritation. "And Loretha Green and Gurlie Klemmer shouldn't spread tales like that where impressionable children can hear them."

"Aw, Mom." Bucky reached across the table to get another roll from the basket. "Everybody knows all the stories about Nance Dude anyway."

"Well, all that happened in 1913, and that poor old woman has been dead for years now. Who knows what hardship she experienced that caused her to do such a harsh thing to her own granddaughter." Mary Beth frowned. "She spent fifteen years in prison for second-degree murder for leaving that child up there in that cave, too. I'd say she paid for any wrongdoing she did before she died."

Billy Dale's eyes lit up. "So, since she's dead, it could be *her* ghost at Drop Off Ridge, Mom. You don't know. She lived over near Utah Mountain and that's not far. Maybe her ghost is sad about what she did and can't rest in peace. Davy's big brother,

Nalin, said she might be searching the mountains for the grand-daughter she buried alive in the cave."

Mary Beth's face reddened. "I think we've all had just about enough talk about ghosts at this table." She looked around her. "Daddy, I think you and Manu should do a search around the area near the lodge and Drop Off Ridge tomorrow to see if you can figure out who's doing these ghost pranks on our land. I don't like my boys being involved in frightening things like this."

"It does bear looking into." John scratched his chin in thought. "I don't much like ghost sightings happening so near our farm-land, either."

"What if that ghost had snatched us or something?" Bucky waved his piece of buttered roll as he threw his thought out. "We might be buried in some cave now or pushed off that ridge and be dead."

"That's highly unlikely." Mary Beth gave them a warning glance.

Lydia tried to suppress a smirk, but John saw it and winked at her. At least all this ruckus over the ghost had helped Lydia's first dinner with the family to be less awkward. The ghost had become the center of focus instead of her.

CHAPTER 6

The next morning, John and Manu met with Officer Lester Sexton about the ghost sightings of the day before. Lester brought his shepherd dog, Phebus, to help search the area for any clues not immediately evident.

"I guess we really couldn't expect Sheriff Sutton to come out and investigate a ghost," Manu said to John, while watching Lester and Phebus explore around the rustic hunting lodge on the Upper Farm Road. "But I lack a certain confidence in Lester Sexton, I don't mind saying."

John grinned. "Yeah, I know what you mean, but maybe he'll luck into something. Phebus being here might help."

The two men chuckled, and then Manu gestured toward the big lodge sprawled under a canopy of tall pines. "John, I went through the lodge myself last night, checked all the rental cabins on the road above, even walked up the hiking trail toward Garretts Gap. I couldn't find any evidence of a squatter on the property, nor could I see any tracks in the area where the boys said they saw the ghost."

"It's a puzzle and that's a fact," John said as the police officer reappeared from behind the lodge.

Lester crossed the road to join them, shaking his head. On the pudgy side in appearance, Lester waddled more than he walked, and although not the brightest bulb on the tree, he tried hard and always meant well. "I can't find a sign of fresh tracks or any evidence of a break-in, John." He clucked at the shepherd to sit down. "You'd think if all this ghost business was caused by a prankster, it would have settled down by now."

"How many ghost sightings have you been called in on, Lester?" John leaned over to pet Phebus's head.

"I reckon three before this." Lester counted on his fingers. "First one up Indian Creek Drive on the back road that circles under Sheepback Knob. Gurlie Klemmer reported it—heard a moaning sound and saw a ghostlike form as she cut through the woods to Loretha Green's place one evening. The second came from a couple of men hunting in the ridge area, across the creek from your place. Next, the Plemmons came down to the police department in Maggie, all torn up 'cause their little girl Amy got near scared to death seeing the ghost while playing by Indian Creek." Lester turned to look down the road in that direction. "That was less than a quarter mile from here, John, and now your boys say they saw the ghost on this side of the creek. Sure can't figure what to think of all this."

"The boys also told us that Alo Youngblood's wife, Reena, saw the ghost," Manu added.

Lester scowled. "Well, she didn't report it. But then, that family stays close to itself. They don't step out much—probably in part from living on Silas Green's land. He's a hard man to work for." Lester rubbed a boot in the dirt. "Used to beat up on his own girls, I hear. Didn't surprise us none when them girls took off soon as they grew up."

"Twisted man." Manu spit in disgust at this news. "Ela says his wife, Loretha, is real glad every time he goes away traveling with his farm equipment sales. Guess there's no love lost there."

John brought them back to the subject. "Has the police department found any clues or information about who they think is behind these ghost tricks?"

Lester shook his head. "Nope. We go out and look, but we don't find nothin'—just like here." He pulled a notebook from his pocket. "Either of you think of anything else I need to write down before I go?"

"No. I think we already told you everything." John followed Lester to his police car, shutting the door after he and the dog climbed in. "Thanks for coming, Lester. Let us know if you learn anything more."

He and Manu watched Lester drive away. "Guess we didn't learn much from that visit," John said.

"Oh, I don't know." Manu pushed his hat back on his forehead. "We learned the names of the folks who reported the other ghost sightings, and we learned that all the sightings happened in this general vicinity above the Drop Off ridgeline. It's not like ghosts are popping up all over Maggie Valley. Just here around the creek, ridge, and knob."

"And?" John raised an eyebrow.

"*And* it's something to keep an eye on." Manu looked down the road toward the creek. "I think I'll do a little exploring on the other side of Indian Creek, if you don't mind—go talk to some of the folks Lester mentioned. Maybe stop by the Youngbloods' place, too. See if I can learn anything more. It's my guess the police department won't do much about a couple of ghost sightings unless property damage or violence is involved. I'd personally like to get to the bottom of this before anything like that happens."

"I agree." John nodded. "I'll ask around when I go into town today. See what I can find out at the local spots. Maggie's a small place—there's bound to be talk."

A few hours later, John found himself flagged down by Tolley Albright as he pulled into the parking lot of the Maggie Valley Restaurant. "Going in for lunch, John?" Tolley asked.

John glanced down at his watch. "Guess I could if I thought I'd have some good company." He grinned at his longtime friend.

"Well, let's do it. I hear country-fried steak is on the menu today and that it's real good." Tolley patted his ample girth.

The two men soon sat at a table by the window with two plates of food before them. As they ate, John filled Tolley in on the ghost sightings and what he'd learned about them while poking around downtown.

"Gossip is really spreading about this ghost, Tolley." John cut a bite of his steak and then forked it up with a mound of mashed potatoes.

"People love something like this to talk about." Tolley paused between bites. "But it's adding up to more than talk now. One of my clients who owns rentals in that area is complaining about profits falling off. This business might affect my realty sales—and your lodge and cabin rental business, too—if an end doesn't come to it soon."

"I'm more worried about someone getting hurt."

"Well, let's hope it doesn't come to that." Tolley plunged into a new subject. "Hey, Rebecca told me Lydia's back, and she wants us all to get together one night. I bet the Alexanders will feed the four of us free barbecue at the Cataloochee Ranch tonight if we'll clog a little and entertain the guests. I hear they've got a big group staying there this weekend." He wiggled his eyebrows at John. "Free dinner date for a little dancing—just like old times. What do you say?"

John drummed his fingers on the table. "I'm not sure if Lydia will go, Tolley. There's a lot of old angst floating between us."

Tolley mopped up the last of his gravy with his roll. "Well, dancin' might help to work some of that out. You know how much Lydia used to love clogging up at the ranch. I'll bet you can talk her into it. Just show up later on at her place carrying that red cowboy hat and her red dancing shoes. Tell her Rebecca and I and the Alexanders are counting on her coming."

John hesitated.

Tolley smoothed a hand over his bald head before scratching his short beard, where most of his hair seemed to have migrated. "Come on, John. You gotta create ways to get this woman back in your life. You and I both know you've never gotten past her, not even dated another woman all these years. Take a chance, man. This used to be something the two of you liked doing together."

By the time he and Tolley parted, they'd called the Alexanders to arrange to clog for their Friday night outdoor barbecue, and now John stood at Lydia's door, mustering up the courage to ask her out. He knocked and she opened the door after a few minutes.

"John?" she asked. He watched her eyes drift over his red, white, and blue cowboy shirt, and then down his jeans-clad legs to his red cowboy tap shoes.

A smile twitched at the corner of her lips. "Well, it's been a long time since I saw you in that costume."

"The Alexanders need some cloggers to entertain the guests tonight after the outdoor barbecue. They've got a big crowd in. Tolley and Rebecca asked us to come along with them."

He handed her the bag he'd held behind his back. Her eyes widened as she rummaged in it, seeing her old red tap shoes, the matching cowboy shirt to his, and a red cowboy hat on top.

She started shaking her head slowly. "John, I haven't done this in a long, long time."

"It's like riding a bike," he said. "You never forget what to do."

"Listen, it's nice of you to ask me—"

He stopped her. "It was Tolley and Rebecca who set this up. They wanted to do something special with you home to the valley. Tolley called and set everything in place, then asked me to come by and pick you up. A number of old friends will be at the ranch tonight—all glad to see you again. The Cross-Creek Boys with their pickin'-and-singing group, the Aldridges, the Alexanders. Probably a few others helping with the barbecue." He paused. "I figure you can tolerate my company for a night in order to make a lot of old friends happy."

She held the door open. "You have a persuasive way of pulling me back into the past, John Parker Cunningham."

He followed her inside. "I'd like to leave much of the past in the past and walk out into the future with you instead. Find some happier times together."

She turned her green eyes to his. "This isn't a date, John. It's a get-together with old friends."

He nodded, deciding not to push his luck further.

"Okay. I'll go get ready," she said, taking the bag and heading toward the back bedroom.

"Whew." John heaved a sigh of relief when she left, pleased she'd actually agreed to go.

A happy evening began after that. Lydia filled out her cute cowboy shirt and snug jeans as sweetly as John remembered. And after a few awkward moments, she moved with skill and ease into the remembered *double toe ball, heel ball, heel step* movements of clogging that had always been such a pleasure to both of them.

"Come on, liven it up," Tolley called beside them, where he and Rebecca danced in colorful matching outfits of their own. "Let's add in some slides, kicks, and stomps now. Whoo-eee!"

"You slow down, Tolley Aldridge!" Lydia warned. "I haven't done this in a very long time."

"Ah, you're a pro. Look at you." He grinned, moving into a *hop-double hop* movement to the rhythm of the Cross-Creek Boys. "We're all dancing about as fine tonight as that Maggie Valley clogging champion, Burton Edwards."

Lydia laughed, kicking at him in fun as she and John danced around the other couple in a well-remembered movement, their heels tapping on the concrete floor with clean, sharp sounds.

After several numbers, the four friends sat at a picnic table recuperating and working on a big plate of pit-smoked barbecue and fixin's.

Lydia looked out across the night and sighed. "I'd forgotten how much fun this can be and how beautiful it is here on Fie Mountain. It's like being on top of the world."

"We're at five-thousand-feet elevation here, and come wintertime skiers will be zooming down those slopes nearby." Tolley gestured behind him.

Rebecca smiled, reaching across the table to squeeze Lydia's hand. "I'm so glad you could come tonight. It's like old times, the four of us dancing together again. I haven't had this much fun in a month of Sundays."

One of the Alexanders came by carrying a plate of food. "Eat all you want, folks, and don't be backward about it," he said, winking and joking. "We got plenty and it's shore good."

"That goof," Rebecca said. "Did you know this ranch is in its third generation now? And growing more beloved every year? The lodge is still warm and inviting, serving those wonderful family-style meals, all the cabins rustic and cute, and there's always something to do here—horseback riding, wagon rides, swimming, croquet, fishing in the lake, great entertainment, or hiking up to the Cataloocheee Divide Trail." She sighed, resting her chin on her hand. "I read that Cataloochee means 'wave upon wave'—like the waves of blue mountain peaks rolling away in the distance there."

Tolley laughed. "You're starting to sound like those tourist flyers we give away at the realty office, Becca."

"Oh, hush. I'm simply havin' a good time. And I can wax poetic if I want to." She punched at him playfully, then leaned over to kiss him, making John envious. "You know you love me just the way I am, Tolley Aldridge."

The evening flew by, John enjoying every minute with Lydia and their friends. She greeted their old acquaintances with warmth and affection and talked with humor and interest to the visiting tourists.

Vance Coggins, the lead singer of the Cross-Creek Boys, dropped by to give Lydia a kiss during a short break.

"Wish you'd have brought Mary Beth to sing a number or two with us," he said to John. "She's got a fine voice."

"I'll tell her you said that." John clapped him on the back with affection.

"Is Mary Beth still singing?" Lydia asked, after Vance walked away.

John nodded. "Yes. She sings around the valley with bands like Cross-Creek sometimes, occasionally for weddings, and always at church in the choir on Sundays. Will you come to church to hear her?"

Lydia hesitated before saying, "I'm sure I'll visit one Sunday."

"Pastor Reilly, the stuffy minister that Mother had in her coat pocket is gone now, Lydia. We have a new minister at Fairview Methodist named Reverend Oliver Wheaton. A mid-years man.

Kindly sort. Good preacher. Has a strong tenor voice and is a fanatic bird-watcher."

John sipped at a glass of cold lemonade. "Perhaps Reverend Wheaton is too much of a bird-watcher, now that I think on it." He grinned. "The man glanced out the window last Sunday, spotted some sort of rare bird sitting on the cemetery fence rail, and completely lost his train of thought right in the middle of his sermon."

Lydia giggled, and the sound teased up John's spine. Being with Lydia all evening, touching her in the moves of their dancing, sitting near her, hearing her voice, and catching the scent of her, had been heady stuff for John.

"Let's go dance some more," she said, reaching across to catch his hand. "The band's started up again."

Later that evening, after saying good-byes to their friends and driving in the dark down the mountain, John put his hand under Lydia's elbow to walk her to the door of Hill House.

"I had a good time, John," she said, dropping her eyes. "Thanks for persuading me to go."

He leaned in, slipping an arm behind her back. "It was my pleasure." He let his lips drop to hers, savoring the good-night kiss, yearning for more as he felt her softness against him. "Let me come in, Lydia."

She stiffened. "No, John." Her eyes grew troubled and she bit at her lip, drawing away from him.

His mouth tightened. "Can't you let the past go?"

"Just like that?" Her eyes flashed. "Simply forget everything—walk into a new tomorrow? Not hardly." She stamped a foot in annoyance.

He gave her a quizzical look as she continued.

"You still don't understand how much pain I went through in the past here. How your mother hurt me with her subtle insults, digs, and haughty looks every day. Always criticizing me, finding fault with me. Wearing my soul down to the quick." She turned to look out across the dark yard, hugging herself with her arms as if chilled. "It took me years in Atlanta to begin to feel good about myself again. To like myself. To realize I was a decent and likeable person."

He frowned. "You always took Mother too seriously."

She whirled to face him with angry eyes. "And you never took her ongoing attacks against me—and then against the boys—seriously enough. You always said to 'look the other way,' 'turn the other cheek,' 'don't let her get under your skin.' It made me always feel in the wrong. As if it was my problem and not your mother's."

John felt uncomfortable. "Mother was a difficult person, I agree."

"*Difficult?*" Lydia's voice grew almost shrill now. "You still don't see that she was abusive. Verbally abusive. She wounded people with her words and ways. She wasn't simply difficult."

John felt himself stiffen. "I don't see any point in maligning her now that she's gone, Lydia. It doesn't seem respectful."

She lifted pained eyes to his. "Here's where our problem is, John. You still don't understand what I went through, how it felt to me, and why I gradually grew so wounded and hurt that I had to leave. Do you think I wanted that? Wanted to leave my home and break up my family?"

He didn't know how to reply. "You didn't have to leave."

"Yes, I did. I was dying here—like a person being gradually, daily poisoned to death. And you couldn't see it. You didn't help me, either, except to tell me to buck up. To toughen up and not let her bother me."

"That's how I managed it." He clenched his jaw, finding her criticism difficult to take. "You always thought I should somehow be able to change my mother, but you can't change others much in this world. You just have to change yourself to get along."

Tears welled in her eyes. "You're still doing it, John. You're still saying that somehow I should have found a way to get along with your mother. You still don't see why I couldn't—how hard I tried, but how I simply couldn't." She sniffed. "Then when your mother went at the boys later, you expected the same accommodation from them. You told them to buck up and find a way to get along with her. To understand she was 'just the way she was.' "

Irritation needled up John's spine. "What could I have done differently? Beat up my mother? Thrown her out of her own home after I promised my father I'd care for her? Should I have walked away from the farm and all my responsibilities?"

Lydia shook her head. "No, John. All I wanted, and all the boys wanted, was for you to stand with us sometimes. To stand up for us. To not pretend it wasn't happening. To not lock your heart away from our pain."

"That's overly harsh, Lydia. I never locked my heart away. I always loved you and the boys."

"Yes," she said softly. "But not enough. If you love someone, you don't let another person hurt them again and again, while you stand by and do nothing. There is something inherently wrong with allowing someone to hurt those you love—while you watch and do nothing."

He rubbed a fist in his palm in annoyance. "You make it sound like I stood by and let her beat on you and my sons."

"Didn't you?" she asked, the tears sliding down her face. "John, the wounds of verbal abuse hurt as much as the wounds of physical abuse sometimes. Both are forms of bullying."

John's heart hurt from her harsh words. "You always over-dramatized the situation with my mother."

She opened the door and let herself inside. "And you always underdramatized—and overlooked—the situation." She paused, looking at him with tear-filled eyes. "For the boys and me to come back into your life, you have to find a way to see that."

Lydia shut the door, clicking the lock behind her, leaving John feeling, once again, shut out and misunderstood.

CHAPTER 7

Lydia spent the weekend quietly—settling into the house, working in the yard, writing e-mails to friends and family in the evening. She talked to the boys, but didn't tell them about the swirls of mixed emotions she'd encountered.

"I hope I haven't made a mistake coming back here," she told her aunt Martha on the phone Sunday evening. She sat snuggled into a corner of the sofa as she talked, both of the kittens sleeping on her lap.

"Now, now, Lydia. You just told me earlier of all the good times you've enjoyed—getting together with old friends, clogging up at the ranch, working in the flower beds, and hiking up the mountain trail yesterday afternoon."

"It is beautiful here." Lydia sighed. "So different from the city—"

"And as for this business with John," her aunt interrupted, "I'm delighted to hear the man is trying to win you back. It shows he has good sense."

Lydia shot back, "Yes, and he's kissed me twice and without even asking."

Martha snorted. "Personally, I've never liked those namby-pamby men who ask if they can kiss you first before they do it. Give me the take-charge kind any time over the timid ones."

"Honestly." Lydia rolled her eyes.

"Just because I never married doesn't mean I haven't known my share of men over time, girl. I just never found one worth marrying or giving up my freedom for." She paused. "But you and John were always different. You two fit together like two peas in a pod. I saw you belonged together from the first. Even after all this trouble, the love is still there."

"Maybe." Lydia shifted in discomfort. "But there's so much trouble and misunderstanding."

"Yes, but at least the old harridan's gone now. You have a new chance to talk and work things out." She grew silent. "That's why I encouraged you to go back, Lydia. Surely you know the boys and I would prefer to keep you here in Atlanta with us. But I saw that a part of you still yearned for John and missed your life in North Carolina. Even after ten years, you never really transplanted. You know it's true."

"I guess." Lydia shifted the kittens to the couch beside her and curled her legs under her. "But why can't John see his part in why everything went so wrong?"

"I don't know, but you keep talking to him. Keep telling him how you feel, what you want of him. What you need from him. A lot of men can't figure out emotional issues without some help." Martha paused again. "I think women get raised up more as nurturers, sensitive to the needs and feelings of others. They become naturally more empathetic by nature. You've read the research on that."

"I suppose."

"There's no I *suppose* about it. You've seen much of the same kind of behavior in your boys. We've talked about it often enough together." She laughed. "Many times we both got purely frustrated and exasperated with those boys, but we never gave up on them. Don't you give up on John, either."

"It's good to talk to you, Marthie." Lydia used her pet name for her aunt and godmother. "You're the only one who really knows I came back to North Carolina, not just for the job, but to see if there might be a way for John and me to get together again."

"Well, I'm glad you're admitting it at last. You denied it long enough after the first time I brought it up to you."

"I guess." She smoothed back a loose strand of hair. "I miss you, Marthie. I miss our Sunday afternoon teas and our talks over lunch at the school."

Martha shifted the conversation. "That reminds me. Have you been over to the campus at Western yet?"

"No, but I'm going tomorrow and then into Waynesville for errands and to see John's sister, Holly. She wants me to have lunch."

"That sounds good. I always liked Holly. Strong, sensible woman. I guess she had to be strong to grow up as Estelle Cunningham's only girl. That couldn't have been easy."

"No. She's made allusions to that effect." Lydia chewed on her nail. "You know, John made a comment the other night that let me know it wasn't easy for him, either."

"What did he say?"

She tried to remember. "I fumed that he always advised me to handle his mother by toughening up and by not letting her bother me. John sort of harrumphed and said that's how he'd gotten through. How he managed. He said he couldn't change his mother, so he changed himself to get along."

"Couldn't have been easy for him. You need to find some way to get John to talk more about his childhood. He probably repressed and buried nearly half his feelings, growing up the way he did. By talking to him, you might get more information and some insights about why he handles things the way he does."

Lydia laughed. "That's what you always say: Get more information. You've given me that advice about on-the-job problems, too."

The older woman chuckled in response. "It usually works when you do it, too, doesn't it?"

"Most of the time it does—I admit it." She considered the idea. "Maybe I can get some information from Holly tomorrow that might help."

Martha yawned into the phone. "Dear one, it's getting late, and unlike you, I am not on vacation and I need to head to the office early in the morning. That career center won't run itself, you know. Plus, I'm having to train and work with your replacement."

"Pamela is wonderful. You know she'll do a good job."

"Yes," Martha replied with her usual businesslike tone. "I expect you to do a good job down there at Western, too, with my old director's job from long ago. You know I stuck my neck out recommending you."

Lydia smiled. "I know. I'll give it my best."

"That a girl." Lydia heard the smile in her voice. "You do the same in trying to work out the strained relationships with your family, you hear?"

Lydia recalled these words of encouragement as she visited the Western Carolina University campus the next day. She met with the vice chancellor of undergraduate studies, who would be her direct supervisor, renewed old acquaintances, and made several new contacts. Her job appointment didn't start officially until September first, but she planned to work scattered part-time hours in August to begin to acclimate—especially toward the latter part of August as the students began to return.

"I don't feel anxious about beginning my work with Western," Lydia told the outgoing director when they met. "I worked here for many years as a student and later as a support staff member. I feel I already know the career center and the college well."

"Yes, and I've only heard good things about you from others at Western whom you worked with in the past—and from Martha Howard."

Lydia smiled. "Well, Martha might be a little prejudiced since she's my aunt."

"Not when it comes to business, if I know Martha. Plus, we had only strong praise from others on staff at Georgia Tech who worked with you there. You come to us with excellent recommendations, Lydia. I feel confident that I am leaving the center in good hands as I move on."

Lydia knew the current director had accepted a new job directing a career counseling center in a larger university, much like her aunt Martha had done when she moved to Georgia Tech to a higher position and salary.

"Have you met all the staff at Western?" the director asked.

Lydia nodded. "I met my administrative assistant, the main counselor in the center, the coordinator of special events, and the work-study coordinator today. Also, as you know, I met with the vice chancellor earlier. It's a good beginning."

The two shook hands, and Lydia moved back through the career center and down the steps of the Killian Annex Building to head for her car. She looked around with pleasure at the solid brick buildings and at the impressive clock tower rising high above the lawn. Western was a beautiful campus, nestled in a rolling mountain setting.

"Thanks, God, for opening this opportunity for me. I'm truly grateful." She sent a glance skyward. "Help me to do a good job with it and to find a way to mend relationships with my family. I especially need Your strength and help to do that."

Lydia continued her prayer in her car as she headed to Waynesville for her lunch with Holly. "That confrontation with John at the door Friday night was less than pleasant, Lord, and both my encounters with my daughter have felt formal and strained—first at dinner and then at the store. I hate feeling like such a stranger with my own child, the two of us tiptoeing politely around each other."

Coming into Waynesville, Lydia began to focus on looking for a parking place near Holly's store. After graduating from college, Holly had lived and worked in Asheville for years, but then returned to Haywood County to open a small bookstore on the historic main street in downtown Waynesville. Lydia had maintained a casual correspondence with Holly over the years, and she looked forward to seeing her store.

Walking down Main Street, she saw the green awnings that Holly had told her to watch for. As she pushed open the store door, she spotted John's sister right away at the front register.

Holly waved and made her way over. "It's good to see you, Lydia," she said, offering her a quick hug. Stepping back, she laughed that deep, throaty laugh Lydia remembered so well. "I saw you pause and wince when I first looked up. I know, from looking in the mirror every morning, that I'm the spitting image of my mother in many ways—except for being taller—but I assure you I'm nothing like Estelle Cunningham in temperament."

Lydia dropped her eyes.

"Oh, come on. Don't start feeling guilty on me." She put an arm around Lydia's shoulder. "Let me show you around the store, and then we'll walk down the street to the City Bakery for lunch. It's a cute place for sandwiches and soups, or good quiche, and the ambience is wonderful. We can sit and catch up. Then we'll come back here for dessert in the coffee shop. Having you visit is the perfect excuse to ignore calories today."

They soon sat at a cozy table on the back patio of the City Bakery, Holly tucking into quiche with a side salad and Lydia enjoying homemade chicken salad.

"When did you open Barbers' Books?" Lydia asked. "It's charming. I love the layout of the store and the little coffee shop in back."

Holly stirred a spoonful of sugar into her tea. "When I left the farm and went to college, I studied retail management. I worked part-time at Barnes and Noble during college, and they offered me an under-management position after graduation. I stayed with them, moved up in position, and lived in an apartment as a happy single, until I met Wade Barber." She laughed. "It's funny that what got us talking the first time we met is that both of us grew up around apple farming in Haywood County."

"So, Wade is related to the Barbers who started the orchard outside of Waynesville?"

Holly nodded. "Yes, and both of us had left our farm origins and developed an infatuation with books. Wade worked as a book rep for one of the major book companies then." She stopped to eat a few bites. "When we met we were already in our forties, if you remember."

"And then you *didn't* come home and get married in the family church." Lydia smiled. "I heard about that often enough."

"Well." Holly rolled her eyes. "Giving Mother an opportunity for an event wasn't one of my priorities. We got married on an Alaskan cruise ship—much more our kind of thing. We cruised for our honeymoon, saw the Northern Lights and watched whales." She smiled. "Then, eight years ago, Wade and I started the bookstore here. Wade recently retired from Pearson and is now helping me in the store full-time. We make enough together to stay ahead, and we both love having our own place."

Holly asked Lydia questions then about the boys in Atlanta and about her new job at Western. Then she leaned back and crossed her arms. "Well, we've been nice and social up until now, Lydia, but I can tell by how you've stirred your salad around so many times that you have something else on your mind. Why don't you just spit it out? You know I'm very direct. Are you having regrets that you moved back to North Carolina? Are you and John having problems living near each other?"

Lydia wrinkled her brow at Holly's questions. "I don't regret coming back to the mountains, even though I miss the boys, Aunt Martha, and some of the friends I made in Atlanta. I feel much more contented and at home here." She paused. "As for the job, I'm excited about that and I still think it's a good opportunity for me. All my visits to campus, including the one today, have been positive."

"And John?" Holly lifted an eyebrow in question.

Lydia sighed. "That's the part I have questions about."

"He hasn't been hard on you, has he?"

"No. No." Lydia waved her hand. "If anything, I've been hard on him. I keep pushing to talk out problems from the past, and John just wants to pretend they never happened. 'Let the past be the past,' as he says."

Holly nodded. "Yeah, John likes to sidestep difficult situations and relationships. As he says, 'Tend to the apples and move on.' "

"Why does he do that, Holly?" Lydia put a hand on her hip. "Sidestep around problems like they're not even there? Say, 'It'll work out,' or 'It'll get better with time' about everything?"

Holly pushed her empty plate aside. "It's how John learned to cope when he was a boy, I think, with a home life that was never healthy." She signaled to the waitress for more tea. "Things were better in my younger years. Daddy's parents lived in Main House, and they ran the farm at that time. They were both gracious, warm, hardworking individuals. They set the tone for the farm and were beloved in the community. Mother never really fit into what I like to refer to as the 'Cunningham mold.' As she candidly told me one day during one of her famous hissy fits, she'd married Daddy to 'marry well,' to combine two well-respected Haywood families—and she reminded me that I needed to take a proper pride in our heritage, always keeping in mind my place in the community." She shook her head. "All this lecturing was due to my infamous infraction of daring to date a local boy Mother considered unsuitable."

Lydia closed her eyes. "That sounds so much like Estelle. I can hear her voice in my mind."

"I bet you can still see that finger she always shook at you when she got on one of her bandwagons." Holly laughed, wagging her own finger in the air.

"How can you laugh about it, Holly?" Lydia said and winced.

"You have to find defense mechanisms in order to live with an autocratic, domineering sort of person like my mother. A child—and even an adult—needs to find ways to cope and stay sane. I coped by staying out of Mother's way when I was very young. Later I learned to laugh and be defiant." She stopped, pushing her glasses up on her nose. "I often think John coped by looking past the difficult times and choosing not to see them, by never rocking the waters, by always going along to get along. When you live in a no-win environment as a child, you learn to find ways to function in that environment. Basically, you either submit or you fight. And with Estelle Cunningham, fighting never accomplished much."

"How well I remember." Lydia sighed.

Holly smiled at her. "You fought, Lydia, and I fought. And eventually we had to leave because we wouldn't submit. John didn't fight. He went along, and so he was able to stay."

"But isn't that cowardly?"

"Not really in the situation. It was more a form of realism."

She grinned. "I had psychiatric counseling, and it helped me get free of believing I could have changed things by my behavior. I couldn't have."

"That sounds like what John said—that you sometimes need to realize when you can't change someone, so you change yourself."

Holly spread her hands. "You see? John got it figured out long before we did. He realized Mother wasn't a person you could reason with in a normal way, so he learned to sidestep her."

"He compromised, Holly." Lydia leaned forward in irritation. "He let her get her way even when she was wrong."

"And you're still angry at him for the way he coped." Holly reached a hand across the table to take Lydia's. "If John had fought, Lydia, he would have needed to leave as we did. And he loved the farm deeply, like a man loves a woman."

Holly's face softened. "When I look back, I see how things changed the most for John at two pivotal points. The first was when Stuart died."

Lydia well remembered stories of John and Holly's brother, who died at nine of lockjaw.

"A tragic death and hard on all of us," Holly continued. "But especially on Mother. In an odd way, Stuart was the only one of us Mother truly loved. The first son, the heir, and named after her father, Judge Stuart Whitmeyer. He even looked like Grandfather Whitmeyer." Holly smiled at the memory. "Stuart coped by flattering and joking his way around Mother—and it worked. He was the only one of us who seemed able to get his way with her. Stuart was funny, charismatic, and a natural charmer. I shudder to think of the ladies' man Stuart might have become if he'd lived. He could wrestle money and favors out of Mother with sweet talk and smarmy compliments. He even talked her into keeping a dog in the house, and you know how she felt about animals indoors." She paused, looking away in thought. "Whenever Stuart came around, John and I might have disappeared into the woodwork for all she noticed. Stuart lit up the day for her."

"John never told me that."

"I doubt he saw it. I was eleven when John was born and Stuart was eight. A year later, Stuart died. Mother grieved for him for years. She didn't even want to care for John, who was only a baby then. My grandmother Mary and I raised him." She smiled. "I always think that's why John turned out so well. Mother hardly noticed him until he started his teens. Then she realized more children weren't forthcoming and that John would be the heir. During that same period, our grandparents passed away, and Mother and Daddy moved from the Manager's House, where the Sheppards live now, to Main House. That's when Mother really morphed into another being."

"What do you mean?"

"She became the Grand Dame of Cunningham Farm, taking over our Grandmother Mary's role as mistress of the farm and easily moving into a role of dominance over my father. Dad could never see fault in Mother, you see, and he always expected John and me to work to see that Mother 'didn't get upset,' as he called it. In short, he expected us to find a way to get along with her even if she acted unreasonably. If upsets occurred between us, Mother always won. It was rare that my father asserted his will over hers in matters of the home."

Lydia's mouth dropped open. "So your father set the example for John of going along, of not rocking the boat, and of letting Estelle win in all matters?"

"I suppose so." Holly tapped her chin. "I never thought about it that way, but John did begin to adopt Daddy's ways of coping with Mother's temperament without argument or dispute."

"Do you think John sees this? Do you think he understands the situations that led him to think and act as he's done?"

Holly shrugged. "Probably not." She sipped at her tea. "I know Mother paid little attention to your boys, or Mary Beth, either, until Daddy died and she suddenly realized the boys would be the future of the farm."

"You're right, Holly." Lydia stared at her, knowing her mouth had dropped open as she did. "It was when Grandpa Will died that Estelle suddenly focused her attention on J. T. and the twins, grooming them, as you say, to be potential Cunningham Farm heirs."

"Mercy, I pity them that time." Holly shook her head. "I can remember how Mother focused on me when I hit my teenage years. She started critiquing every action I took, every garment I wore, every word I spoke." Her eyes caught Lydia's. "She went after you like that, too—to some degree from the very first when you married John, but more so after Daddy died and you and John moved into Hill House. I saw it every time I came to visit."

"And I remember you stood up for me." Lydia smiled at her. "That's when I started to love you so much, Holly."

"Well, I wasn't around often." She shrugged off the compliment. "But I felt proud of you when you took a job at the college to help the farm recover and to help John. Mother gave you a fit for going out to work, I know, but I thought it was wonderful you chose to do that. You could have loaded up the kids and left right then, gone back home to your folks. Some women do when hard times hit. That's when I knew you really loved John and the farm."

"Thanks for that, Holly." Lydia looked down at her plate. "But don't be too complimentary. Working orchestrated a way for me to escape from Estelle every day, too."

"No." Holly waved a hand at her. "Work became rewarding to you, Lydia. Don't condemn yourself for finding a place of meaning for yourself while you worked to save the farm. I always thought it fair justice that you discovered yourself during that time—forged new goals and a purpose for your life. Started working on your master's while you could get your classes free at Western. Began to make a career niche for yourself."

"Did you fault me when I took the job working for Martha at Georgia Tech, when I moved to Atlanta and left John?"

She shook her head. "Not me, Lydia. You ask Wade. I predicted the day would come when you'd jump at a chance to get away from Estelle. It tickled me when the boys decided to go along with you. How did that come about? I never knew exactly."

Lydia smiled at the waitress who stopped to refill their tea and to ask if they wanted dessert before continuing. "J. T. was a junior in high school then. He wanted desperately to go to college and study architecture after graduation. Billy Dale, like his grandfather Howard—my father—was interested in engineering and Parker in landscape design. Georgia Tech had wonderful programs in all these areas." Lydia added sweetener and lemon to her tea and stirred it, remembering. "Estelle refused to consider the boys leaving the area to attend college after graduation, and she adamantly opposed any career interest they voiced except working on the farm in some way. Contentions and fights became daily patterns in those years, and J. T. started threatening to run off and join the army as soon as he turned eighteen. The twins soon began to make similar threats."

Lydia bit her lip. "The boys felt angry at their father, too, for not supporting them more in their career leadings and for not defending me when Estelle lit into me—or them—daily about one thing or another." She stopped to sip her tea, remembering again. "Estelle blamed me that the boys entertained career aspirations other than farm management, and she attacked me in some way nearly every day—calling the boys 'out of order,' 'rebellious', 'ungrateful,' or 'defiant.' Things had really come to a head in our home."

"Where did Mary Beth stand in all of this?"

Lydia grimaced. "Most of the time she stood with her grandmother. She wanted peace in our home. She wanted her brothers to not be mad anymore and to not leave the valley. In a surprising way, she and her grandmother became close through the years when I worked outside the home at Western. Estelle kept Mary Beth every day while I worked, you see, and Mary Beth's gentle temperament and malleability didn't create difficulties between the two."

Holly crossed her arms. "Let's be honest, Lydia. Rebecca Albright told me Estelle poisoned the girl against you as soon she got her off to herself. She convinced her you didn't really love her or you 'wouldn't have gone off and left her in order to work at that college.' I can just hear her saying it, too, because she said it to me on several occasions. She never appreciated all you did through those years to help pay off the pile of debts that had accumulated during Daddy's illness and repeated hospital stays."

"She didn't help my relationship with Mary Beth, that's true." Lydia spoke the words with a tight nod.

"So, what's that relationship like now?"

"Strained." Lydia let out a long breath. "We seem to artfully avoid saying all the things we're both thinking whenever we get together."

"So bring it out in the open." Holly's eyes met Lydia's. "In loving honesty, Lydia, you simmer everything inside too much and often fail to express yourself as you should."

"I know, but I am getting better. Living on my own all these years has strengthened me."

"Good." Holly pushed back her dark, short hair, graying now just as Estelle's had. Holly's resemblance to her mother still jolted Lydia, although Holly stood taller than the more petite Estelle had and possessed a fuller figure.

While Lydia's thoughts drifted, Holly returned to their former subject. "So, when you went to Atlanta, you had in mind that J. T. could follow and get his education at Georgia Tech while you worked."

"That's it exactly. It was one reason Martha called to offer me the job—to give that chance to her nephews." She tapped a nail on the table. "The other was because she knew how unhappy and miserable I'd become."

"And I well remember heck-fire broke loose when you accepted that position and told John and Estelle you planned to move to Atlanta."

Lydia nodded. "I told John the move was to pave the way for the boys to go to college and to break the rising tension at the farm. I admitted to him, too, that I'd been unhappy and that my parents, Aunt Martha, and I all agreed a separation and a change for a time might be good for everyone."

"That's a much nicer way to put it than to tell them to eat dirt."

Lydia laughed. "Heavens, I love to be with you, Holly. You help me to laugh about the most awful things."

"Not everyone would understand what you went through, but I do." Holly took the check from the waitress. "I felt like I was reliving my earlier life every time I visited and watched my mother go at you and the boys. I hated that there was so little I could do about it."

Lydia pulled out her purse to look for her billfold, but Holly waved her off. "No, this one's on me, dear. I invited you to lunch and am delighted you came." She reached a hand across to pat Lydia's. "We're Estelle-survivors, you and I—John, too, although I'm not sure he sees it the same way we do." Holly paused. "You know, from what I hear from friends in the valley, I don't think Mary Beth had such a sweet go of it with Estelle when she returned with the twins, or later when she nursed Estelle through the cancer that took her life. When you get some time with your girl, you may find she's more in tune with you, and with all you endured from her grandmother, than you might think."

Lydia's eyes brightened. "Do you think so?"

"I'd say it's a strong possibility." Holly put some cash on the table with the ticket and stood up. "Come on, Lydia. Let's go back to the store and get a piece of red velvet cake to top off a nice day. A lady in the area bakes every day for the coffee shop, and I promise you, her red velvet cake is a delicacy to die for. On our way, we can swing into the Mast General Store. I want to get the twins a couple of toys to send back with you."

CHAPTER 8

Monday morning found John, Mary Beth, and the twins, along with Ela and Manu, at breakfast at Main House, getting ready for another day.

"Billy Dale, do *not* slurp your juice." Mary Beth glanced up from the section of the newspaper lying by her plate.

He grinned. "I can make even better slurp sounds if I want to."

"I'm sure you can, but don't, okay? It's not nice manners to slurp or to let people hear you drinking or eating."

"It's not nice manners to put corn on your teeth, to make smiles with orange slices, or to play with your food, either," Bucky added with six-year-old authority, waving his cereal spoon in the air.

"That's right." Mary Beth's attention shifted to her father. "Daddy, there's an article in the paper today about the ghost sightings."

"Cool!" Billy Dale leaned across the table, trying to see the paper. "Are there pictures?"

"Awww. You can't take pictures of ghosts," Bucky told him. "Everybody knows that."

"There are no such things as ghosts." Mary Beth spoke each word slowly and emphatically. "There are spirits, good and bad, and angels, good and bad—and sometimes people discern or see these. However, good spirits and angels never flap about trying to frighten people. If you remember in your Bible stories, one of the first things an angel usually says is 'fear not.' However, spirits from the dark side are likely to say or do anything—having no good intent and originating from the father of lies."

"That's the devil." Billy Dale stuck two fingers up over his head.

"Yes, and evil spirits from the devil probably get a big kick out of frightening and deceiving little boys and getting people to believe in ghosts."

"Aww, shoot." Bucky wrinkled his nose. "So, you don't think ghosts are dead people?"

"Absolutely not, although you hear people talking as though ghosts are dead people floating around trying to get revenge or find peace."

Billy Dale paused around a large bite of pancake. "I see ghosts of dead people on TV all the time."

John laughed. "Well, surely you boys know that half or more of what you see on television is made up to entertain people. On TV, dogs dance and talk. Butterflies sing. People have supernatural powers and can fly. And athletes tell you they love a certain kind of cereal for breakfast or a style of athletic shoes to run in, when they may not like either—and all for a big paycheck."

"Daddy John is right." Mary Beth poured herself another cup of coffee. "Television is all about making money and providing stories and fantasies to entertain people."

Billy Dale puffed out his lip. "You guys are taking all the fun out of this. It's cooler to think the ghost is that Indian, mad because he got murdered up on the ridge, or Nance Dude out to get little kids."

"There are no such things as ghosts in the Christian view." Mary Beth sent Billy Dale a sharp glance. "People don't become ghosts when they die. They may 'give up the ghost,' meaning their spirits leave their bodies, but then their spirits go on to heaven or to hell. They don't hang around causing trouble, trying to take revenge, or haunting places or buildings."

"Your mother is sharing wise words with you." John took a last sip of coffee and stood up. "And the more likely explanation of the ghost sightings around here is that someone is playing a prank for some reason. If that's so, that individual could be dangerous. Maybe mentally unstable. I want you boys to promise me you won't go to the Upper Farm around the area where you saw this ghost again, or go across Indian Creek above the ridge where other folks have witnessed these sightings. It might not be safe."

Mary Beth folded up her paper, got up, and walked around the table to give both boys a kiss. "Daddy John is taking me to work at the store, since Clyde is fixing my car. You boys be good while I'm working today and you mind Ela and Manu."

"Okay." Bucky sent Ela a devilish grin. "Maybe we'll go watch *Ghost Hunters* on TV."

"Merciful heaven." Ela rolled her eyes. "I'll sure be glad when all this ghost business is resolved."

Heading down the Farm Road in the truck a short time later, Mary Beth asked, "Daddy, what do you think is really behind the ghost sightings?"

He shook his head. "I don't know, Bee," he said, using her childhood nickname. "The police department is looking into it, but they haven't found any clues to lead them to affirmative answers yet."

"Well, I don't like any of it."

Pulling up at the store, he followed her out of the car and inside the building. "While I'm here, I'll bring in those boxes from the back storeroom that were delivered yesterday."

"Thanks." She tucked her purse into a cabinet under the register. "Most of the boxes contain apple-related gift items. I'm gearing up for the apple season to come."

John smiled. "I think we'll see a good crop of Early June apples this year. That will give you some apples to sell sooner than usual. I'll go check the rows later today and see how they're coming along."

Mary Beth put a hand on his arm. "How are things coming along with you and Mom?"

John's eyes narrowed and then he stiffened.

"Oh, don't get all defensive, Daddy." She leaned a hip against the counter. "I just meant in general. I know you've been to Hill House a time or two and that you took Mom to Cataloochee Ranch to clog Friday night. I wish I could have seen that. I used to love watching the two of you dance."

"We had a good time. She enjoyed herself." His lips twitched into a smile. "Vance Coggins said he wished you'd come along to sing with him and the band."

She smiled. "I'd like to do that again soon. I promised him I'd sing with the group the next time they got scheduled at the Stompin' Ground."

"Let me know when that is." He selected a Tootsie Roll from a candy barrel and tucked it in his pocket. "I'll bring your mom down one night. She said she'd like to hear you sing."

Mary Beth drummed her fingers on the counter. "I still feel strained with her. I wish I didn't, but it's been so long since we were close."

"Go up and talk to her at Hill House on your own one afternoon. See if you can break the ice, get her to sharing." He reached over to touch his daughter's cheek fondly. "I talked to her a time or two like that, and I think it's helped."

"Do you think Mom will be mad when she finds out we're really not having financial problems and didn't need her to rent Hill House to help us out?" Mary Beth bit her lip.

John shrugged. "She might get whipped up at first, but I think when you explain that you and Rebecca cooked the idea up so you could spend time with her again, she might work herself past it. Might even feel flattered."

"I hope so." She slipped on a red Cunningham Farm Store apron, reaching around to tie it in back. "I need to open the store, Daddy." She looked toward the big clock on the wall. "Ela said to remind you to take that basket of fresh vegetables by the church for the minister."

"I'll remember," he said, heading for the door.

A quarter mile down Black Camp Gap Road, John looked for the turn to Fairview Methodist Church, sitting like a beacon on a hilltop at a rise in the road. The historic redbrick church, with its high, Gothic steeple and lovely old stained-glass windows, had been built with the same brick used for Cunningham's Main House. The Cunningham family had donated the land and much of the money for the construction of the church, as well.

Mother certainly told me that often enough. John rolled his eyes at the memory.

He walked across the church lawn, after parking the car, to let himself in the iron-fenced cemetery, scattered with small and large monuments of church members gone by. The Cunningham plots lay near the back boundary of the cemetery, in almost a miniature cemetery of their own with so many markers now.

John took off his hat at his parents' graves, the joint stone of Mary and John Cunningham's standing next to them. Stuart's monument stood a space or two away, with a white granite angel atop it. It always made John sad to see it.

"Hello, John." Pastor Oliver Wheaton called his name as he walked across the cemetery to join him. He reached out to shake John's hand.

"I saw you as I went out the door to put birdseed in the feeders." He pointed toward an array of feeders near the side of the church.

John laughed. He couldn't help himself. "Maybe you'd better not put those feeders so near the windows by the pulpit area."

A flush ran up the minister's young face. "You may have a good thought there." He looked toward the feeders. "I guess you saw my attention drift the other Sunday. Right in the middle of the sermon, I looked out and saw a yellow-throated warbler. It's a rare bird for this area. Bright yellow throat and distinctive birdsong." He paused, looking toward the feeders again. "I'm fond of birds."

"Nothing wrong with that, Oliver," John said. "Country folk, like here in the valley, understand a love for wildlife."

A tall man, nearly John's own height, the young minister looked directly into John's eyes. "But I need to keep my avocations and my vocations separate. Is that what you're trying to say?"

"You're just starting out here, Pastor. You preach a good message, are liked by all the people in the church. No sense in giving folks something to talk about."

He considered this, straightening his belt as he did. "You know, I think those feeders would fit nicely near that side fence covered in vines." He pointed to the area. "I could easily see any bird visitors from my study window on the back side of the church, but *not* from the pulpit." He grinned.

"Good plan." John smiled. "Maybe you could use something about birds in one of your sermons. There's a lot of references in the Good Book to birds, flowers, and trees. You might even make a series of it. Turn something that caught folks' attention into a message."

"Hmmm. You might have a good thought there, too." He glanced at the grave below them. "Your brother?"

"Yep. Died just before his tenth birthday. Hard on all the family."

"Hard on you?"

"Not in the way you mean. I was a late child and only a baby when Stuart died. But it left me the only son to carry on with the orchard."

"Did you have other aspirations?"

"Not really." John rubbed his jaw. "But my mother wasn't an easy woman to live with. That caused problems with my family after I married."

"Is that why your wife and boys left?" Oliver asked candidly. He lifted his hands. "As you say, it's a small valley and people talk."

"Yeah, I reckon that was the main reason why."

"I hear she's back and folks are wondering if you'll reconcile. Is that what you want, John?"

John closed his eyes. "I never stopped wanting that from the day she left, but it's hard getting back to a place of trust after all that's happened. She keeps wanting to look back, rehash the past. I feel that what's past is past. Isn't that biblical?"

"Perhaps, but things still need to be talked out, even old issues, in order to move on. Especially with women."

"You been married?"

"No, not yet." Oliver laughed. "But I've pastored and counseled a lot of women in the ten years I've been in the ministry, in two different churches. They like to talk things out more than men, need to talk things out to move on." He grinned. "You might want to change your plans about where to locate your own feeders, too—decide to put them out more in the open."

"I get your point. But I'm not a man who likes to get all analytical. I'm more a man who likes to deal with today and move on."

"Even if it means moving on alone?"

"Ouch. You're direct."

"Sometimes it pays to be." Oliver ran a hand over the top of the angel on the grave. "And sometimes we don't like to talk about things of the past because we don't want to remember them. We want to bury them, even from ourselves. I'm not sure that's always healthy. Here's a scripture related to that idea you might want to think on from First Corinthians 13: 'Love is patient . . . and rejoices with the truth.' When hope and trust are lost in a relationship, you have to be willing to give the patience and love to restore it, even if that means dragging up some old memories you'd as soon bury and forget." He glanced down at the graves. "These loved ones have gone on, but the ones who remain are precious. And time is short."

"Nicely put, Pastor, but what about the scripture in Philippians that advises to 'forget those things which are behind, and reach forth to those things which are ahead'?"

"Very good." Oliver smiled. "I like a man who knows his Bible, but let me add that there's a comma after those words in Philippians 3, and the next part of the sentence urges to 'press toward the mark for the prize of the high calling of God in Christ Jesus.' I believe that scripture in full refers primarily to moving on in the Lord and onward in our walk in God." He clapped John on the back. "But that was a good save, John. You showed quick thinking there."

John couldn't keep from grinning, but then as he looked toward the graves before him, the grin slipped from his face. "You'd think Lydia could at least meet me halfway."

"Let me ask you this, John. Did you ever go after Lydia when she left, tell her you wanted her to come back?"

"Well, no." John kicked at a rock on the ground. "She's the one who left. I didn't ask her to."

"And she's the one who's come back." Oliver put a hand on John's arm. "A woman who had no interest in reconciling would never return to the place where her husband lives, John, and especially to a rental house right on his farm property."

John jerked his eyes up.

Oliver's gaze grew tender. "She's already met you halfway, John Cunningham. Now you have to walk the other half distance—and do whatever it takes—if you want to win. Do you?"

John frowned, stepping away from him. "You're a dang meddling man, Oliver Wheaton."

"I might have said the same about you, coming here and hinting I move my bird feeders and keep my mind on my Sunday sermon."

John laughed. "You're right there. When are you going to come over to the house for dinner? I'd like for you to get to know the family better."

"I'll gladly come anytime. Ela Raintree's cooking is legend around here."

John clapped the minister on the back. "Speaking of which, that's why I stopped by. Ela sent you a basket from the garden, and I think she tucked in one of her poppy seed breads, too. I have it in the truck for you."

The men walked back to John's truck, laughing.

CHAPTER 9

Tuesday, Lydia spent the day quietly at Hill House. She took pictures around the property, including photos of the growing kittens, and shared them online with her sons. Lydia fed the kittens, Trudi and Ava, soft, canned cat food now, mixed with a little milk. She enjoyed training them and watching them romp and play together. They entertained her, made her laugh, and kept her from becoming lonely in the evenings.

She sat on the front porch in the late afternoon now, curled up in a wicker chair reading, the front door propped open to tempt the kittens to come outside. They needed to learn to navigate the outdoors, but Lydia knew they also needed supervision until they felt comfortable and safe outside. Ava and Trudi crept tentatively out on the porch to begin sniffing and exploring the area, but when an unexpected noise interrupted the afternoon silence, they jumped in surprise and scampered back into the house.

"Silly cats." She laughed at them. "That was only a crow you heard. See it sitting over there on the fence? He's supposed to be afraid of you—not the other way around."

Wide-eyed, the two slunk back out on the porch after a few minutes, fears soon forgotten as they started batting a small pinecone between them. However, the sound of a car coming up the driveway sent them scurrying into the house again.

Lydia looked up to see Mary Beth getting out of a small pickup truck. She lifted a hand to wave as she caught Lydia's eye.

"Hi." She stopped at the bottom of the porch steps. "I thought I'd stop by and bring you a loaf of Ela's poppy seed bread. She went on a baking spree yesterday." She walked up to bring Lydia the offering.

"Thanks." Lydia set it on the small table beside her. "Do you want to sit down?" She gestured to the wicker chair across from her. "I can make some iced tea, cut us a slice of Ela's bread. I'm eager to sample it."

Mary Beth shuffled nervously as Lydia stood up. "If it doesn't sound silly, maybe we could have hot tea—like we used to."

Lydia smiled, glancing at her watch. "What a good idea. It's four p.m., and as your thoroughly English grandmother Howard would say, exactly the right time for afternoon tea." She held open the door for her daughter. "I'll make Earl Grey Lavender tea, dig out my bone-china teacups, and open some boxes of biscuits to accompany our bread. You can help me make the tea and set the tray."

Her daughter's face lit up in a smile. "You brought your tea things to Hill House?"

Lydia felt her heart catch. "Of course. I have too much English blood to forget something that important." She moved into the kitchen, putting a kettle of water on the stove to boil and retrieving a chintz teapot from a shelf over the stove.

"Oh." Mary Beth caught her breath. "It's your Chatsford teapot, the one Grandmother gave you. You still have it."

"I do." Lydia smiled, and turned to get floral-patterned teacups and a matching bone-china tea tray from the china cabinet. She set two teacups, saucers, and spoons on the tray, adding white cloth napkins beside them and a two-tiered silver tea tray. From the cabinet, she took down two boxes of biscuits, one vanilla cream, the other chocolate-raspberry.

While searching for the loose tea on the kitchen shelf, she said, "Mary Beth, you can cut slices of the poppy seed bread and put that and some of those biscuits on the tea tray. Once you open those biscuit boxes, there's a metal tin on the shelf you can use to put the extra biscuits in." Lydia gestured in that direction. When she turned around, she found Mary Beth holding the floral-patterned tin box, tears streaming down her face. "Oh Bee, whatever is the matter?"

Mary Beth's shoulders shook. "I've missed you so much, Mother. I am so sorry about everything."

Lydia moved to gather her daughter into her arms, smoothing her hair with loving hands, weeping now herself. "Me too, darling. Me too."

"I know I acted awful to you and the boys before you left. Said such horrible things." She sniffled, laying her head on Lydia's shoulder. "But I didn't understand why you wanted to leave and I didn't want you to go. Later, when I grew older and began to understand things better, I didn't know how to get back to where we'd been." The words poured out. "I started so many letters and then tore them up. I didn't know what to say."

"You were very young when I left. Only thirteen."

"That doesn't excuse me for being mean." Mary Beth sent Lydia an anguished look. "I wouldn't talk to you on the phone all those years or answer your letters. I wouldn't come visit when you invited me." She pulled away, lifting wet eyes to Lydia's. "Grandmother encouraged me not to write or talk to you. She said you didn't love any of us anymore, that you'd turned the boys against us."

Lydia felt herself tense. "I imagine she did. Your grandmother had no fondness for me from the start, Mary Beth. I regret that. I hoped I'd win her affection in time, but I never did. In fact, the more time went on, the more she seemed to dislike me. I never understood it. I spent years and years trying in every way I could to build a loving relationship with her, but I never succeeded. Eventually I gave up trying."

She turned to the teapot, starting to measure out the spoons of loose tea into the infuser, then pouring the hot tea into the pot over the tea.

Mary Beth sat down at the kitchen table. "I came today, hoping we could talk. Hoping to break the awful strain that's been between us." She started opening the packages of biscuits. "Have you felt it?"

"Yes." Lydia set the timer and then came to sit beside her

daughter while the tea steeped. "I hoped things would get better with time."

"This is better, isn't it? Even with the crying, it's real." Mary Beth pulled a paper napkin from the holder on the table and blew her nose. "Can I stay awhile and talk? Having afternoon tea with you feels so much like the happy times we shared when I was a little girl." She touched the cups on the china tray lovingly. "When I saw the old tea tray, cups, and the tin, I simply broke. Maybe it was a good thing." She raised wet eyes to Lydia's. "You don't hate me, do you?"

"How could I ever hate you?" Lydia reached a hand across to stroke her daughter's cheek, starting a singsong rhyme. "*I love you as much as peaches love cream. I love you as much as a king does his queen—*" Her voice softened over the words that she and Mary Beth used to make up together.

Mary Beth interrupted, her eyes brightening. "*I love you as much as daisies love showers. I love you as much as bees love flowers.*" She laughed. "I remember we used to lie on old quilts under the Old Oak and make up those silly rhymes while the boys climbed in the branches."

Hearing the timer, Lydia got up to pour two cups of tea. "Is Old Oak still standing?"

"It is, and my boys climb into its branches now, like we did when I was little." She stirred a little sugar into her tea as Lydia sat down. "Daddy measured that oak last month, and it's over eighteen feet around the base. Some of the limbs spreading out from it are huge now."

Lydia sipped her tea, smiling at the memories.

Mary Beth leaned forward. "I have some things I want to tell you, but first I want to ask about my brothers. Catch me up on them. Please?"

Lydia finished swallowing a bite of Ela's bread, and then went into the living room to retrieve a photo album to bring back with her. She opened it to the first page, turning it around for Mary Beth to see. "Here's a photo of the boys and me that your aunt Martha Howard took this spring. There's J. T. and there's Parker and Billy Dale." She pointed to each one. "Billy likes to be called Will now. All his friends and work colleagues call him that, but I often forget."

"They've grown so much." Mary Beth touched the picture lovingly. "But I'd still have known them."

Lydia turned the page. "Here's our little bungalow in Atlanta near the Botanical Garden. That's your aunt Martha on the porch of her house that sits beside ours." She put a finger on the next page. "These are pictures of Georgia Tech and the building where I worked at Career Services with Aunt Martha." She laughed as Mary Beth studied a street photo. "That's the multi-lane freeway I crossed every day to get to work—and to get practically anywhere. I certainly don't miss that."

Mary Beth studied the pictures, nibbling biscuits and drinking her tea.

"This is J. T. with his wife, Laura." Lydia flipped to another page, filled with photos of her tall son and his trim, blond wife.

"She's very beautiful and looks very sophisticated."

Lydia smiled. "She's both. She majored in visual merchandising and after graduating did window design for a large corporate retailer. When the babies came, she started her own business out of her home, Urban Visual Merchandising and Design. She does window dressing and design for small shops in the Atlanta area that don't have their own in-house window dressers."

Lydia touched a colorful photo of a towheaded little boy and a small toddler with a mass of fair curls. "These are J. T.'s and Laura's two children—Jack, four, and Rachel, who just turned two."

"I can't believe J. T. is a father." Mary Beth shook her head. "Look at him, he looks so mature and polished."

"He works as an architect for Harrison Design. The company creates custom residences and town houses. J. T. started part-time with them as a gofer, running errands and doing low-level tasks while in school. He did his internship with them after graduation, and then moved into a full-time position. Two years ago, he took the Architect Registration Examination to become a licensed architect." Lydia smiled. "He's doing well. He and

Laura lived in Aunt Martha's garage apartment when they first married but later bought a small home."

Mary Beth turned the page to pictures of Will. "And here's Billy Dale." She pointed. "I know he's a civil engineer, like Grandfather Howard."

"Yes." Lydia smiled at the picture of Will in his construction hat. "Will works as a construction engineer and surveyor for Valentino and Associates in Smyrna. The company does boundary and topographical surveys, construction staking and layout, and design mapping. In two years, Will can get his license to be a professional engineer and surveyor in the state of Georgia."

"He must love working outdoors."

"Yes, J. T. can handle a lot of time inside drawing plans, but Will is never happier than when trekking over some wilderness area surveying."

Mary Beth smiled. "Sounds like him."

Lydia saw Mary Beth's eyes drift to soft-faced Amelia, dressed in a lace blouse and period skirt. "That's Will's wife, Amelia, a lovely, sweet girl," Lydia explained. She reached over to the kitchen counter to grab her purse. "She made this purse for me, did the lavish embroidery herself, created the design. She's a very gifted girl—majored in textile design—and she clerks at a vintage clothing store right now. Like Laura, she's developing her own business on the side, creating embroidered and decorative items. Several stores already carry her work, and she's developing a Web site to show her designs."

Mary Beth studied the pictures of Amelia and Billy Dale. "They live in Aunt Martha's apartment now, don't they?"

"Yes. Like J. T. and Laura did, they're saving for a house and hope to find one by next year. In the meantime, they're close to Parker, who's still in the bungalow where he and I lived before I returned to Maggie."

"Can he afford to keep it on his own?" Mary Beth looked worried.

"He can now." Lydia smiled. "He just got a nice raise at the Botanical Garden. You remember Parker always loved growing things, and he majored in landscape architecture. Through his last years of high school and all through college, he worked at the Atlanta Botanical Garden near the house. By the time he graduated, he'd developed a real love for the gardens there, and when they offered him the job as the exhibition coordinator, he took it. It's not exactly in the field Parker studied for. As the co-ordinator, he develops, plans, and implements the exhibition program, and he organizes and manages any events, like the many community and educational activities held at the Garden all through the year."

"And he likes it?"

"Actually, he loves it." Lydia smiled. "We all love the Botanical Garden. It gave us a green sanctuary near our home in the big city. The boys and I walked, played, picnicked, and went to the parks and pool there whenever we hungered to see flowers, green grass, trees, or the lake. It's a truly beautiful oasis right in the heart of the city."

"Daddy said Parker is engaged now."

"Her name is Marie Carroll." Lydia pointed to a picture of a dark-haired, smiling girl. "She is a first grade teacher at Morning-side Elementary, and she met Parker when she brought a class of students to the Garden. They plan to get married at the end of summer. Marie's rental lease is up then, and she'll move in with Parker now that I'm leaving. Before that, they planned the op-posite, for Parker to move in with Marie."

"You'll go back for the wedding?"

"Absolutely! I can hardly wait. I'm very fond of Marie. She makes Parker laugh and keeps him from becoming too serious. They're a nice match."

Mary Beth dropped her eyes, fussing with her teacup.

"Bee, I think you and your boys, and your father, should go to the wedding with me. Maybe even Ela and Manu."

Mary Beth's eyes widened. "Do you think they'd want me to come?"

"Yes, I think they would." She put a hand over Mary Beth's. "The boys never meant for you to be hurt when they went to

Atlanta with me." She laughed. "Parker always hoped you'd come down and join us, maybe go to school at Tech, too."

"I sort of cancelled my chances of going to college when I married Sonny."

"Did you have any special career plans before that?" Lydia asked gently.

"Only foolish ones." Mary Beth shook her head. "I didn't have anyone to help me with sensible plans, to guide me on a career path, or to acquaint me with options based on my interests." She laughed, a sad, hollow sound. "Of course, my mother was good at all those things, but I was too proud and angry to ask her for help. I thought I knew everything myself." She blew out a long sigh. "In senior year I fell in love with Sonny Harper, and I got caught in his wake, dated him, sang with him and the Flat Ridge Boys. I felt special around school being a singer. I began to think I might make it big, go to Hollywood or something. That's what Sonny and the band wanted, to take off and go after their big break in California after graduation."

"Your father said he didn't realize you and Sonny were growing serious."

"Don't blame Daddy for anything I did. I hid from him, and Grandmother, that Sonny and I were even dating for a time. I told them I only sang occasionally with the band, and I lied about where we sang sometimes, too. They wouldn't have approved of most of the places. Or of my thoughts or plans." She frowned. "I knew I'd be doomed if Grandmother ever imagined I wished for anything beyond marrying locally and staying on or near the farm. She counted on me marrying a farmer to join Daddy in the orchard, you see, to have sons to work and carry on the Cunningham legacy. As she reminded me often enough, everyone else had abandoned their duty."

Lydia winced.

"Don't feel bad. I had started to understand more about my grandmother by then. In my own way, I'd grown angry and begun to see how she helped drive you all away." She traced her hand across the photo book. "And look what my brothers have become. They got their chance to find their own dreams and had someone to encourage them."

She raised her eyes to Lydia's. "I know you wrote and asked me to come to Atlanta. You told me I could stay with you and go to college, with free tuition like the boys. I did read the letters that you sent me through Rebecca." She bit her lip. "I guess you know Grandmother tore up a lot of your earlier letters before I could ever read them. Didn't you?"

Lydia nodded.

"I figured that's why you started sending letters through Rebecca later." She crossed her arms. "Rebecca has been a good friend to me."

"I'm glad." Lydia got up to pour two more cups of tea from the Chatsford teapot. Then she sat down and showed Mary Beth the last of the pictures in the album before closing it at last.

"Bee, tell me why you married Sonny and what happened."

"It's embarrassing." She twisted her hands.

"Then you don't have to tell me about it." Lydia smiled at her, reaching over to cut another small slice of the poppy seed bread to nibble on. "I'm just happy you're here, to have us talking."

"No, I want you to know." Her eyes shifted in memory. "It's not a long story. I went to the senior prom with Sonny. We went to a party afterward, drank a little too much, got silly, ran off, and got married." She put her fingers over her eyes for a moment. "I was so young, and it was prom night. Sonny looked so mature and handsome in his tux, talked about all the wonderful things we could do together after graduation. His plans sounded so exciting—traveling with the Flat Ridge Boys, singing in other cities."

She shifted in her seat. "I had no real plans, no ideas about what I would do after graduation. All my friends had plans for college or starting jobs. And I was in limbo—working around the farm, knowing I didn't have a ghost of a chance to leave to try anything else." She paused, remembering. "Holly worked in the bookstore in Asheville then. She said she'd get me a job over there and that I could come and live with her and Wade until I saved enough for my own place. Grandmother went totally ballistic when I brought up the idea. She freaked out and screamed at me, then practically snubbed me for a week, withdrawing her affection, making cutting comments at the table." She shrugged. "You know how she could be."

"I do." Lydia remembered all too well how Estelle had made her pay when she stepped outside prescribed expectations.

"I felt trapped. Sonny seemed to understand. He called Grandmother 'the old bat,' said I needed to get away from her. He told me he'd take care of me, love me. I believed him. At first, we were happy. We moved into the basement apartment below his parents, and we had fun fixing it up. His mother started letting me help her do hair and nails in her salon, and I started to think, for a while, that maybe I'd become a beautician like her."

"But?" Lydia sipped at her tea.

"It sort of bored me after a while." Mary Beth shrugged. "Wilma is wonderful at her job. You know that. Everybody likes her, and she does good hair and is terrific with people."

Lydia smiled at her. "Often we learn the work that's happiest for us by trying different jobs. There's nothing wrong with that."

"I suppose not, but I felt guilty that I didn't love it like she did." She paused. "Then it started making me throw up every time I came into the shop and we realized I was pregnant. I swear, I couldn't even go in that shop the whole time I carried the twins without the salon smell making me simply green."

Lydia laughed. "For me, it was the smell of gasoline. I had to practically hold my breath every time I got the car filled up."

"Anyway, because I felt bored, I started walking down to the highway from the house to help out at the Harpers' upholstery store." Her eyes fired with enthusiasm. "Sonny's father, Ray Harper, acted so sweet to me. He knew Sonny was traveling a lot with the band and that I felt at loose ends. At first he contrived little things for me to do just to be nice, but I quickly made a place for myself at the store. I organized the office, refurnished the reception room, sorted out all the files, brought order to the shop. You should have seen how awful it looked before I did."

"I remember." Lydia grinned. "Ray and his son Eric did exquisite upholstery work, but their store was a pit."

"Not anymore. I got it clean and organized, started answering the phones, handling the incoming customers. Everybody began to notice, and business picked up for them. Ray started paying me. I worked for him full-time until the twins were born and part-time after, sometimes taking the babies down to the shop or getting Eric's wife, Faye, to watch them."

She dropped her eyes. "It really helped me. Sonny started traveling more and more with the Flat Ridge Boys." Mary Beth twisted her hands. "He wasn't happy I got pregnant, and he hated how I looked when I started showing. When the babies came, he complained when they cried at night or demanded so much of my time during the day. He began drinking and came home really drunk some nights. He didn't act sweet to me at those times."

Lydia leaned over in concern. "Did he hit you, Bee? Hurt you?"

"He never hit me, but he hollered at me. Seemed angry at me all the time, like it was all my fault I'd gotten pregnant. He really freaked out when he learned I was carrying twins. And, of course, I got huge."

She sighed deeply. "Sonny took every opportunity to go on longer and longer trips after that. And he changed more and more. His brother, Eric, told me once that he thought Sonny and some of the boys in the band had started using drugs. Sonny often asked me for what little money I made working for his father." She frowned. "Other times he just stole it. Sonny worked doing deliveries and pickups of furniture for the store, when he wasn't on gigs with the band, but he started getting unreliable with everything. He acted so different, Mother. It scared me sometimes."

"Why didn't you go to your father?"

She hung her head. "I couldn't. Grandmother was already mad at me for marrying Sonny. He wasn't a farmer and he'd ruined her plans. When I tried to talk to her once—troubled about things with Sonny—she told me I'd 'made my bed and had better learn to lie in it.' " Tears formed in her eyes. "She called me a disappointment, said all her grandchildren had failed in their responsibility to the farm and to the family, turned their backs on their legacy. Those words felt so harsh right then when my life was falling apart."

Lydia's heart hurt over her daughter's words. "I'm so sorry I couldn't have helped you more."

. "You tried. Your letters meant a lot to me in that period. Even if I didn't answer them, I appreciated them. If only because you said you loved me."

"I never stopped, not even for a minute." Lydia reached across to touch her daughter's cheek again.

"Mother, I thought so many times of our teas and how we talked and talked over the lovely Yorkshire or Earl Grey teas that your mother sent us. How we shared our hearts while nibbling homemade scones, pastries, or English biscuits—like these."

Lydia smiled. "I order my tea and biscuits through a little import company online now. They have nice things. I'll make you homemade scones again soon, the ones you like with the raisins."

"I can almost taste them."

Lydia leaned back in her chair. "Did Sonny stay in touch with you and the boys after he left? Does he come to see them or help you financially?"

"No to all. And when Daddy learned he deserted me, he came and brought me and the boys home. Billy Ray and Bucky weren't even two yet, and Sonny simply took off to California and left us."

She twisted her hands. "It was awful in some ways coming home to Main House and Grandmother, but it would have been worse to stay with the Harpers. They acted sweet to me, of course, but the whole situation grew terribly embarrassing. Sometimes I worried that they blamed me because Sonny had changed so much and took off from his home and family."

"Oh, surely they didn't." Lydia rewrapped the loaf of poppy seed bread to keep it fresh. "I remember the Harpers being a nice family. It must grieve them that Sonny treated you as he did."

"Yes," she admitted. "But having me and the boys in their home proved to be a constant reminder. A constant hurt."

"I was very proud to learn your father came to get you."

Mary Beth rolled her eyes. "Yes, but you should have heard

Grandmother rant and rave. But Daddy was clever. He told her the Cunninghams would get a bad name in the valley if they didn't take care of their own in a crisis. That it might hurt the family business and our reputation."

Lydia raised an eyebrow as Mary Beth continued.

"He pointed to the boys, sitting at the table in their high chairs, and told her, 'Don't be foolish, Mother—here are your heirs for the orchard. Surely you want these boys growing up on the farm. They're our legacy.'" Mary Beth laughed. "That gave Grandmother a totally new perspective, and she quieted down. She started working to charm her way into the affections of those twins like she'd done to me once. Like she did with my brothers before they started talking about careers beyond farming— wanting to explore something different with their lives."

Lydia thought back to what Mary Beth said about Sonny. "Have the boys seen Sonny at all since he left? Doesn't he ever call or write?"

"Once he came through town on a holiday, dropped in to see his family, and I took the boys there to see him. The boys were three. They barely remember the visit. They do know and understand that their father and I are divorced." She paused. "I divorced him based on desertion after he left me and wouldn't send child support. He's supposed to do that now according to the court, but he never does. Instead, he writes and asks me for money sometimes."

"What?" Lydia felt anger slice through her. "You haven't sent it?"

"Sonny can talk sweet, be very convincing. Apologize and tell me he's turning over a new leaf. That he wants to be a better father to the boys. That he's right on the edge of a once-in-a-lifetime opportunity or is in an unexpected pinch. Needs me to wire him money. Temporarily, of course. As a loan."

"Do you ever get any of this money back?"

"No. Daddy says not to send him any more ever, but sometimes Sonny sends me threatening letters. He calls and threatens things about the boys if I won't help him."

"Oh, Bee." Lydia reached across to take her hand. "Have

you talked to the police about this, or to an attorney? This is serious."

"Daddy did once. But you see, no one really knows where Sonny is right now. Not even his parents. Sometimes he says he's in Vegas, sometimes in California. Once he told me he was in Chicago. He said he'd gotten stuck in an airport in the winter, that he and the band needed a little money to rent a car to get to their next gig. This time, even Devon—one of the other boys in the band—got on the phone and said it was true. He begged me to wire them some money."

Mary Beth sighed. "I guess it was another lie. I never heard back from them, even though I asked them to call me when they got to the next city safely. They never sent back the money, either."

"Oh, Mary Beth, I'm so sorry. It hurts to trust and to be let down."

"It does, but it worries me more that I got another letter from Sonny today." She fished it out of her pocket and unfolded it. "He says he might come through this area on his way to Florida, that their band is going there for some engagements that their manager arranged. He writes that he might want to see the boys, that they ought to know their father."

Lydia scanned the one-page letter Mary Beth laid out for her to see. "It's very vague, isn't it? No specific mention about where he is now, when he will arrive here, or where his band is playing in Florida."

"I know." She crossed her arms. "I feel uncomfortable about him coming through, Mother. The boys have seen a few pictures of their father, but they don't remember much about him. Daddy has basically been their father. They know their Grandad Harper, too, of course, and Sonny's brother, their uncle Eric. They've been happy, despite all that's happened."

"You're worried about them meeting Sonny and how that might affect them."

"Yes. And something doesn't feel right about this. He's never planned a visit like this before. I casually asked Eric the other day if they'd heard from Sonny lately, and he said no. So, he's written me, but he hasn't written his family about stopping through. That seems odd. It makes me feel like he's up to something."

Lydia looked back over the short letter. "Well, he doesn't ask for money here."

"No, and that's a first."

"Have you told your father about this?"

"No," she admitted, twisting a loose strand of hair around her finger.

"Well, tell him. You know I don't keep secrets from your father. You've shared with me, but you need to share with him, too."

Mary Beth smiled. "It sounds funny to hear you say that when you and Daddy have been separated for so long."

Lydia stood and started putting the cups and dishes in the sink to wash. "I've always tried to be honest with your father."

"I know." Mary Beth stood up to help her.

"Don't worry over the dishes. I'll wash them up later." She turned to her daughter with a smile. "Let's sit out on the porch until you need to go. I want to let the kittens go outside again if they will. I'm trying to train them to get used to the outdoors. I want them to be indoor-outdoor cats. Right now the silly things don't even know how to climb a tree or pee in the grass yet. I'm taking them out in the yard and hanging them each on the side of a tree to teach them to climb."

Mary Beth giggled, gathering up both of the kittens in her arms as they headed outside. "How will you teach these two fluffballs to pee in the grass?"

Lydia frowned. "I'm not sure. Hopefully, they'll figure that out. If not, I'll put a little soiled cat litter in a dirt area outside to give them the idea."

Cuddling the kittens, Mary Beth asked, "What did you name them?"

"Ava for the one you found on the store porch, and Trudi for the fluffier one with the black streak on her nose."

"Good names." She put them down gently on the porch so they could explore.

"Where are your boys today?" Lydia asked.

"With Ela. I don't know what I'd do without her. And when she's busy, Nevelyn keeps them. Or Sam's wife, Doris." She smiled. "I'm lucky to have so many helpers, especially since I opened the store."

"You've done a good job with that store—in setting it up, arranging it, and making it successful, from all I hear. I'm proud of you for that."

"Thanks. I remember how you used to talk to Dad and Grandmother about opening a store in that old building. You used good reasons and even had little drawings of what you thought it might look like, why you thought it might be successful. You took me to explore through the building once when you were plotting and planning. I remembered all that when I resurrected the idea to Dad."

Lydia snorted. "I'm surprised your grandmother let you do it at all."

"I threatened to take the boys and leave if she wouldn't give me the opportunity to try it. I told her I needed something to do besides sitting around the house all day. I even threatened to get an apartment in Waynesville and work for Holly or to go to your parents' place in Boone to stay until I could save for a place for my own."

Lydia looked shocked.

Mary Beth just rolled her eyes. "Grandmother and I weren't getting along very well by that time."

"I see."

A flash of irritation crossed Mary Beth's face. "She interfered too much in how I raised the boys. She never wanted us to have any fun, to go anywhere or do anything unrelated to the farm." She flounced in her chair. "If we even played cards or worked a jigsaw puzzle spread out on the table, she'd walk by and make subtle comments about how much time we wasted on foolishness. If I climbed trees with the boys or played tag with them, she said I acted unladylike. If we danced or sang in the house, she frowned and started the vacuum." Mary Beth turned to Lydia. "Ela said she used to do the same things to you, Mother. I remember it a little, but not much."

Mary Beth pulled a piece of string across the porch for the kittens to chase. "Even something like playing with a couple of kittens would be something she'd frown over. Grandmother always acted like having fun, laughing, or cutting up were sins or something. I can still hear her clearing her throat and huffing around with her chin in the air. I got tired of it. I needed something outside the house to do, a way to get out from under her constant eagle eye."

"I'm so pleased she let you open the store." Lydia watched Mary Beth dribble the string down the porch steps so the kittens would venture into the yard.

"Funny." Mary Beth smoothed back a strand of hair, tangled by the summer breeze. "The one good thing that happened from marrying Sonny was that I learned I loved to run a business. I really loved working at Harper's, even in that mess when I first started. I loved arranging everything to function efficiently and to look nice. I loved ordering supplies, dealing with the public, even doing the books." She looked up from where she sat on the porch steps to smile at Lydia. "I'll tell you something if you won't laugh."

"I'll try not to."

"I'm going to school online, working on my degree in business. I don't want to be the only Cunningham without a college degree."

"And why would I laugh at that?"

"Oh, because I'm not doing it the traditional way, I guess." She petted Trudi as the kitten rubbed up against her leg. "But as a working mother, taking courses online works well for me."

"Most colleges are initiating or expanding their online programs for just that reason today."

"Can I ask you something, woman-to-woman?"

Lydia tensed. "What?" she asked.

"What do you think of Neal?"

Lydia relaxed, having expected a personal probe. "Bee, you should know that I love Neal. I practically raised him at our house, playing with J. T. as much as he did. Why do you ask?"

She looked off down the yard. "I think he might be interested in me."

"You think?"

"Okay, I *know* he's interested in me, but it feels weird."

"Why?"

"Because I've known him forever, because he was J. T.'s best friend growing up. Because he's older than me."

"Only four years older. That isn't much difference for adults. Only for children."

She shifted uncomfortably. "It scares me thinking about getting involved with someone after all I went through with Sonny." She patted the letter in her pocket. "And because of the problems I still have with Sonny."

"From what John told me, Neal had a failed relationship, too. He got hurt and betrayed. Perhaps you have something in common there."

She pulled the string along for the kittens again. "He's talked to me about that."

"That's good." Lydia's lips twitched. "Has he kissed you?"

"Mother!"

She shrugged. "Just a question."

A flush touched Mary Beth's cheeks. "Not before this weekend. And even then, we were playing night tag with the boys. We raced out into the bushes to hide. I stumbled and tripped. Neal caught me and it just sort of happened." She turned to look at Lydia and wrinkled her nose. "Now I'm going to feel weird when I see him again."

"Meaning this has kicked the friendship up to a new level."

"Yes." She sighed. "And I don't know whether I'm ready for our friendship to go there yet."

"Then talk to Neal about it. He'll give you time." Lydia smiled. "He may feel weird about what happened, too."

"No. He feels smug. I saw it in his eyes."

Lydia tried not to grin. "What do you want now, Mary Beth?"

"I'm not sure." She played with her rings, eyes downcast.

"Was Neal a good kisser?"

Mary Beth looked shocked.

"It's important," Lydia prodded.

She blushed, then grinned. "Better than I might have expected."

"Well, that can sometimes be a big factor in things. Maybe you ought to test that aspect again in a more deliberate setting."

Her eyes twinkled. "I'll give that some thought."

Lydia wisely refrained from any more comments.

Mary Beth glanced at her watch. "You know, I hate to go, but I need to get back and help Ela with dinner." She skipped up the stairs to give Lydia an impulsive hug. Lydia hugged her back with warmth, then watched her daughter walk with a light step out to her truck.

"Love you and see you again soon!" she called out as she climbed in.

Her heart full, Lydia whispered softly to her departing car, "Love you more, Mary Beth. Love you more."

CHAPTER 10

Later in the week, John saw Lydia heading down the driveway at Charlie and Nevelyn Sheppard's house. He was working with Charlie today in the Upper Orchards along with Charlie's son, Chuck; Charlie's father, Sam; and Eugene Sheppard. Too much work waited to go and talk to her, but his eyes followed her.

John noted that she'd caught Eugene Sheppard's attention, too. At eighty-two, he sat on an old barrel under a shade tree, in the supervisory role more common for him these days since he'd passed eighty.

"There goes Lydia," he said. "Nice to see her back around the place." His eyes shifted to John. "You reckon you and she will get back together?"

"I can't rightly say, Eugene." John split open another bag of fertilizer with his knife. Based on Neal's soil tests, they were applying fertilizer in a circle around each tree in this section of the orchard today, six inches out of the drip line. Earlier, they'd weeded around the tree roots.

The old man nodded. "Yep. That Lydia's always been the kind to have a mind of her own." He grinned. "Pretty woman, though. Always was a looker."

John followed Lydia's progress along the drive as he stopped to mop sweat off his face with the bandanna stuck in his back pocket. The sun blazed down relentlessly today, not uncommon for mid-June.

Lydia wore those capri pants she seemed to favor now, in a bright strawberry color with a long, breezy checked shirt over them. She swung an aluminum bucket in one hand. Looked like she might be heading to the ridge area to look for blueberries and blackberries after her visit at Nevelyn's.

"John." Sam Sheppard interrupted his thoughts. "I think we need to upgrade the rodent guards around those young trees we put out in the Side Orchards this spring."

"You seen problems there?"

He nodded, standing up to glance toward that direction of the orchard, while dusting fertilizer off his knees. "Looks like rabbits might be getting through the outer fencing. It wouldn't be much of a problem in itself if the trees weren't so small."

Eugene laughed. "Yeah. We don't need no Peter Rabbit munching up all those new trees, that's for sure. We got some young Rattle Cores started in that orchard—that's one of them real old apple varieties. Don't want to lose those." He warmed to the subject. "You know them apples have a hollow core, and the loose seeds will rattle around inside the core if you shake 'em."

Sam smiled at his father. "I remember, Dad. John and I used to play with Rattler apples as kids."

Chuck propped an arm on his rake and pushed back his bill cap. "My little Dillon enjoyed playing with those Rattler apples last fall. He rolled them up and down the floor listening to the seeds rattle around inside."

"He sure is a cute one." Eugene chuckled. "It's a treat to me and his great-grandma Ozetta to watch him play, especially riding that stick horse of his around the yard. Ozetta made the head of it from an old sock and I whittled up the stick to size. You know, despite all them fancy toys of his, I think the boy loves his old stick horse the best."

Attention moved back to their work then, but John's eyes drifted thoughtfully to Chuck, his shirt off in the heat, only twenty-one years old and already a father of two. He and Vera Scanlon married in high school, with a child on the way, the two of them only kids themselves. Charlie Sheppard and his wife, Nevelyn, supported the couple, moving them into their big house to join them and their two younger daughters, Sara and Kristen, embracing Vera into their fold with warmth. She needed support, coming from a family filled with quarrels and alcoholism.

As if reading his thoughts, Eugene said, "We all appreciate how Mary Beth is letting Vera work down at the store part-time."

John measured out a six-inch line around the base of a Jonagold apple tree. "Mary Beth and Nancy are glad to have her. The store's growing, getting busier. They needed more help."

Chuck pricked up his ears. "We're savin' the money to build our own place."

Eugene waved a finger at him. "You remember John showed you that area on the Upper Farm Road where you can build if you mean to stay working at the farm. It's a good spot with a fine view over the farm. We could use someone living closer to the lodge and rental cabins, too."

"I aim to stay, Grampa Gene." The boy said the words with pride. "There's been Sheppards managing Cunningham Farm since the eighteen hundreds."

John smiled. "I'm glad to hear that, Chuck. And since that's the case, I don't think you'll need to build. I talked to the contractor who built the rental cabins only last month. He has a plan for a larger log home that will blend in with the lodge and rentals in looks. I'll build the house if you and Vera plan to stay on the farm. You can work on the farm and manage the lodge and rental properties for me, too, if you want more salary. You can take care of the tube rental slopes and the business there in the winter, as well. I need someone living on that part of the land. This ghost business has shown me that."

Chuck's mouth dropped open. "Mr. Cunningham, that's too generous."

"Don't be looking a gift horse in the mouth, boy," said Eugene. "Sounds fine to me."

"Well, there is a catch." John gestured the men toward the big coolers in the back of the truck for a water break. "Jim Reeves, the contractor, said he'd reduce the house costs considerably if we do a large portion of the construction work. Everything we're capable of."

Chuck's eyes brightened as he sluiced cold water over his face to cool off. "I'll do anything I can to help."

Sam grinned. "John, you know you can count on all of us to help. Manny, too, I'm sure, and even the women when there's painting, papering, or landscaping work to do."

"Well, good. We'll start work on the house as we can. You know we won't get much time after the apples start coming in this fall, but over the winter and spring, things lighten up a little. Maybe we can get you young folks into your own place by this time next year." John clapped Chuck on the back. "I'm pleased you want to stay on the land, Chuck. I'll call you and Vera to come and look at the house plans when Jim comes to the house next. Let you put your input into the design."

Chuck's eyes glowed. "Man, I can't wait to tell Vera."

John looked toward the sun, slipping lower in the sky. "Well, why don't you go do that now? I think we've all put in enough work for today. Besides, it's moving toward dinnertime."

He turned to Sam. "Let Charlie, Chuck, and Eugene clean up here. You walk down to the Side Orchards before heading home and see what work needs doing there tomorrow to put wire around those young trees. Then check to see if we have the materials in the sheds. If not, one of us will go into town early tomorrow to get what we need. We can finish here with the fertilizing first thing in the morning and then start the cages for the young trees in the afternoon."

Looking up the Farm Road, John's thoughts strayed to Lydia. If he hurried home and showered, he might be able to walk up to the ridge in time to walk her home. Or if not, he could stop by the house a minute to see her. With this in mind, he headed for Main House, whistling as he went.

Thirty minutes later, in clean jeans and a dark green shirt, he headed back up the Farm Road, Cullie loping along happily at his side, ears pricked and tail waving.

"We're going to see if we can run into a pretty lady, Cullie," he said to the dog.

Near the intersection, where the road branched right toward

the lodge and left across the Upper Farm, John stopped abruptly, the hairs on his arm prickling. A scream rent the air, and before he and Cullie could make it even a few feet toward the sound, Lydia came streaking up from the woods area above Drop Off Ridge, running hard.

She plowed straight into him as she gained the road. "John!" Alarmed eyes rose to his. "I saw the ghost. I swear I did."

Unlike the boys, John knew Lydia wasn't prone to fancies. "Where?" he asked, looking over her shoulder from the direction she'd come.

A hand still bunched in his shirt, she turned to point. "In that direction, a little below where the ridge starts to drop off below the lodge. Not far from the ledge. In the spot where the blackberries grow thick. You know the place."

"Let me go look, Lydia. You stay here until I get back."

"No!" She wrapped her arms around him. "Don't leave me here by myself." She looked down the road toward Hill House. "I want to go home, John."

"I know." He rubbed her back, holding her close. "But I need to go check and see if there's still someone there. I'll leave Cullie with you. The two of you start walking on toward Hill House if you're afraid to wait. I'll catch up with you."

She looked down at the collie. "I'll wait with Cullie—unless I see something else. John, I am not kidding about this." Her breathing was ragged, and her face still pale with shock.

"I know." John ran a soothing hand down her cheek. "I'll be right back."

He quickly took the path down to the rocky ledge above the ridgeline. He saw nothing, even after tromping through the brush all around the area. Crossing the ridge again, he located the blackberry bushes where Lydia had been picking, before she panicked and ran. Her pail still lay turned over in the brush. Circling the area, he looked for tracks. All he found was a small section of dirt where it looked like someone had wiped out a track with a branch.

"Clever," he said to himself.

Finding nothing else, he climbed back up to the road. Lydia sat on an old log under a shade tree, watching for him, Cullie sitting obediently—if somewhat impatiently—by her side.

"Good dog." John ran his hand down the collie's back. Only good training would keep a dog waiting as Cullie had when the scent of danger and excitement hung in the air.

John pulled out his cell phone and called Manny. "Lydia just saw the ghost, Manny. We're at the Farm Road where it forks to the lodge. Can you come up? Call Sam and Charlie to meet us here, too."

They came quickly and let Lydia tell them what she'd seen.

"I saw a shrouded, ghostly form exactly like the boys described. Back in the woods area near where I picked berries." She stomped a foot in annoyance. "Dadgumit, I'd picked a whole bucket of blackberries and I dropped my bucket when that thing appeared, moaning and flapping around."

"We'll look for the bucket." Sam grinned. "And for the ghost."

John told Manny about the dusted print he found.

Manu nodded. "You take Lydia on home. She's had a shock. We'll take Cullie and thoroughly search the area. Maybe find something else with all of us looking. I'll call the sheriff's office and make a report after we look around. It's as likely we'll find something as Lester." He grinned.

John looked at Lydia's hand, clasped in the material of his shirt again. "Good idea, Manny. You call and give me a report later on. Take Cullie back to the house with you, too, when you finish."

He told Cullie to stay with Manu, then put an arm around Lydia and started down the Upper Farm Road toward Hill House. "Do you need me to go get the truck, or do you think you can walk the distance back?"

"I can walk. But a little help won't hurt. I still feel shaky." She wrapped her arm around his waist gratefully, leaning against his side as they walked, coordinating her steps to his in a unified rhythm.

After a distance, she loosened her grip on him at last. "I thought those boys were making up that ghost sighting the other night. Or at least exaggerating it." She shook her head. "They certainly weren't, John. Whoever is perpetuating this prank has conceived a very convincing costume, too—blood on the ghost's garments, and a convincing, raspy, threatening voice." She turned her eyes to John's. "Why would anyone do this? Hide out and frighten people in this way?" She stomped her foot in anger again. "When I think of that little Plemmons girl, seeing that thing while out playing by the creek alone. It must have terrorized her."

John thought back on the ghost sightings Lester had told them about. "There must be some logical explanation for all this."

Lydia stopped walking to glare at him. "And just *what* is logical and sensible about ghosts moaning around in the woods in bloody garments, John Cunningham?"

He chuckled and took her hand to walk on, seeing her less shaky now, the color returning to her face. "I meant that behind it all probably lies some logical explanation. People seldom do things without some reason, even dressing up like ghosts and frightening people."

She snorted. "Well, I can't think of any sensible explanation for what's happening."

Once they were at the house, John followed Lydia inside. "You sit down now." He headed for the kitchen. "What can I get for you—water? A cola?"

She looked at the couch longingly. "I want hot tea, and I doubt you remember how to make it."

"No." He smiled. "Not if you still make English tea from loose leaves. I only know how to do the tea-bag kind."

She wrinkled her nose. "Let me brew it then."

He followed her into the kitchen, the kittens coming out to scamper around their legs. "Mary Beth said you made afternoon tea when she came here earlier this week."

A soft look passed over her face. "We had a lovely time." Lydia glanced at the kitchen clock. "It's too late for afternoon tea now, John, but we can have high tea."

"Kind of like supper?"

"Yes, very much like supper." She put on water to boil, put

food down for the kittens, and began to rummage in the refrigerator. "I baked a beef tenderloin yesterday with new potatoes, carrots, and green beans. I was feeling extravagant, having all this time on my hands. I can heat everything up in the microwave in a few minutes if it will suit you."

He watched with pleasure as she fussed around the kitchen.

"I have homemade bread I bought in Waynesville and I even made scones yesterday, thinking Mary Beth might drop by again."

"You've had a bad fright, Lydia. You don't need to make me dinner."

She turned to him. "It will give me something to do to busy my mind. You know that always helps me calm down."

"Yes, I remember." He leaned against the kitchen table. "In that case, what can I do to help?"

"Set the table and talk to me. Divert my attention so my mind won't keep replaying that awful scene."

John moved with familiar ease to the cabinets where Lydia had always kept her dishes in the past. Finding plates, he put two on the table, then hunted for silverware and got down cups and saucers for the tea. Out of the corner of his eye, he watched her spoon loose tea into the old teapot she'd had since they married, pouring hot water over it afterward.

"What?" she said, turning to catch him watching her.

"Nothing. Just enjoying, like Mary Beth did, watching you make English tea again. Not many people do that sort of thing anymore."

Lydia put the top on the teapot and set the timer. "You know my mother came from the UK and that I lived there in my youngest years. I lost the accent when we moved to the States, but I remember the customs. And, of course, Mother continued them in our home here." She turned back to her cooking. "It just feels right having tea. I miss it on the days when I can't make time for it. It's a small luxury I truly love."

"Tell me what you remember about living in England."

"Not much, really. Mostly impressions. Little remembrances." She turned to smile at him. "I remember having afternoon tea in London with my grandmother Howard at a very elegant restaurant. I have odd memories of row houses in quaint little towns and castles on lush, green lawns. I recall leaning over bridges to look down on the boats on the Thames, hearing Big Ben chime, and seeing the guards walk in front of Buckingham Palace, never giggling or smiling—even when I made faces at them."

He laughed. "Where did you live in England?"

"In Leicester near the university, in a town house near where Daddy worked on the engineering project that took him to the British Isles." She whisked one dish out of the microwave and put in another. "He met Mother there, you know. Married her and later brought her home to the small farm and·rural property his parents owned outside Boone, North Carolina. His sister, Martha, still lived at home then, and that's when Mother and Martha developed such a bond."

"I've been to their farm many times." John sat down at the old kitchen table, in the same chair he used to sit in when he and Lydia lived at Hill House. "In fact, I drove up there last year to help your grandfather with a problem he was having with his orchard."

She turned around in surprise. "I didn't know that."

"I visited your parents, too. Thanked them for the flowers they sent for Mother's funeral."

"I didn't send any flowers." She frowned. "It somehow seemed awkward to do so."

"Your parents added your name with theirs."

She lifted her eyebrows. "Mother never told me that."

"Well, she told me I'd lost a prize to let you go. I agreed."

John watched her blush as she turned to get the tea. "Here, John Cunningham. Everything is ready. Eat while it's hot."

He dug in, finding his hunger rising at the sight of the food. It had been a long day.

They ate in silence for a short time, John remembering how they'd eaten here so many times when they first married, loving their little house situated above the farm, private and to themselves. So delighted in each other's company.

John ran his foot up the inside of her leg. "Penny for your thoughts, Lydia Ruth."

She flushed. "Well, I can assure you they don't match yours!"

He laughed. "I was just remembering the good times when we first married." He reached to get another slice of beef. "We did know happy times here."

"Yes. And I remember how crowded it was with the two of us and four small children around this table—"

John's cell phone interrupted her words. He pulled it out of his belt clip. "Yes, Manny. Did you find anything?" He listened as Manu filled him in briefly. "Yes, I'll share with Lydia, and yes, thank you, she is better now. Tell Ela and Mary Beth I'm eating with her and keeping her company a little longer."

"What did he say?" Lydia asked as he hung up.

"Manu found some footprints this time, mostly wiped out, as from a branch, like the ones I found. But they discovered no other evidence, nor did they find anyone hanging around the area."

Lydia sighed. "Oh well."

"Actually, it's more than the police have found before. Sam called the sheriff's office. Lester Sexton came up and they showed him the tracks, filled him in on what you saw." John speared green beans with his fork. "At least there are footprints for once. Ghosts don't leave footprints."

She waved a hand. "Some people would argue with that."

"Well, to me finding footprints means 'person'—and a clever person, too, who knows how to cover his tracks."

Her mouth dropped open. "Oh, I hadn't thought of that. A real ghost would hardly bother to sweep out his tracks."

John told her about the other sightings as they finished their dinner. She cleared their plates and warmed the scones she'd made for their dessert, setting out butter, honey, and several pots of preserves to lavish on them. Pouring them both more tea, she settled back into her chair.

"Here's your touch of English tea to close the meal, John." She spread a smear of blackberry jam on her scone.

Noting the picture of berries on the jar, he smiled at her. "Manu found your bucket of blackberries. He said only a few spilled when you dropped the pail. He took them down to Main House for Ela to keep for you."

"Oh good." Her face brightened. "They're delicious with scones and cream at breakfast. And I thought I might try making some homemade jam." She looked toward the window. "There's a full moon, John, and with dark just falling we might see lightning bugs. Let's go sit out on the porch." She picked up her teacup. "You can bring your tea and another scone if you want."

She started toward the porch. He followed, after adding more hot tea to his cup. Personally, he preferred hot coffee after dinner, but tea would do.

"There!" Lydia pointed into the night as he came outside. "The lightning bugs are out. What little miracles. You know Mother says they don't have lightning bugs in the UK. She never saw them before she came to the States. Many places on the earth don't have them, and I read their numbers are dwindling."

"Hard to believe, when there are over two thousand species of fireflies."

"How do you know that?"

"I pick up and remember trivia. You should know that."

She huffed. "I remember I always lost playing those trivia fact games with you—or with the children. The boys, in particular, got your fact-recall genes."

"Tell me about the boys, Lydia."

Lydia filled John in, as she had Mary Beth, going into the house to get the photo album so he could see the pictures she'd shown his daughter.

"I'm proud of them," John said when she was done. "I hope they know that."

"How can they, when you've never told them? Never written, never called them, and never gone down to see them."

His temper flared. "I figured they could drive up here to see me if they wanted to."

"Oh, John. You know the boys—or I—could hardly come to the farm for a cordial visit after our angry parting with Estelle.

Don't you remember how horrible those last days were before J. T. and I left?"

"They didn't improve after you two left, either." He scuffed a boot against the porch floor. "Then Billy Dale and Parker packed up one night and drove to Atlanta to join you. They didn't even wait to finish their junior and senior years at the high school here. They finished in Atlanta with you."

Lydia put a hand on John's, where he sat in the swing beside her. "Estelle made it impossible for them to stay. You know what they went through—the incriminations, the rantings and ravings, the accusations and insults against J. T. and me after we left. They couldn't handle the anger and bitterness. The pressure to change. To choose sides. They felt miserable."

"I kept hoping it would blow over. That Mother would calm down, settle back to normal. Let up on everything." He looked out into the night. "She often did after a time."

"I don't think she would have, that time." Lydia kept her hand over his. "It was good of you, John, to let them stay with me after they ran away. You could have legally fought me to retain custody. Unlike J. T., Parker and Billy Dale were underage."

He pushed the swing into a soft rhythm. "It was early summer when they left. I thought they'd come back. Start missing their friends, want to get back to school." His voice dropped. "I thought they'd miss the farm, realize apple season was starting. I don't think I really understood at the time that none of them wanted anything to do with this life here."

"Oh, John." Lydia took a deep breath. "That's too harsh. If the boys had felt that you and your mother supported their dreams and goals, I think they might have come back and forth as they made their way through college and into adulthood. Maybe, like Neal, they'd have found their way back in time. But they grew so angry and bitter."

He sat quietly, thinking that over. "I tried to be a good father to them. I loved my sons—and Mary Beth—with all of my heart." John turned his eyes to Lydia. "I didn't mean to fail them."

Lydia's voice whispered across the night to him. "You need to tell them those things. You need to tell them and not me."

He ran a hand through his hair. "Surely they know how I feel about them. Surely, as men, two of them married now, they know a man can have divided loyalties between the people he loves. Divided loyalties about issues in his life."

She turned to touch his face. "John, we can work on fixing the issues between ourselves. But you must resolve the issues between you and your sons yourself. I continued to tell them through all these years that you loved them, that you felt torn between your loyalties to us and your loyalties to the farm and your mother. I explained that your father had asked you to take care of your mother on his deathbed, made you promise."

"But they didn't understand?" He searched for the answer in her eyes.

"No." She shook her head. "Sometimes I didn't, either."

"Oh, Lydia." He put his arms around her and laid his head against her forehead. "I always felt so torn with the battles between you and my mother, and then with the dissension between the boys and Mother. I never knew how to handle it best. What to do."

"So you did what you've always done?" Her question floated out softly into the night.

John pulled back to look at her. "What do you mean?"

"How did you handle problems with your mother as a boy? What did you do when you had controversies with her growing up, or as a teenager, or when it was time to go to college?" She kept her eyes on his. "You sidestepped the problem, or waited it out, didn't you? Or you gave in, went along, because it was easier, made peace. Because you hated the conflict, it seemed easier to bend. To go along."

"And what's so wrong with that? Is fighting and arguing so much better? Isn't making peace supposed to be the Christian way to handle things instead of stirring up more contention?"

John could see her thinking about this, sipping her tea before answering. "The big difference comes when the bending and going along compromises something important to you. In many ways, you never had that problem, John. Your major focus was on the farm and on the orchard, just as your mother wanted for you. You wanted to go to school near home. You wanted to stay near the farm and planned to come back to the farm after graduation. You told me that when we met. You blended comfortably into the fabric of everything Cunningham."

"And your point is?"

"I didn't always blend. I was different—and your mother never liked that. She had a hard time appreciating anyone different from herself. You know it's true. To her, her own particular ways, ideas, thoughts, beliefs, and interests were the right ones. She could never appreciate my differences. As the boys grew and began to develop their own ideas and goals, different from what she wanted to impose on them, she made life difficult for them, as she'd done to me for a long time before."

"She wasn't very flexible." John scowled. "With Mother you had to learn how to go along with her, to humor her, to keep from making trouble. My father taught me that early on."

"Did you hear what you just said? That's what you expected from yourself and so that's what you expected of us in regard to your mother. But our personalities were such that we couldn't do it. Our interests, beliefs, and dreams were such that we couldn't throw them out to go along." Lydia twisted her hands in her lap. "Holly said that you, she, your father, and even Stuart, all developed your ways of coping with your mother's difficult, autocratic, and inflexible personality. In a sense, Holly helped me to see that each person who lived in the close wake of your mother had to choose whether to bend, conform, and stay or to fight and eventually leave. You needed to stay, and you had to bend and conform to do so. We couldn't conform and so eventually we had to leave."

"Holly could never learn to go along with Mother, and it got worse as she grew older." John searched his memory. "The more she tried to assert herself, to be her own person, the more problems she had with Mother."

"That's what she said."

John looked at her. "You're saying it was the same way for you." He shook his head. "I never thought of it like that."

"What if someone had fought you when you were young,

made you feel foolish to want to run the orchard, ridiculed you for your love for it, your interest in it. Tried to keep you from the dream of continuing it, giving your life and heart to it. Or made you feel stupid for any interest in farming you had, called you disloyal to your heritage for even holding that interest. Would you have found it easy then to go along with that person?"

He straightened. "You know I wouldn't have."

"Your sons felt that you should have fought more to see that that type of behavior wasn't imposed on them. They felt that you—by not doing anything—allowed your mother to bully them and bully me unnecessarily. They resented you for never taking a stand for them. Or for me. They felt you didn't protect me or them from your mother's emotional abuse."

John stood and walked across the porch to stand by the rail. "I had no idea they felt that way about me. I knew they had troubles with Mother, but I didn't realize they also blamed me." He turned to look across at Lydia on the swing. "Did you feel that way, too?"

She nodded, turning her eyes away. "I'm sorry, John, but I often did."

He came back and dropped down to his knees before her. "You should have told me, Lydia. You should have told me." He took her hand. "I loved you more than life itself. I thought I helped you best by not making it worse, by not escalating the arguments by getting into the fray, by keeping the balance. Later, when things grew so bad between you and Mother, and between Mother and the boys, I couldn't seem to see how I could help."

John looked up at her. "I tried to talk to Mother, urging her to try harder to get along with you, with the boys, but I guess that wasn't enough." He leaned over then to lay his head in Lydia's lap. "I'm so sorry I failed you. I didn't mean to. I did-n't try to."

She stroked his hair, not making a reply.

John got up to sit beside her in the swing. "Can you find a way to forgive me? I can't go back and do things differently now."

"No, we can't go back."

He sought her eyes. "But you said if we talked, that maybe we could move on. I'd like that, Lydia Ruth."

"I think I would, too, John Cunningham." She leaned over to give him a small kiss. "Not everything has been resolved tonight, but we've talked out a lot of things. It's a good beginning."

He moaned. "You mean there's more?"

"Probably." She laughed. "And with the boys, there's certainly more. But for tonight, let's put the past behind us for a little while and simply enjoy the night, this wonderful full moon, the lightning bugs flashing in the darkness, the sounds of crickets and cicadas in the air."

John tucked his arm around her on the swing, gathering her close against him. "I can go there."

"Thanks for saying you still love me, John." She nuzzled her head against his shoulder. "I love you, too, you know."

He searched for her mouth then, enjoying the wonder of having her here, back in his arms and back in his life.

CHAPTER 11

The next morning, Lydia walked down to Main House to collect her blackberries from Ela. She felt good about her talk with John the night before, about the love and apologies he had expressed.

The kissing wasn't bad, either. She grinned at the thought, feeling girlish and young.

Letting herself in the back door, Lydia followed the sound of Ela singing in the kitchen. "You're in a good mood," Lydia said to her, walking into the large, sunny room. "I don't remember you singing over the stove when I lived here."

Ela made a rude noise and sent Lydia a sideways glance. "Mrs. Cunningham disapproved of singing when you were supposed to be working."

"I see." Lydia leaned against the counter.

Ela poured a bowl of cake batter out into two floured pans. "Let me put this cake into the oven, then we'll sit down and have a cup of coffee together." She paused. "Or I can fix tea."

"I'll make the tea while you finish the cake." Lydia headed for a cabinet. "Do you still keep leaf tea?"

"Bought some the day I heard you were coming home." She grinned at Lydia, wiping her hands on the apron wrapped around her waist. "Got it at the Mast General Store in downtown Waynesville. They carry loose teas there, sell teapots and such, too."

"I love to explore in the Mast store." Lydia took down the bag of Earl Grey tea from the shelf, found the teapot, and put a teakettle full of water on to boil on the stove. "Blue Ridge Books has good Rishi Teas, too."

Ela popped the two cake tins into the oven, then washed her hands at the sink before sitting down at the table with Lydia. "My, my, it's good to sit here and look across the table at you again."

Lydia smiled. "Thanks. It feels good to me, too." She looked around and sighed. "Visiting or working in the kitchen with you was one of the places I could feel happy for a while when I lived here."

Ela frowned. "Estelle Cunningham was a hard woman."

Lydia leaned her chin on her hands. "How did you deal with her as well as you did, Ela? She was so disrespectful to you."

"No, that's not true." Ela shook her head. "Estelle set the relationship between us from the first day Manu and I came to work here. We were the help and she was our employer. She drew the line firmly and stated with clarity the boundaries and expectations in that relationship. In her own way Estelle respected me—and Manu—for our work and dedication as helps to the family. I recall times she complimented me, and times when she didn't, but we had our ways together that worked. I always hurt more for you than me in living with Estelle. It was different with you."

Lydia got up to pour their tea. "Why was it so different for me? Why could Estelle never like me?"

Ela checked the cakes before answering and then brought back a tin of fresh oatmeal cookies to sit on the table. "Ozetta Sheppard said Estelle saw you as a threat. You reminded her of her predecessor she'd only recently supplanted, Mary Cunningham—a tall, gracious, warmhearted, and kindly lady, beloved by all. Estelle was her polar opposite—short, squat, harsh in nature, and not easily liked or sought out in friendship. Estelle knew this, but her position as matriarch of Cunningham Farm gave her respect and a position of authority here and in the community. From the first, your ease and joy vexed her, Lydia. She wasn't a happy person within herself, and she resented happiness and pleasure in others."

Lydia dipped a cookie into her tea. "Holly talked about how lovely Mary was. She called the farm a happier place before Mary and John died and Estelle came to Main House."

"Holly would remember the change."

Lydia pushed her hair back behind her ear. "I tried so hard to make Estelle like me."

Ela shook her head. "Yes, and Estelle saw it a sign of weakness to try to please others. I heard her make remarks to that effect often enough—making derogatory comments about someone being too nice or too accommodating, showing no backbone. Pride ruled Estelle versus thoughtfulness or love, and she capitalized on position, duty, proper role, and appropriate conduct. She learned that in the Whitmeyers' stuffy home where she grew up—her parents hung up on ancestry, prestige, and right standing in the community, always looking and acting just so. I don't think I ever saw Estelle Cunningham simply let down and be herself, kick off her shoes, laugh, and have a good time. She was always proper, stuffy, and critical."

"The critical part I certainly remember. I don't think I ever did a thing that pleased her." Lydia blew out a breath of regret.

"Few people did, child." Ela got up to take the cakes out of the oven to cool. "Estelle had few real friends. She couldn't risk truly close friends because she didn't dare let anyone get that close. She always feared revealing a weakness, letting her guard down. At heart, she was a lonely woman, and deep down she envied your loving ease with your children, with John and with others. She resented your joy in life, your spontaneity and creativity, your inventive ideas. You were a freer being than she could ever be. . . ."

"Yes, and she tried to squash me into her own mold. Always pressuring me to change and be like her, criticizing and picking at everything I did—at my clothes, my cooking, my mothering, my interests." A wash of harsh memories swirled across Lydia's mind.

"She was hard on you." Ela walked over to look down at Lydia. "But she's gone now, and you need to let the past go. You need to realize that she owned the problem, that she was a troubled person. You need to move on. Forgive and forget."

Lydia looked around. "That's especially hard to do here—in this house, where I still feel her presence so strongly."

Ela made a tut-tutting sound. "Generations of Cunninghams, Sheppards, and others have lived on this farm, loved it, and built it. Fine, good, decent people. You can't judge this old farm or house based on one woman who was a little twisted. In a way, your heart ought to reach out to John and Holly, who came out as strong and well as they did with Estelle for a mother, and to the Sheppards, who stayed on the farm and put up with her high-and-mighty ways toward them. Your heart should remember others around this area, too, who moved on despite Estelle and who built their lives, loved, and thrived, despite her."

"You sound like John." Lydia felt a flicker of annoyance. "Saying I should have gotten along better."

"No, I never meant that." Ela shook her head. "Estelle put you through a daily hell she had no right to inflict on anyone. You had every right to resent it." She pulled out a large bowl to start to mix cake icing in. "But Estelle is gone now. And it's time for healing."

"I'd like to experience more healing. Surely you know that."

Ela turned to her with a hand on her hip. "Well, you'll have to work at it for healing to come. Maybe fight a few battles to get to a new place."

"What do you mean?" Lydia felt confused by Ela's comments.

"Purpose to go and make your peace—in every area." She walked over to smooth a hand over Lydia's hair like she would a child's. "Begin with the house. Go through every room. Confront the old memories and purpose to get past them. If need be, speak to the rooms, to the shadows in the rooms. To the lingering spirits. Get free, Lydia. This house is only a house, and Mary Beth and John have made a lot of changes since Estelle died. But you've felt fearful to even walk around in it. Let old memories keep a power over you instead. Cowardice can never step free of the past, Lydia, only bravery can."

She sat down at the table to look in Lydia's eyes. "When you've finished with the house, you need to go to the woman's grave at some point, too. Make your peace there."

Lydia shuddered.

"Until you move forward in bravery, the past will hold you, and continue to hurt you, control you, and keep you from future happiness and freedom. You have to face your ghosts, your fears, and banish them. You have to establish yourself, to free and separate yourself from the hurts of the past."

"Where did you learn these things, Ela? And how do you know if they will work?"

Ela smiled. "I'm Cherokee. We are more interconnected with the earth and life than white men. I was taught these things and I know they are truth. I reverence the wisdom of my ancestors."

Lydia looked toward the kitchen door leading into the main house. "Will you go with me?"

"No. You must go alone. The Great One will be with you and He will help you." She made a shooing gesture toward the door. "There is no one here but us today. This is a good time."

And so Lydia found herself wandering down the hallway of Main House intent on facing her past to make a new beginning. Anxiety slowed her steps and for a moment she considered simply sprinting out the front door. Gathering her courage instead, she walked into the formal dining room, where Estelle Cunningham had reigned at the head of the table, making each evening meal an unbearable ordeal to get through.

Stopping in surprise at the doorway, Lydia noticed changes immediately. The dark flocked wallpaper and formal oil paintings were gone, the heavy silver tea service put away, and the room lightened from its excess of ornate furniture and decorative china. The walls were painted a clean, clear blue now above the wainscoting, the table no longer encased in padding and lace tablecloths, the formal chairs reupholstered. A light, happy feeling pervaded the room, helped by the heavy draperies gone from the windows.

"Wow." Lydia couldn't help the exclamation. Everything looked and felt so different.

After a few moments, she walked through the room trying to decide how to confront her past constructively. Uninspired, she sat down at her old place at the dining room table and dropped her head to pray for guidance. After a time, she lifted her eyes and looked toward the head of the table. "Estelle," she said. "I know in my heart I did everything I could to love you and to try to make you love me. I'm sorry I failed to please you, and I'm sorry about the personal problems that caused you to be unable to love me and care for me. I'm a nice person, Estelle. I believe you'd have seen that if you'd ever let yourself try. I'm sorry you felt so repressed that you had trouble letting anyone know joy, and I'm sorry for all the unhappiness and issues you couldn't get past to enjoy life more and to love more."

Lydia paused, frowning. "I'm not sorry, Estelle, that I resisted letting you change me to be like you. And I'm not sorry I tried to make a happy, warm, loving home for John and our children. I know things grew less happy for you after John, the children, and I had to move here with you after Grandpa Will died. I wish things could have been different." She took a deep breath. "But today is a new day, and I am moving on, purposing to be happy in life, purposing to let the past go to embrace the future. Like Ela said, I'm going to go through every room, and face and banish old memories in order to start looking forward instead of backward."

She stood to put her hands on Estelle's old chair. "I forgive you by faith for all the old hurts and pains, Estelle. I think truly a dark force warred in you to create so much unhappiness in others. And I don't want that old darkness hanging around me, or in me, anymore." She took a deep breath. "Lord, help me let it go and set me free from all the bad memories and sorrows associated with unhappy, past times. I ask it in Jesus's name. Amen."

Lydia walked around the room, feeling lighter and freer. It surprised her how much better she felt. With rising confidence, she set off through the rest of the house to make her peace in every room as Ela had suggested.

She returned to the kitchen later with a smile, to find Ela frying chicken for the family's lunch, her caramel cake now iced and sitting on the counter.

"Smells good in here," Lydia said.

Ela turned to look at her carefully. "You look good. Spirit lighter. Eyes clearer. You found some healing."

"Yes, I did." Lydia walked over to hug the small woman. "And you helped push me in the right direction to do it. Thank you."

"You're welcome. Now, set the table since you're here. John, Manu, and the boys will be in soon for lunch. Mary Beth, too, I think, since Nancy's at the store today. You can join us. I put fresh-picked cabbage in the slaw, there's early sweet corn and field peas from the garden ready to put on the table, and you'll find a fruit salad with strawberries and blueberries—one of the twins' favorites—in the refrigerator. There's plenty. You can help me set everything out."

Lydia began to get plates down from the cabinet.

Ela turned to her. "How'd you find the house?"

"Very changed, more so than I expected."

"Nice, isn't it?" Ela smiled. "I always say a house takes on the personality of its mistress, and you can certainly see the joy and happiness of Mary Beth in every room, can't you?"

Lydia smiled. "Yes, I can."

"Well, you be sure and tell Mary Beth how much you like it. It will mean a lot to her. She and your father put hard labor and work into every room."

Before Lydia could respond to this, the twins came barreling into the door ahead of John and Manu.

"We saw a big snake, Ela—" Billy Ray called out as the door banged shut behind him.

"Yeah, but it wasn't a poisonous one," Bucky interrupted. "Manu just picked it up and snapped it dead." He demonstrated with a whipping motion of his hand.

Bucky pushed his hands under the faucet with Billy Ray's to wash them for dinner. "We think it was trying to make a home around Old Oak and Manu didn't want that. He said it might scare folks."

"It would scare me." Lydia smiled at her grandsons, finding it easier each time she saw them to tell them apart.

Billy Ray's eyes brightened. "It was *big*, Nana Lydia." He emphasized the word and spread his arms to show the length. "Manu called it a rat snake and said it could climb trees. It was coiled around a branch in Old Oak."

Bucky climbed into his seat at the big kitchen table where they ate their breakfast and lunch meals. "Manu needed to kill it because it could also get into the chicken eggs, which isn't good. He said it could even kill and eat little animals, like maybe squirrels or our cats."

"Is its bite poisonous?" Lydia asked.

Manu finished washing his hands at the sink and sat down to join them at the table. "A rat snake can bite, but it's not poisonous. But its bite can hurt and be painful. I didn't want to take the chance of leaving the snake around Old Oak since all the children play there so often and climb in the tree's branches."

"Yeah." Billy Ray leaned toward Lydia, his brown eyes animated. "I'd just started climbing up the tree, and I'd probably have got bit if Manu hadn't seen the snake and called out to me."

Ela raised her eyebrows at Manu.

As if in reply to her unspoken question, he said, "I looked up from the grapevines nearby, where I was working, and saw the snake hanging on the tree limb. About four or five feet long— hard to miss."

Ela nodded, satisfied that Manu had been keeping an eye on the boys while he worked. "Let's eat," she said. "While everything's hot."

Mary Beth let herself in the back door. "Looks like I'm just in time." She smiled at her family, her eyes especially lighting up with pleasure to see Lydia at the table. "Mother, what a treat." She leaned over to give Lydia a quick hug as she moved to take her own seat. Then, of course, she had to hear about the snake episode before grace could be said.

As Lydia passed a dish of vegetables to Mary Beth after the blessing, she caught her daughter's eye. "I took a tour of the house before lunch to see all the work you've done." Lydia smiled at her. "I can't believe how different everything is—it looks wonderful."

"Yeah," Bucky added. "Mom took down all the pictures of the mean ol' frowning people. They always scared me."

Lydia saw John smirk.

"I'm so glad you like the changes." Mary Beth's face brightened. "I remember how you used to wish you could change some things and I used some of those ideas—like putting the rose-spritzed wallpaper in the upstairs guest room—"

Lydia interrupted. "And the rich, deep blues in the living room. I love the feeling in there now." She remembered the room before—stuffy, ornate, and full of uncomfortable antique chairs and high-back settees.

"I helped reupholster a lot of the furniture from what I learned helping out at Harper's."

"And we got dinosaurs in our room." Billy Dale beamed. "Grandmother wouldn't let us have dinosaurs before. Did you see our room?"

"I did, and I love your bedspreads with the dinosaurs on them and the big cabinet with all the dinosaurs inside it. You'll have to tell me their names. I don't know them."

"We know *all* their names and all about them." Bucky jumped into the conversation. "We'll teach you."

As lunch finished and Mary Beth got up to leave, Lydia asked, "I was wondering if it would be all right for the boys to come and visit with me for a few hours this afternoon? I thought we might take a walk up one of the trails behind the house and then bake cookies afterward."

"Can we? Can we, Mom?" they both asked at once.

"I suppose." She smiled. "It will give Ela and Manu a break from watching out for you. But don't give your nana any trouble, you hear?"

"We'll be good," they parroted.

And so it was that Lydia had a lovely afternoon with her grandsons that day. They took a small hike behind Hill House to a sweep of cascades in the creek on Strawberry Knob, baked chocolate chip cookies, and then took the kittens out on the porch to play.

"I liked our hike," Bucky said, trailing a string across the porch for Ava to chase.

"Me too," Billy Ray added from the porch swing. "Can we go again sometime and do a long hike?"

"What did you have in mind?" Lydia asked.

"We want to go to Cataloochee and maybe see the elk." Bucky looked up from playing with the kitten. "Tommy Simpson's daddy took him and they saw calves last week—that's what you call baby elk. He said they were cool."

"I haven't been to Cataloochee Valley in a long time. We'll have to plan a day to go over and explore the valley, pack a picnic and hike one of the trails." Lydia saw John's truck pull up as they talked. He'd promised to come pick the boys up toward the end of the day.

"Daddy John," Bucky called out to him. "Nana Lydia's taking us for a hike in Cataloochee and maybe we can see the elk."

"You need to watch these guys or they'll be making all sorts of plans for your life, Lydia Ruth," John said, walking up the flagstone path to the porch.

"Actually, I haven't been to Cataloochee in years and years. I'd love to take a day to drive over and hike one of the trails I remember."

"Can we go this week, please?" Bucky asked. "While the baby elk are still there?"

"I tell you what," John put in. "How about if you two, Lydia, and me drive over to Cataloochee together? Maybe Friday. I think I can get caught up on the farm over the next few days to take a day off by then. I'd hate to see Lydia have to keep up with both of you two wild men by herself."

"Can we really go?" Billy Ray's eyes lit up. "That would be so fun."

"We'll ask your mother tonight." He looked at the clutter of milk glasses, cookie plates, and toys scattered around the porch.

"On condition that you guys police the area here before we leave."

"Okay." Bucky jumped up to start collecting glasses and Billy Ray followed, carrying cookie plates into the kitchen.

"Where did you find these old cars?" John asked, noting the pile of Matchbox cars.

"I found them in the attic and thought they might come in handy one day. They were J. T.'s and the twins'."

"I remember," he said, leaning over to pick up a green convertible. "The boys knew the make of every vehicle here, if I remember correctly."

Lydia smiled. "I enjoyed spending time with the twins today."

"Did they bombard you with a lot of questions?"

"Of course, like all normal six-year-olds would." Her eyes caught John's. "I showed them all the pictures of their uncles in the photo book and told them all about them. I hope you don't mind."

"Of course not." He studied her. "Did they ask you anything they shouldn't have?"

She laughed. "If they did, I handled it well. It's natural they should be curious and have questions."

The boys came back out from the kitchen, and John stood to avoid being stampeded.

"What time are we gonna leave on Friday?" Billy Ray asked, nearly running into him.

"How about around ten in the morning?" John gestured to the cars on the porch, and the boys squatted down to load them into the wooden box. "That will give us time to have breakfast, pack a lunch, and still get to the valley in plenty of time for a good hike and exploration."

Bucky looked up from plunking a handful of cars into the box. "Mama says we have family that came from the Cataloochee Valley."

"We do." John leaned a hip on the porch rail. "We have kinship links to the Palmers who used to live in the valley. We'll stop and see the church named after them when we're there."

"I wanna see the Caldwell house, too," Billy Ray chimed in. "Neal said one of his great-great-granddaddies built it. He told us stories about him and said when the park took the land in the Cataloochee Valley, a lot of the people moved over here to Maggie."

"That's true." John agreed. "We'll go see the old Caldwell place, too. It isn't far off the main road."

The boys bubbled with plans until it was time to go.

"You sure you're up to this?" John grinned at her as the boys launched off the porch heading for the truck.

"I look forward to it." She paused. "What was the name of the trail following the creek that went over so many log bridges? I think the boys would love that hike. It has so many places along the water where they can stop to jump on rocks or wade. And they'll love crossing all the log bridges over the stream."

John grinned. "That's the Caldwell Fork Trail, and it's a great trail to take the boys on. We'll do that one on Friday. It's a broad trail to walk on and a moderate hike. We can walk a few miles up the trail, picnic, and hike back out easily. We'll also drive up the valley to see the Palmer Church, the old schoolhouse, and the Caldwell place before we begin."

"And the elk." Lydia smiled. "I do hope we see some elk. The boys are counting on it."

John stepped closer and traced a finger up her arm. "I'm looking forward to a nice day with you, too—even more than with the boys." He leaned over to pick a Shasta daisy from beside the porch and then tucked it behind Lydia's ear before he headed to the truck. "I'll see you Friday—if not sooner."

Lydia felt a flutter around her heart. Things were moving forward positively in her life, with this a good day to remember, but a small caution light still flickered in the back of her mind. She needed to be careful.

$\mathcal{C}$HAPTER 12

The week flew by, and John had little time with Lydia before Friday. A storm blasted through the area that they needed to clean up from, and June drop started in the orchard.

"What's June drop?" Bucky asked, as he and Billy Dale followed John and Sam around the orchard.

John smiled at the twins. "It's a natural phenomenon, when apple trees begin to drop some of their young fruit as the new fruit is being formed."

"Can you make it quit?" Billy Ray stopped to pick up a handful of small ripening apples that had fallen from a Jonagold tree.

John stifled a laugh. "Actually, June drop is good for the trees. In fact, we're going to help the thinning process today by removing more of the overload of apples forming."

The boy frowned up into the tree. "But wouldn't you always want all the apples you could get?"

"Not if it overtaxes the tree." John put his hand on Billy Ray's shoulder. "We experienced a heavy flowering spring, and so the trees are creating more fruit than they need to. In a natural way, the trees drop some of the fruit they don't need in June, usually the inferior apples. Too much fruit would strain the trees' resources and make the branches weigh too much later on."

"Is that why you told Sam you're gonna thin more off of the trees today?" Bucky asked.

"That's right." He reached up to pick a young, ripening apple to examine it. "We often need to go through all the orchards to help the thinning process. It makes for a stronger, healthier crop of apples."

"Can we help thin?" Bucky's eyes lit up as he asked.

John glanced at Sam, who nodded.

"Sure. We could use some extra help." John smiled at the boy.

"Me and Billy Ray are going to run your orchard one day when you get old. Is that okay?" Bucky slipped a hand into his.

"Yeah, Sam's daddy, Grandpa Sheppard, said you'd need someone since your own boys are doing other stuff." Billy Ray crowded against his other side affectionately. "Do you think you could teach us all the stuff we need to know?"

John found it hard to answer around the lump in his throat.

Sam ruffled Billy Ray's hair, answering for him. "I think we can teach two smart little boys like you to be fine orchard farmers." He grinned at the boys. "But maybe I'd better give you a little quiz to see what you know." He paused for emphasis. "First question: Billy Ray, what are the two varieties of apples that Cunningham Farm created on its own from grafting and experimenting?"

"The Cunningham Red and the Cunning Sweet," Billy Ray recited, pleased to know the answer.

"Pretty good." Sam turned to Bucky. "How about you telling me a couple of the farm's earliest fruiting apples?"

Bucky wrinkled his nose in thought. "The Early Joe, the Parmer, and the Lodi—that last one's a yellow apple."

"The Pink Pearl comes early, too," Billy Ray put in. "Ela and Mama like it because the insides are pink and it makes pink applesauce."

Hearing Cullie barking, the boys forgot the quiz for the moment and raced ahead to catch up with the dog.

"Do you think they'll really want to stay on the farm, Sam?" John watched them run up the road.

Sam pushed back his hat. "I don't see why they wouldn't. They've loved the farm since they could toddle along beside you through the orchard rows." Sam picked a ripening fruit off a Strawberry Pippin tree to examine it. "Sometimes the love of the land skips a generation. And their mother, Mary Beth, loves the farm." He turned to grin at John. "Neal Caldwell does, too. You think something might work out there?"

"I guess just about everybody has noticed Neal's interest," John replied. "But time will tell if it goes further than that."

John was thinking back on that comment Friday morning when Neal stopped by Main House as the family finished breakfast. "I hear you guys are going hiking today." He tousled the twins' heads.

"Yeah, Nana Lydia and Daddy John are taking us." Bucky waved a fork in the air with enthusiasm. "We're gonna see the elk and your family house, too."

The twins babbled on with excitement, but John noticed Neal's attention kept shifting to Mary Beth. "Bucky, you and Billy Ray better run and do your chores so we can get ready for that hike and leave for Lydia's on time."

They flashed a look at each other before hustling out of their seats to head for the door. "See ya later, Neal," they called.

Mary Beth smiled. "They're so excited about this hike."

Neal shuffled his feet. "I heard you might be singing a few numbers with Vance Coggins and the Cross-Creek Boys tonight down at the Stompin' Ground."

"They want me to come." She shrugged.

"What if I take you down and tag along with you tonight?" Neal propped a foot on the rail of a kitchen chair.

Mary Beth dropped her eyes. "I'd like that, but I made plans to go with Daddy and Mother already." Her eyes moved to John. "Mother did say she'd come, didn't she?"

John fidgeted, knowing he'd dragged his feet in asking Lydia to go. "Well, I expected to finalize that on our hike today. The week got busy before." His glance moved to Neal. "Mary Beth, why don't you plan to go with Neal for now, and then if I can talk Lydia into coming, we'll join you there, have a double date?"

A panicked look crossed Mary Beth's face at the word 'date.'

"Let's just call it an evening with friends, John." Neal picked up on Mary Beth's panic. "We'll sit together, maybe clog a little, share a fine time. I don't think Lydia has heard Mary Beth sing with the Cross-Creek Boys. It will be a treat for her. The Ivy Hill Band will be there, too, and a couple of local clogging groups Lydia will enjoy."

"That sounds good." John smiled at his daughter. "I think your mother will enjoy an evening at the Stompin' Ground. She hasn't been there in a long time. It will be a treat."

"Well." She hesitated. "But it will create a late night out for the twins. . . ."

"Manu and I will sit with the boys," Ela put in. "They'll be worn out after that hike and no trouble."

"Okay, thanks. But I need to get down to the store now." Mary Beth glanced at the kitchen clock as she pushed back her chair. "An early shipment is coming in and I want to unpack it before I open the store."

"I need to get to work, too." Neal opened the back door to head out, then turned back. "I'll stop by about seven thirty. That will give us plenty of time to get there before the doors open at eight o'clock."

Later that morning, as John arrived at Lydia's with the boys, he corralled her to tell her that Mary Beth would be singing that evening. "Neal and Mary Beth really want you to come," he said. "Mary Beth will be singing with Vance and the Cross-Creek Boys, which she often does, but I think she's a little nervous about having an evening with Neal totally on her own." He grinned. "I wish you'd seen her face when the word 'date' got thrown out."

Lydia's face flushed as she leaned over to tighten the laces on her hiking books. Obviously, the word 'date' made her a little nervous, too.

"Neal assured her it was just an evening with friends, a chance to hear some good music, clog a little, and enjoy some fine dance groups." He picked up her waist pack to hand it to her, shooing one of the kittens off of it first. "I hope you'll come along with us," he added. "Mary Beth would never admit it, but I know she's wanting you to hear her sing. It was you who always encouraged her to sing—even paid Molly Simmons to give her lessons on the sly."

Her eyes flashed. "All of Mary Beth's singing had to be done on the sly because your mother didn't approve of it."

"Mother did let Mary Beth take piano. She made her practice, too—even after school when you were working."

Lydia rolled her eyes. "She considered the piano an appropriate accomplishment for a young girl, John, and she only let Mary Beth play classics, hymns, and the pieces in her exercise books."

"Funny, I seem to remember her playing boogie-woogie and rock 'n' roll songs." He grinned at her. "You and I even showed the kids how to jitterbug one evening while Mary Beth played."

"If you'll check your memory, John Cunningham, you'll realize that all those times happened when your mother went to committee meetings at the church or to one of her civic clubs or gatherings." Irritation threaded her voice. "Most of our fun occurred when your mother was gone."

Before he could reply, Bucky pulled open the screen door. "Hey. Come on. Me and Billy Ray are ready to go. What's taking you guys so long?"

"We're on our way." Lydia picked up her waist pack before turning to John. "Did you pack all those lunch items into your backpack?"

"I did," he said, draping one of the straps of the backpack over a shoulder, glad the subject of his mother was past. "And everyone is carrying their own bottle of water and other personal items they need in their waist packs." He tapped her nose. "Did you pack some sunscreen?"

"Yes." She lifted her chin. "And I hope you remembered to pick up a hiking map."

He pointed to it sticking out of a pocket of his backpack, then reached to open the front door for her. "Looks like we're ready to go."

They headed east from the farm on Highway 19 through Maggie Valley and then onto Rural Route 276 at Dellwood. Soon, they sped through the small community of Jonathan heading toward Cove Creek Road, which would take them up over the mountain and down into the Cataloochee Valley.

"How come Maggie Valley is named after a girl?" Bucky asked.

"Well, there's a story there," John answered. "Back in the late 1890s, when the valley was first getting settled, Jack Setzer wanted to establish a post office. He submitted several names for the post office that got rejected. He sent in more, but had the same thing happen again."

"Why did they reject them?" Billy Ray asked.

"Because another post office was already using the names he sent in."

"I guess they can't have two with the same name," Bucky said.

"That's right, so, getting kind of desperate for name ideas then, Setzer sent in the names of his three daughters as backups the next time he submitted possibilities." John slowed to follow a farm tractor onto the highway. "In 1904 he got a response back from the government telling him their new post office and town was to be called Maggie, North Carolina, after one of his daughters."

"Cool. I'd like to have a town named after me." Billy Ray waved at the farmer on the tractor as they passed him.

John laughed. "Actually, I always heard that Maggie Setzer got real upset and embarrassed that the post office and town was going be named after her. Old stories say she even burst into tears over it."

Bucky wrinkled his nose. "Sounds like a dumb thing a girl would do." Then he glanced at his grandmother. "Sorry, Nana Lydia."

Lydia smirked at John. "Just imagine—if the town had been named after you, Bucky, it might be called Buckyville, or Bucky Town, or Buckner Dean Township today."

While Billy Ray and Bucky giggled over this, Lydia launched into an old 1960s "Name Game" tune, singing in the light, familiar voice John remembered and inserting Bucky's name over and over into the repetitive lyrics. Then she turned to John with a grin as the boys laughed, looking for a new victim and moving into a new verse using his name.

The boys were bouncing in their seats by now. "Do me!" Billy Ray begged. "Do me!"

Lydia tweaked his nose and launched into yet another sing-song chorus using Billy's name. She soon had the boys giggling and singing along with her, substituting all the names of their friends and family members into the song's lyrics. Then, just as the boys began to tire of the rhyme song, she moved them on with ease to other tunes.

John felt transported, listening to her—remembering car trips with her and their children, filled with singing, games, and laughter. So different from the formal car trips of his childhood, traveling with muted conversation or silence if they went anywhere at all. He hadn't grown up with laughter. It was Lydia who had brought joy into his life.

"You're not singing, Daddy John," Bucky chided him.

Lydia sent him an arched look and John, with his deep baritone, joined in singing the familiar words of "Kookaburra."

The Cove Creek Road, winding over and down from the Cataloochee Divide, was a rough gravel road that led, surprisingly, to a lovely, well-paved road through the base of the Cataloochee Valley. John had never heard an explanation that made sense to him of why North Carolina had paved the flat valley road but not the rocky access road across the mountain to it.

At Lydia's insistence, John stopped to buy two tour booklets near the entrance of the valley. She kept one and gave the other to the boys to share, telling them which page to turn to as they passed the historic structures along the Cataloochee Valley Road. They stopped to explore the old Palmer House and the Palmer Chapel, both built in the later 1800s. And the boys were fascinated with the white, one-room Beech Grove Schoolhouse, its old, battered desks still in place.

Passing through a long stretch of grassy valley, they spotted a herd of elk grazing. John pulled over to let the twins jump out to watch.

"Look! Two little calves!" Billy Ray pointed toward two

small, stubby calves cavorting near their mother. "And look at those giganticous antlers on that big elk."

Bucky giggled. "Elk look kind of like Santa's reindeer, don't they?"

"The males do." Lydia leaned on a rough split-rail fence to study the herd in the field. "It's good to see the elk here. I read the park service reintroduced them to the Smokies and that they're doing really well—thriving and reproducing."

John put a restraining hand on the boys' shoulders to keep them from climbing under the old fence. "In the fall the males bugle to attract the females, or cows, and to make challenges to other bulls. They often rut with their antlers then." John pointed to the two young males poking at each other with their antlers. "Those two young ones are practicing for the real thing later."

"Ouch." Bucky frowned. "I bet it hurts to get stuck with one of those antlers."

"Yes, and that's why the rangers warn that you should always keep your distance from the elk. Like bears, they are wild animals and unpredictable."

After the boys tired of watching the elk, John drove them through the rest of the valley. They skipped walking the half mile up Rough Fork Trail to the historic Woody House, but they did trek across the rustic bridge to see the two-storied Caldwell House the boys had asked to visit.

"Neal said Hiram Caldwell, who built this house, was one of his great-great-granddaddies or something." Bucky peeked into all the rooms of the old whitewashed home with interest.

Billy Ray pushed out his lip. "I think it was mean the park made everyone move out. Neal said lots of people didn't want to give up their houses or land."

"That's true." John ran a hand along the top of the old rock fireplace. "But the timber companies were moving in and if the park hadn't saved and bought the land when they did, we might have lost all the forest and wildlife here. Timber companies didn't know how to be conservative in those days."

Quickly losing interest in too much historical talk, like most young children, Bucky headed toward the door. "Let's go do our hike now. Okay?"

John loaded them back into the truck and then drove to the parking area near the trailhead of Caldwell Fork Trail. The start of the trail began by heading across a long, split-log footbridge spanning high above the Cataloochee Creek.

"Cool! Look at this!" Billy Ray's face lit as they came to the beginning of the bridge.

John moved to block him from starting across the bridge. "This is a high and long bridge, boys—twenty-five feet in length. It's said to be the longest bridge in the whole park. Out in the middle, the bridge has a little bounce to it. Because it crosses so high above the creek, we need to cross the bridge very carefully, holding to the rail and not fooling around." He made eye contact with both the boys. "Do I make myself clear?"

They nodded, recognizing his no-nonsense voice.

John continued. "I want one of you in front of me and one in back." He gestured toward Billy Ray to go first. "Put one hand on the bridge railing and the other out for balance, Son." He looked toward Lydia. "Lydia, you follow and keep an eye on Bucky behind me."

The water cascaded in a riot below them, and John felt relieved when both of the boys had crossed safely.

"That was awesome." Bucky literally danced in place. "Let's walk back over it again, okay?"

Lydia shook her head. "Absolutely not. That's quite enough for me. Besides, there are more bridges up the trail as we walk on, and we'll get to cross this one again on our way back."

Billy Ray grinned at her. "Were you scared, Nana Lydia?"

"Absolutely terrified." She shivered for effect. "But I felt better when I stopped looking down."

Laughing, they started up the trail, a happy group of hikers.

CHAPTER 13

Lydia had forgotten how much pleasure she found in walking a quiet backwoods trail in the mountains. She'd hiked some of the pathways behind Hill House leading toward the Smokies boundary, but she hadn't dared to venture too far on her own.

Here the trail wove deep into the wilderness on an old settlers' roadbed with the tumbling Caldwell Fork ever alongside. To the boys' delight, the trail crisscrossed continually over the creek on rustic log bridges. At each crossing, the boys begged to stop to jump on the rocks, to take off their shoes to wade, or to dig for salamanders near the streamside.

Pleased to still find summer flowers in bloom along the trail, Lydia pointed these out to the twins. "That's a white bloodroot by that old log, and the small blue flowers growing beside that pile of rocks are woodland bluets."

"What's the name of those red ones on the hill by that big tree?" Bucky asked, pointing to a cluster of vibrant, star-shaped crimson flowers.

"Those are fire pinks."

The boy wrinkled his nose. "How come they didn't call them fire reds? They're not pink."

Laughing, John answered, "The term *pink* comes from the fact that the ragged petal edges look as though they were cut out with pinking shears—you know, like the scissors your mother uses when she sews."

"I guess." Bucky romped off, unimpressed.

Lydia walked closer to study the flowers. "I didn't know that, John. That's interesting."

He chuckled. "I'm glad someone thinks so."

"Oh, they remember more than you imagine." She started back up the trail beside him, keeping an eye on the boys walking ahead of them.

"Come look!" they shouted a short distance later. "Bunches and bunches of butterflies!"

Catching up to the boys, Lydia saw dozens of swallowtail butterflies clustered all over the ground. They'd gathered right in the middle of the trail, creating a dazzling sight with their bright yellow wings edged in black, each one glittering in the afternoon sunlight.

"How lovely," she exclaimed.

"You mean yucky." Billy Ray made a face. "They're sitting on horse poop." The twins squatted down for a closer look.

"Super gross." Bucky stuck his finger into his mouth in a mock gag. "It looks like they're eating the poop or something."

"They are eating it, in a sense." John laughed. "Butterflies cluster on horse piles to pick up minerals and nutrients."

Billy Ray made another face. "Well, I wouldn't eat horse poop to get my vitamins," he threw out before he and Bucky started up the trail again, eager to move on.

Lydia lingered to watch the mass of lacy-winged creatures gathered on the trail, their delicate wings flashing in the sunlight. She frowned. "It does seem hard to understand why something so lovely would cluster on excrement, John."

He leaned closer to whisper in her ear, "If the boys had rubbed horse manure on their arms and hands, the butterflies might have gathered all over them. But I decided not to tell them that."

Lydia's eyes flew open. "Please don't. Those boys would probably try it just to see if you're right—they're such daredevils at their age."

He looked ahead. "And we'd better move on to catch up with those daredevils."

At about three miles from the trailhead, they all paused to

enjoy McKee Branch tumbling down the mountain into Caldwell Fork. Soon after, they crossed yet another log bridge before coming to a trail intersection with the McKee Branch Trail.

John gestured around, as they paused at the trail intersection. "The Caldwell Fork School used to be here, although there are no remains of it now. Quite a community of folks once lived in this section of the valley. There was even a gristmill near the bridge we last crossed."

"What's a gristmill?" Billy Ray asked as he coaxed a caterpillar to crawl up his finger.

"A gristmill is a water-powered mill used to grind corn or grains into flour and meal. You saw a working gristmill when we visited Cades Cove."

"And we saw one at Dollywood," Bucky chimed in.

Looking around, he changed the subject. "Did Neal Caldwell's relatives live here, too?"

"Yes, I'd say so."

"Then I can tell him we came here." Bucky raced ahead then to catch up with Billy Ray, who'd dumped the caterpillar and moved on.

"I think the boys like Neal," Lydia commented as they followed them over a slight rise in the trail.

"Yeah. Neal's got a way with them."

A mile and a half later, 4.6 miles from the beginning of the trailhead, they stopped for their lunch at their hiking destination at another trail intersection where Hemphill Bald Trail dropped down from the mountain above.

Settled on a rock by the stream, Billy Ray waved his peanut butter sandwich toward the intersecting trail. "Is that the same trail that goes along the ridgetop above our farm, Daddy John?"

"The same one." John fished out a ham and cheese sandwich for himself.

"Can we hike back that way?" Bucky asked.

"Well, you could, but our farm is still a long way from here," John answered. "First you'd need to hike this section of Hemphill Bald Trail three miles up to Double Gap. You know that part of the mountain. It's about four or five miles from Purchase Gap, where you visited the Science Learning Center with your kindergarten class, and less than a mile east, heading toward our farm, to Hemphill Bald. You've ridden horses to that bald from the Cataloochee Ranch."

"I remember." Bucky nodded. "It was way high up on the mountain and you could see forever."

"Yes, Hemphill Bald is over five thousand feet and one of the highest elevations in this area." He took a swig from his water bottle before continuing. "After the bald, you'd hike downhill about two miles more to Sheepback Knob above our place. From there you could head straight down the trail at Buck Knob and come in right behind the lodge and cabins on the Upper Farm. You know that area well."

Billy Ray wrinkled his nose. "How far is that altogether?"

John stopped to add the mileage in his mind. "Probably about eight and a half miles from this intersection down in the Cataloochee Valley. If we hiked it today, we'd need to get someone to drive us back to the valley to get the truck."

"But maybe someday we could do it?"

"Sure." John smiled. "Or someday we could just hike across Hemphill Bald Trail from the back of our farm to the bald. There's a stone table for picnicking there under a tree with great views. Then we could walk on and cut over to Cataloochee Ranch farther up the trail, if you can make it that far. The whole distance would only be about five or six miles, maybe ten to eleven miles round-trip."

"That would certainly be enough for me until I get more conditioned," Lydia put in. "This round-trip hike of over nine miles is taxing for me. I'll probably have sore legs tomorrow."

"What's 'conditioned'?" Bucky frowned.

John grinned. "It means until Lydia has hiked some more and gotten in better shape."

"Oh." Bucky studied her. "Are you not in good shape 'cause you're getting old?"

John laughed. "You did set yourself up for that one, Lydia."

She lifted her chin. "Everyone can hike farther distances when they hike often, Bucky. I've been living in the city a long time, that's all."

After wolfing down their sandwiches, the boys begged to pull off their shoes and wade in the creek while John and Lydia finished their lunch.

They sat in silence for a time, except for the sounds of the creek and the shrieks of pleasure of the boys, until Lydia spoke.

"John, I want to ask you something."

He turned his gaze toward her. "What?"

"Did Mary Beth talk to you about the letter she got from Sonny?"

The flash of anger that flicked across his face gave her an answer before his words did. "Yes, and she told me she talked with you about it." He took a swig of his water. "It worries me that Sonny plans to come through this area and wants to see the boys."

He crossed his arms. "I don't know if you've been told this, but Mary Beth legally took back her maiden name after Sonny deserted her. She and I had the boys' names changed to Cunningham, too. We thought it would be too confusing for them to be raised as Harpers when they were growing up on the Cunningham Farm."

"I remember Billy Ray told me his full name was William Rayfield Cunningham, and I wondered about it." She thought about this. "Do the boys understand their names have been changed?"

John nodded. "Mary Beth and I explained it to them before they started school. We wanted them to be able to explain it to anyone who asked questions."

"Did Sonny agree to this?"

John snorted. "Mary Beth got him to sign the papers by sending him money one time when he wanted it. Apparently, the money meant more to him than his kids."

"How sad." Lydia shook her head. "That boy comes from a nice family. It's hard to believe he's gotten so messed up."

"I know." John finished his sandwich. "He's troubled in some unnatural way, and I've heard through a few sources it might be drugs. That makes me more worried for him to spend time with the boys."

Lydia felt her eyes widen. "You don't think he would hurt them, do you?"

John kicked at a rock. "I don't know, but I wouldn't put it past him to use the boys to threaten Mary Beth to give him money. She's told Sonny she won't send him any more and he hasn't been happy about it."

Lydia watched the boys jump from rock to rock in the mountain stream. "Well, maybe he won't come through here at all. He's visited so few times over the years. Perhaps he'll change his mind."

"I hope so." John sighed. "The boy is their natural father and they have a right to know him. But I wish they were older first so they'd understand his problems more."

Lydia slipped off her socks and shoes and splashed her feet in the cold water of the stream. "I think you need to talk to them. Tell them what you know about their father."

He scowled. "The boys go to visit the Harpers—their other grandparents. They also visit Sonny's brother, Eric, his wife, Faye, and their kids. They know Sonny lives out west somewhere, has his own life there, and isn't interested in any of his family anymore."

She pulled her feet up on the rock again. "That must be hard for them to understand."

He shrugged as he packed the lunch remains back into his backpack. "They ask questions sometimes, but they have so many people in their lives who love them and that helps. Both understand, too, that some people have problems and are harder to live with than others."

Lydia dropped her eyes as she started putting her socks and shoes back on. "Yes, I guess they learned that early, living with Estelle."

John lowered his voice and Lydia felt him tense beside her. "I never let Mother give the boys a difficult time. I stressed to her that if she did, her only chance for future heirs for the farm would be toast."

Her eyes met his. "Do they want to be heirs?"

"They say so, but they're young. Only time will tell."

She put a hand on his. "I'm glad you see that, John. And because you are offering them the freedom to choose, they are more likely to stay."

"I'm trying to change, Lydia."

"I know." She gave him a quick kiss on the cheek while the boys' heads were turned.

Later that night, Lydia sat in the loud and boisterous atmosphere of the Stompin' Ground barn remembering that earlier conversation. She'd heard Mary Beth sing twice and she watched her dance now, with joy and abandon, around the huge dance floor of the big barn theater with Neal.

"They sure make a nice couple," Rebecca said, following her eyes. She and her husband, Tolley, had joined them at a large table tonight.

"Yes, they do." Lydia pulled her seat closer to Rebecca so they could hear each other talk. "What was your impression of Sonny Harper?"

"I remember Sonny as a slightly spoiled younger son who got involved too early with a rock band and unhealthy dreams." She shook her head.

"Do you think he's dangerous—that if he came back to the valley he might hurt Mary Beth or the boys?"

Rebecca tapped a nail on her teeth, thinking about this. "It's hard to say. Sonny grew very self-absorbed at the end before he finally left the valley. He didn't care about Mary Beth, his family, his babies. He only cared about his band and running around doing gigs and shows. Folks whispered that he had drug and alcohol problems. Maybe he did. That can go a long way toward ruining a nice young man's life." She glanced at the dance floor, her eyes finding Mary Beth. "It's nice to see Bee finding some happiness with someone good and decent like Neal. She deserves it."

"I know." Lydia felt a catch in her heart, knowing how absent she'd been during the hard years Mary Beth had had to endure.

A voice interrupted her reverie. "Wanna clog a little, good-lookin'?" Tolley Albright held out a hand and winked at her. "I thought I'd steal a dance with you while John is talking shop with that farmer." He gestured across the room.

Lydia agreed and moved to the floor with Tolley as Neal and Mary Beth came back to the table to rest and join Rebecca.

The farmer John was talking with turned out to be a neighbor. He told John about another ghost sighting near Drop Off Ridge. John filled Lydia in on all the details later as they shared tea on the porch of Hill House.

"Two little boys not much older than the twins got scared out of their wits yesterday." John frowned into the dark. "They had pop guns and were playing in the woods. The ghost jumped out from behind a tree, swinging its arms and moaning, waving what the boys described as a bloody knife. They told the sheriff they ran for their lives, with the ghost hollering threats behind them to never come back there again."

"Honestly, this has really got to stop." Lydia pushed the porch swing into a soft rhythm with her foot. "Doesn't the sheriff have any clues?"

"No." John ran his hands through his hair in irritation. "And I don't like that at all. This sighting occurred right near our property line on the other side of Indian Creek below Drop Off Ridge. That's not far from Ridge House above the Upper Orchards where Nevelyn, Vera, and the children stay alone every day while the men work on the farm."

Lydia stopped her swing. "You're right. Charlie and Nevelyn's house isn't far below the ridge woods or from the Indian Creek boundary, either." She paused. "That's near where that little girl got so badly scared before, too."

He stood to walk over to the porch railing, obviously upset. "It takes a sick person to scare children."

She got up to stand beside him, putting a hand on his arm in comfort. "I'm sure the sheriff's office will find who is behind this soon. Maggie is a small valley and someone will come forward who knows something."

"I hope so." John turned slightly, slipping his arms around her in the darkness. "It's good to have you to talk with again, to share with." He traced a hand down her back. "Did you have a good time tonight?"

"Yes." She made an effort to shift out of John's embrace but found herself backed against the porch rail instead.

"Don't pull away. I won't press beyond what you want." His lips moved to hers as he finished his words and the kiss he gave her was soft and sweet.

Reveling in the familiar spicy smell of him, Lydia moved closer, engulfed in old memories and, at the same time, stirred by new feelings.

"I feel like a kid courting a new girl." John spoke the words against her neck, echoing her own thoughts. "But it's a good feeling, sweet and tender but stirring up my blood, too." He kissed her again and Lydia returned the kiss with passion this time, joyous to think she'd come home at last to the man who'd filled her dreams and heart these long years.

"I love you, Lydia Ruth." He wrapped her tight in his embrace until she could feel his heartbeat against hers. "There's never been another woman in my thoughts or another woman I've felt drawn to since I met you."

He stepped back slightly until he could look down into her eyes. "I want you to know I yearn to have you back. I want to be married to you again in every way, to hold you in my arms as we fall asleep every night, to wake up with you every morning, to cherish you in my heart until we're old and white-haired."

"You already have a touch of white hair," she teased him, running her hands along his temple lightly.

He chuckled and then kissed her again with a warm passion that hinted of more, threading his hands through her hair, nibbling on her neck in a delightful way that heightened her breathing and sent her senses yearning.

She clung to him with pleasure, her hands moving over the familiar lines of his back, enjoying the taste and feel of him.

With a heavy sigh, John kissed her forehead and held her back from him at last. "I need to go or I'll urge you for more."

His eyes loomed dark with desire as she opened her eyes to look at him. She wasn't ready to encourage him to stay yet, but it felt sweet to see the yearning in his eyes again. Passion and desire had slipped away from them in those last difficult years with Estelle.

"We can get married a second time if you'd like, Lyddie, to symbolize a new beginning." His eyes moved toward the door. "I can carry you over the threshold like I did the first time."

She giggled and then drew in a ragged breath, feeling another rush of urgent wanting wash over her. "I'll think, John," she told him. "It's all I can give you for now."

"It's enough." He put a hand to her cheek. "Do you still love me?"

"I do." She whispered the words softly.

"That's sweet to hear."

Lydia leaned her forehead against his chest and he buried his face in her hair. They stood there close together for a few moments, hearts beating so loudly that Lydia felt she could hear them in the quiet of the night.

Then John gave her a last quick kiss and walked to his truck, leaving Lydia to drift into her house feeling cherished—that was the perfect word—a feeling she hadn't known for a long time.

CHAPTER 14

As a farmer, working with the orchard, the changing seasons, and the land, John had learned to be patient. It took time and nurturing to grow things well, and John was giving ample time to grow his relationship with Lydia back into a healthy and sweet place. As the weeks passed, he'd watched her trust toward him increase and he knew her feelings for him strengthened daily.

He found her working in the flower bed in the front yard this morning. John often dropped by to see Lydia before his day began, and they shared dinner most evenings now, either here at Hill House or down at Main House with the family.

Lydia stood up, brushing dirt off her knees and hands, her face flushed. "With the heat wave we're having now in July, I decided to get out and weed my flower beds early today." She smiled. "But I'm finished and I'm glad you stopped by. Go in the kitchen and make coffee—or look for something cold to drink—while I shower off."

Despite the heat, he made coffee, nursing a cup afterward and nibbling on Lydia's fresh coffee cake he found on the kitchen table. The wall phone rang and John picked it up automatically, expecting it to be Sam or Manu. They knew he stopped by in the mornings, and few people knew the house number except family.

"John here," he answered.

An angry voice erupted back. "What the devil are you doing there?"

"Is this J. T.?" John thought he recognized the voice. "Your mother's in the shower and she should be out in a few minutes. Do you want me to give her a message?"

"No," the voice snapped back. "But I have a message for you. I don't like it that you're there early in the morning like this, with Mom in the shower. We don't want you getting back in her life and hurting her again, you understand?"

Irritation crawled up John's back. "You have no right to talk to me like that, J. T. I'm your father."

"Some father." J. T. snorted. "And I meant what I said about Mom. I'm not a little boy anymore, and I'm not going to let you make Mom unhappy again. In case you didn't know, Will and Parker and I *didn't* want her to go back to North Carolina."

John bit down on an angry retort. "J. T., I think you and I need to talk some time. I would never willingly hurt your mother."

"Too late, you already did," J. T. snapped back. "And I don't want to *chat* with you any longer." Sarcasm laced his voice. "You let Mother know we have the rest of her things all packed up. Tell her to call if she wants us to ship them or if she can come down to pick them up." He paused. "I don't want you in her life again and I *don't* want you in mine."

The phone slammed down and John stood there in shock for several seconds, his son's angry words sizzling in the air.

"Who was that?" Lydia asked, coming into the kitchen fresh and fragrant from her shower. Her thick hair was pulled up under a clip at the back of her head, and damp tendrils drifted down her neck.

His eyes traveled over her in appreciation. "That was our son—or perhaps I should say *your* son."

Lydia's eyebrows lifted in surprise at the irritation in his tone. "What happened?"

John's hands clenched involuntarily into fists. "J. T. made it clear he doesn't want me in either your life or his." He paced around the small kitchen. "He wanted to know what I was doing here so early with you in the shower. There were insinuations in his voice, as though I didn't have a right to be here or have any right to be with you."

Lydia wandered into the kitchen and poured herself a cup of tea from the teapot on the counter. Then she perched on the corner of a chair. "John, I think you need to calm down."

"Easy for you to say." He scowled at her. "You weren't just insulted by your own son. He had no right to say those things to me. No right. Haven't you taught him any manners over these years?"

She sent him a steely look. "Don't criticize J. T. to me, John. He loves me and is defensive of me."

"And I don't love you?" He tried to bank his irritation.

"He's remembering his last memories. Things were in a bad state then—both of us hurting. He's worried for me. He wants me to be happy." She calmly stirred a little milk into her tea.

John walked over and clenched his hands on the chair back across from hers. "I can't believe you're making excuses for the way he talked to me. He was rude and out of order, Lydia, and he hung up on me."

"He was upset. I'm sure it shocked him to find you here so early in the morning and to hear you say I was in the shower. You have to admit, the situation suggests intimacy."

"So? We *are* intimate," said John. Lydia's patient tone infuriated him.

"We're not intimate in that way." She crossed her arms primly.

"Not for any lack of desire on my part." His eyes narrowed. "Have you not told the boys we're developing a relationship again?"

He saw her eyes drop to her lap. "No, not yet. The boys worried when I came back to North Carolina. They feared I would get involved with you again. I haven't confided to them yet that we're seeing each other, except in casual interactions with family and friends, of course."

"Are you ashamed of caring for me?" She'd pricked his pride and he knew he snapped out the words.

She sighed. "No, I'm just wary. I still remember problems from the past sometimes. Have flashbacks. I wanted to be stronger in myself before I talked with the boys. More sure of myself."

"Well, great. That's just great. Certainly a boost to my ego." A cold chill went through him. "And where does that leave me with my sons?"

Her eyes flashed with annoyance as she looked across at him. "Exactly where you placed yourself with them. It's *your* responsibility to work to restore your relationship with your sons, if you want one again. Not mine."

She got up and walked away from him into the living room. Sensing him following her, she turned. "You've been working to reestablish a relationship with me, John, but you've done nothing to patch up your relationship with your sons. I can't do that for you. It's not my responsibility."

He began to lose his patience. "And you think it's my responsibility to do that?" His voice dropped dangerously as he spoke the words.

"Yes, I do. And quite frankly, I think it's cowardly that you haven't made any effort to approach J. T., Billy Dale, and Parker."

"Cowardly?" He practically roared the word, sending the kittens scampering under the sofa.

Undaunted, Lydia squared her shoulders. "Yes, cowardly—your typical avoidance tendency. Pretending there's no problem and hoping maybe it will just go away by itself."

He grabbed her arm. "You don't think very highly of me, do you, Lydia?"

"In the way you've handled the situation with your sons, no, I don't." She looked at his hand on her arm until he released it, and then she walked over to stand behind a chair, farther away from him. "I made the effort to keep in touch with Mary Beth after I left. I wrote her letters—which I learned your mother destroyed and didn't let her read. Then I sent her letters through Rebecca as I could, trying to keep in touch with my daughter. Loving her enough to want to stay close."

"You *left* your daughter and moved away," he reminded her, knowing the words were deliberately cruel. He saw her wince.

"I had to leave at that time. And now I'm back, in part to reestablish a relationship with her again . . . and perhaps with you." She leaned over the chair, her eyes sorrowful. "But in all this time, John, you have never made one effort to stay in contact with your sons—never sent them a letter, never called them, never sent them a Christmas present or a birthday card, never acknowledged their graduations or drove down to see them."

He flinched. "After they drove off in a huff, they never came back here, either. They never called me, wrote to me, remembered me at Christmas or on my birthday." Seeing her raised eyebrows, he added, "Oh, I know you sent gifts from all of you and you sent cards, too, on special occasions. But I knew they weren't really from the boys."

"Yes, I sent gifts, cards, and I tried very hard to keep up the family ties. But you never even *tried,* John. How do you think that made those boys feel, not to even get an acknowledgment from their father at important moments of their lives or for them to see my birthday come and go without even a card from you? Your behavior was more than cowardly. It was often cruel."

"I sent you a check every month—to buy things the boys needed, to get gifts and special things. Did the boys know I sent money every month to help?"

"Yes, and they appreciated the help, but it's not the same. A check sent in the mail every month is impersonal. They needed to know you still loved them, even though they chose to live with me. They needed to know you cared, and you never let them know that. It hurt, John."

"I'm not good with picking out gifts and cards and such. You know that. You always did those things. Or my mother did."

She laughed. "And well I remember the horrible gifts your mother chose for all of us at Christmas."

John felt his face flush. "They were no different from the gifts I received growing up."

"Well, then poor you—and poor Holly, too—to always get only socks and a plain sweater for Christmas." Her voice had dropped and John hated the sound of pity in it.

"We did all right. We turned out okay."

"Yes, and it's a blessing and a miracle you did and with no less scars than you both have."

His temper rose. "I don't know what you're talking about—scars."

Lydia propped a hip on the chair arm. "Holly told me she went to therapy for years to help her get past her upbringing. You probably could have used some, too. It might have spared all of us some sorrows."

"I don't like this conversation. It's insulting." John stomped toward the door. "And no matter what you've said, nothing justifies how J. T. talked to me today or that he hung up on me."

"John." Her soft voice caught him as his hand pushed open the screen door. "We can have no future together until you work things out with your sons. I want a united family."

He turned to glare at her. "Making threats and conditions now?"

"No." She shook her head sadly. "Just stating facts." She walked toward him and then stopped. "You're happy that Mary Beth and I have reestablished a relationship. I will be equally happy when you work to reestablish a relationship with your sons."

"The street runs both ways, Lydia."

"Yes, that's true." She gave a deep sigh. "But you're the grown-up in this. The father and, supposedly, the wiser one. The expectation is that you will do what is right and set the example. That you will take the initiative. That's what's expected of parents—to put aside their pride and personal feelings to do what is best for their children and for their family."

He banged out of the door without responding, afraid of what he might say next. Wanting to get away from the guilt and condemnation she layered on him.

Needing to work, he drove his truck down to the Side Orchards, where he'd left the men working earlier checking the trees for aphids, scab, or rust and then repairing fence lines after.

Eugene Sheppard saw him get out of his truck and waved. "We've found where them little Peter Rabbits have been getting through the fence to get at the young trees."

John nodded and set to work rolling out fencing and nailing it snug against the posts. He worked furiously, saying little.

During their next break, Sam walked over to John. "I think some of the early Lodis are about ready to pick." He pointed toward a row of mature apple trees on the hillside above them. "Probably the Pink Pearls and the Parmers, too. Why don't you go check? We've got this fencing job about done."

Charlie looked their way with a grin. "Maybe the fence will hold this time. Seems like this is the third time we've fixed this fence since spring."

With the sound of nails still pounding, John walked up through the orchard rows to check on the trees Sam had mentioned. He found some of the yellow Lodis nearly ready to pick, as Sam had said, and some of the Parmers close to season, but not the Pearls yet.

"Them Pearls need a little more time," Eugene said, coming up behind him. "One or two might be near ready but not the bulk of 'em."

John nodded, walking along to examine the other trees in the orchard. With July here, many of the early apples would soon be ready to harvest, although the bulk of the crop wouldn't come in until fall.

Eugene hobbled to catch up with John while he stopped to pull down an Ambrosia branch to examine the ripening fruit. "That anger you're a nursing makes you walk too fast for an old man to catch up to."

John tried to ignore him.

The old man put a hand on his arm. "You stop and let me set a spell on this old stump." He dropped himself slowly to sit on a broad tree stump and sigh. At eighty-two, he tired easily.

"I didn't ask you to come along with me, E. C." John propped a foot on a smaller stump nearby.

"Yeah, but somebody needed to come along with you and see

that you didn't bring yourself to harm." He grinned up at John. "You were whacking away at them nails down there on the fencing so fierce we were afeared to get near you. We all know you only work in a frenzy like that when you're put out about something." He ran his hands down the twisted wood on his walking stick. "You wanna talk about it?"

"Not particularly." John picked a ripe Early Joe off a nearby tree, turning the small red and yellow apple over in his hand.

"That looks like a good 'un." Eugene held out his palm. "Maybe you'll pass it along, seeing as you seem only interested in lookin' at it. I like the flesh of the Early Joe—tender, juicy, and flavorful."

John passed the apple to the old man and watched him bite into it with pleasure. Then he turned to examine the tree again. "I think we can come pick a bushel or two of these today or tomorrow. Mary Beth can sell some in the store and the women can use the rest for pies and applesauce."

Not deterred from his purpose, Eugene caught John's eye. "You used to talk with me, Son, when you had a problem."

"I know." John put a hand on the old man's shoulder fondly. "But this is something I've got to think through and work out on my own."

"Yeah, there's problems like that." He scratched his head under the rim of his battered straw hat. "You might want to take a good walk up toward the mountain to clear your mind. I'll tell the men you went to check around the lodge. It's worrisome knowing that ghost is still on the loose and the culprit behind it not found."

"Yes, it is." John's eyes moved over the rolling hillsides to the wooded ridges above. "Maybe I will walk up above the lodge and check around."

Since the men had picked up on his anger and irritation, he wasn't too eager to rejoin them right now and be quizzed further. "You tell Sam where I've gone, all right, Eugene?"

"Sure." The old man pulled himself up on his cane. "And I'll shoot up a prayer on my way back that you'll get some help from the Big Man on your problem. When you ain't comfortable dumping out your worries to a friend, the Big Man's always there for an ear. You remember that."

"I will." John patted Eugene Sheppard on the back before he headed down the fields to join the other men.

An hour later, after walking the wooded trail past the rental cabins to Garretts Gap up on the mountain and back—and praying at length—John still had found no peace. Coming down toward the Lodge Road, he saw the Crowe boys playing around below the hunting lodge.

He waved to them. "You boys be careful playing around the ridge and creek. The sheriff's had more sightings of that ghost prankster around here."

"You don't think it's a real ghost?" the older boy, Nalin, asked him.

John shook his head. "No, I don't. But someone pretending to be a ghost can be just as dangerous."

Davy walked closer as the boys came out of the woods. "Maybe there really is a ghost—Nance Dude or that old Indian who got killed on the ridge long ago. Maybe the ghost don't want no one messing around this area."

John noted the worried brown eyes of the younger boy. "Well, maybe that's more reason for you boys to head on back toward home. Your mom might be worried."

Waving, they headed off down the Lodge Road toward the creek. John sat on the porch steps of the hunting lodge, trying to settle his thoughts. He kept hearing Lydia's words echoing over and over in his mind, especially some of the ones she said near the end: *We can have no future together until you work things out with your sons.*

Did she mean that? And was it true what she added later, that it was his responsibility to make amends with the boys and not theirs to come to him? He'd always comforted himself that he'd be ready to make peace whenever they felt ready to come home again. But Lydia seemed to think it was his place to take the initiative and go to them. That he'd let them down, let her down, by not going to them all these years.

John dropped his head in his hands. "Dang woman. Makes a man doubt all he's come to believe, all he thought was right."

He thought about J. T., talking so hateful to him this morning. Hanging up on him. He'd have given the boy a long lecture in the past for behavior like that, probably walloped him if his attitude hadn't improved in the process. Now he was a grown man and far away. And saying he didn't want to talk with his own father.

John seethed at the thought. "Well, we'll see," he said at last, getting up from the steps and kicking at a pinecone in the path. "We'll just see."

He set off at a steady pace down the Farm Road. Letting himself in the back door of Main House, he headed up to his bedroom. There he dragged out his travel duffel, threw some clothes and toiletries into it, then changed out of his work clothes into slacks and a clean shirt. He looked up some addresses and phone numbers in a tattered black book in the drawer by his bed, Googled on his computer for map directions, and headed out to his truck less than thirty minutes later.

Manu, trimming some shrubs near the back porch, looked up when he saw John throw his duffel in the truck. "Going somewhere, John?" he asked.

"Yep," John told him, climbing into the front seat of the vehicle. "I'm taking a little trip for a few days. Need to clear something up and check on some things. You tell Ela, Mary Beth, and Sam I'll be gone a day or so. Maybe the weekend, but I'll be back by Monday, I reckon, at the latest."

Manu nodded.

"You've got my cell phone number—Sam does, too—if there's any problem that can't be handled until I get back." John started the truck.

"Drive safe," Manu said, not asking any more questions.

An hour down the road, John punched a long distance number into his cell phone and heard a familiar woman's voice answer, "Martha Howard, Career Services, Georgia Tech."

"Martha, this is John Cunningham. I know you're at work and this might not be the best time for a call, but I need a favor."

"What can I do for you, John?" she asked.

"Could you put me up at your place tonight in Atlanta? And could you get my sons together at your home for a talk? It seems like it's overdue between us, and I thought it might be best if we got together at some neutral place for a visit."

"You can certainly stay at my place, John, and I'll do my best to get your boys over to my house, too." She paused. "If you don't mind my candor, I'd say this visit is long overdue."

"Well, better late than never, like the old saying goes." He slowed the truck around a mountain curve. "I ought to be there about five."

"Fine. I'll make some calls, use some clout. Fib a little if I need to. You be careful in that Atlanta traffic."

He snorted. "I'd rather deal with a rattlesnake."

Martha laughed and it felt good to hear the sound. "I assume you have the directions, but if you need help call me later when you get closer."

"I will. And thanks, Martha."

"Don't thank me too soon. You're on your own with this one. I'm just the organizer."

"I understand." He passed a slow-moving vehicle as he swung onto the highway.

"Oh, and John," she said before he could hang up. "I'm ordering pizza for everyone and you can foot the bill."

"Sounds fair, Martha. Good to talk with you. See you soon."

CHAPTER 15

On Sunday afternoon, Lydia sat in a lawn chair outside with Mary Beth, watching the twins play in a plastic wading pool.

"That little pool you bought proved a hit with the boys and has sure kept them busy this afternoon." Mary Beth pushed down her sunglasses to wink at Lydia across the top of them. "It's given me a needed break, too."

Lydia watched her daughter stretch out her legs in the sun. "Is running the store with the boys so young too much for you?"

"No." Mary Beth smiled at her. "I love the store. I love running it and I love visiting with the customers. And Ela is great about watching the boys for me while I work. But, as you know, two small twins at once can be a handful." She turned to her mother. "How did you manage it with J. T. only a toddler, when Billy Dale and Parker were still small?"

"You adapt." Lydia laughed as she rubbed suntan lotion over her arms and legs. With her red hair and fair skin, she had to use care when out in the sun at any length. "The boys played together well, too, especially when Neal was over at the house so much, making an equal foursome. J. T.'s and Neal's personalities clicked well, like Billy Dale's and Parker's did."

"You're right. J. T. and Neal were like two peas in a pod, and I remember they argued very little." Mary Beth looked thoughtful. "You know, looking back, I think Neal spent more time at our home growing up than at his." She picked at a nail. "I guess that's why it feels so funny being with him like a boyfriend."

Lydia raised an eyebrow. "How's that going?"

She saw her daughter blush. "Pretty good," she answered evasively.

Bucky turned his squirt gun on her and fired a stream of water her way.

Surprised, she gasped. "Buckner Dean, if you or Billy Ray squirt me or Nana Lydia again, I'm taking that squirt gun away from you, do you hear?" She wiped the water off her face.

"Aw, Mom, we were just havin' fun."

She tossed her head. "Well, you have fun squirting each other or squirting at that target we set up." She pointed to the tin cans they'd lined across the fence top.

The boy turned to squeeze off a stream of water toward the row of cans. "When's Daddy John coming home?" he asked, climbing out of the pool to put the can he'd blasted back on the fence.

"He said by Monday at the latest." Mary Beth rolled her legs so she would tan more evenly.

Lydia made no comment. No one knew she and John had quarreled the day he left, or that she'd worried herself sick since he took off wondering where he was, what he was thinking, and why he went off on his own without telling anyone exactly where he'd gone.

Billy Ray looked up from the set of boats he pushed through the water. "He didn't tell nobody where he was going."

"He didn't tell *anybody*." Mary Beth corrected his grammar.

"Anybody," he parroted. "I wish he'd taken me and Bucky. We never get to go anywhere."

Bee rolled her eyes at this typical summer complaint of her boys. She used to voice the same complaint herself when small. "Manu told you Daddy John had to go take care of some sort of business. You can't take small boys on business trips."

She got up to adjust her chair and lay down on her stomach this time. "Besides, you've gone a lot of places this summer. Neal and I took you over to Cherokee to the Oconoluftee Village. You got to see the Indians dance and we shopped downtown. We hiked to Mingo Falls one day, too. And Nana took

you to the arboretum and to the college so you could see where
she's going to work. She and Daddy John took you hiking in
Cataloochee, too. . . ." She would have gone on, but the sound
of a truck coming distracted them.

"Daddy John!" The twins hollered in unison as John's truck
pulled up into the driveway and to a stop. They raced toward
him, dripping water behind them as they ran barefoot across the
grass.

"Whoa!" John said, getting down from the cab. "Don't be
leaping on me soaking wet like that."

The boys danced up and down around him. "Come see the
pool Nana Lydia got us. We've got squirt guns and boats, too."

John nodded at the women and followed the boys to properly
examine the pool and toys and then watched them squirt tin
cans on the fence line.

Mary Beth rolled out of her chair to stand and give her father
a hug as he walked back their way. "Hey, Daddy. We missed
you. Where've you been? Manu said you had some business to
take care of."

"I did, in Atlanta."

Lydia knew her mouth dropped open.

He grinned at her. "I drove down to pick up the rest of Lydia's
things and had a visit with my boys."

Mary Beth's eyes widened. "You visited with J. T., Parker,
and Billy Ray?"

John pulled up a chair. "Billy Ray prefers to be called Will
now. You might want to keep that in mind."

Mary Beth pulled her chair up closer to John's. "Daddy, I still
can't believe you went to see the boys. Are they all right? How
did that go? Where did you stay?"

"That's a lot of questions." He reached down to dig a can of
cola out of the small cooler Mary Beth had tucked beside her
chair.

"Daddy." She gave him an exasperated look. "You know we
want to know everything and you're being purposely evasive."

John took a long drink of the cola and then rubbed his neck.
"I decided it was time I talked to the boys. I think your mother

might have said it would be a good idea, too." He sent her a smug smile.

Lydia wanted to punch him for it. How dare he take off down to Atlanta and not even tell her!

He crossed an ankle over his knee. "I stayed with Martha and she helped me get all the boys together at her place for a family visit on Thursday evening. J. T. brought his wife, Laura—they'd gotten someone to sit with the children, Jack and Rachel. Billy Dale—I mean, Will—brought his wife, Amelia, and Parker brought his fiancée, Marie. We had quite a crowd for pizza and salad. Martha ordered and I paid."

"I can't believe they all came." Mary Beth leaned forward. "How did they act?"

"Angry and testy at first. We all threw our weight around, until J. T.'s wife, Laura, got provoked and took us to task. She'd taken some sort of mediation conflict management training in college, and she made us take turns, one at a time, saying what we wanted to say with no one interrupting. She policed us with an iron hand while we did it—then she let us go around again with a comeback. This helped us talk things out, once we all got into the pattern." He laughed. "That Laura's a strong, powerful woman. I guess she doesn't let J. T. get away with much." He glanced at Lydia.

Lydia's eyes met his. "Laura has a very strong personality and excellent organizational skills."

His mouth twitched. "I saw that. She organized us into finding a constructive way of talking things out."

Mary Beth sighed. "I wish you'd taken me with you. I feel awful about how I acted toward my brothers before they left and how I acted afterward." Her voice drifted off.

John leaned over to pat her leg fondly. "I said some words on your behalf, Bee. Told them some of the things you've shared with me. I hope that was okay." He paused. "They want you to come down, bring the boys." He paused again and grinned. "And bring Neal."

Mary Beth blushed. "You told them about me and Neal?"

Unrepentant, he crossed an ankle casually over his knee. "It came up. You needn't worry. I didn't offer details."

Mary Beth rolled her eyes.

John focused his eyes on Lydia. "We made some peace together, the boys and I. Not that everything's smooth as silk. You couldn't expect that after ten years. But we laid hostility aside, talked out what we wanted and expected from one another. That was a part of all that mediation stuff—telling the other person what you wanted from them to feel good again after everyone aired out and got their say."

Familiar with the mediation process of conflict resolution, Lydia asked, "What did you tell them you wanted in order to feel happy again and have resolution, John?"

She could tell he wrestled with telling her before he spoke. "I told them straight-out I wanted my family back, unified and caring about each other like a family should. I gave my regrets for all the years I didn't make an effort to be more a part of their lives. I told them I was genuinely sorry for all the unhappiness my mother caused and for how little I did to change what came down." His eyes found Lydia's. "I also told them I still loved their mother and wanted to make it up to her for the problems and hurts of the past. That I wanted to create a happy future with her. I expressed my hope that all the anger and resentments in our family could be left in the past."

"Wow." Mary Beth shook her head. "What did they say?"

John ran a hand through his hair. "Well, by that late hour in the day, we'd all about vented out all our rage, anger, and hard feelings, so I think it was taken well."

Lydia put a hand to her mouth, close to tears. "Did the boys talk out all their feelings, too, John?"

"Yeah, they gave it to me pretty good." He winced. "It was overdue. I needed to hear it and they needed to say it."

The twins shrieked around them, chasing each other with water guns, Cullie barking and running along behind them. They laughed happily as they leaped back into the wading pool, both unaware of the tensions circling among the adults.

Lydia paused to watch them and then turned to John again. "You drove down to Atlanta on Thursday and it's Sunday now." She sent him a probing gaze. "What have you done since then?"

He smiled a slow smile. "I went to see where each of my boys worked on Friday and Saturday—out in the field with Will on Friday morning surveying a piece of mountain land, to J. T.'s architectural firm to meet him for lunch and take a tour with him afterward and then over to the Botanical Garden to see where Parker works on Saturday morning." His eyes found Lydia's. "I was proud to see all they've accomplished, to let them show me their workplaces and talk about their plans for the future. You did well guiding them, Lydia. They've found happiness and satisfaction in what they do. That's important for a man."

"And for a woman," Mary Beth chimed in. "Don't get sexist, Daddy."

He raised two hands in surrender. "I wouldn't dare with you two around. My new daughters-in-law—and daughter-in-law-to-be—would hardly let me get away with such remarks, either. They pursue interesting lives and work, too."

Lydia bit her tongue, trying to let John tell about the happenings in his own way, trying not to break in to his account with the constant questions that assaulted her mind. John grinned at her, seeming to sense the effort it cost her. "I got to go to a nice cookout in J. T.'s backyard on Saturday evening," he continued. "Got to play with my two grandchildren and get acquainted with them. Jack looks enough like J. T. did as a boy to take me back in memory easily, and that little curly-haired baby, Rachel, just starting to walk, is as cute as a button. She liked riding horsey on my knee like Mary Beth used to."

Tears started sliding down Lydia's cheeks now. She couldn't help it.

"Aw, don't cry, Lyddie." John went over to drop down by her chair where he could catch her hands in his. This only made Lydia cry more, leaning her head against his.

Mary Beth cleared her throat. "You know, I need to haul these boys out of the pool and take them down to the house for supper." She waved at the twins, giving them instructions to dry off and get ready to leave. Getting up from her lawn chair, she gathered her things and began stuffing them into the large tote bag by her chair.

Lydia made an effort to pull herself together to tell the boys good-bye. They didn't need to see their grandmother crying.

John stood, too, and walked Mary Beth and the boys out to her small truck. "You tell Ela and Manu I'll come on back to the house after I've visited with Lydia a little longer."

"Mom made a big dinner for the boys and me for after church today and there's plenty left," Lydia heard her say. "I'm sure she'll feed you dinner and you two can talk some more."

Mary Beth waved some fingers at them as she bundled the boys into the truck. "I'll expect you both to tell me anything I missed later, you hear?"

John glanced toward Lydia as Mary Beth backed out of the driveway. "That was sensitive of her to clear out."

Lydia kicked at him with annoyance as she stood and started folding up the lawn chairs to take to the shed. "I can't believe you simply took off to Atlanta without even telling me, John Cunningham. I was worried sick all weekend, wondering where you were. . . ."

He jerked her into his arms, making her drop the chairs, and kissed her with ferocity. Lydia made an effort to struggle and then melted into the passion sizzling between them. It seemed shameless standing on the front lawn, practically making out like teenagers, but Lydia didn't care. It felt so good to have John back in her arms, to hold him, to be near him after that horrible quarrel.

"I'm glad you missed me." He murmured the words as his lips slid from hers to move over her face and eyes.

"Oh, John, when did you get so romantic?" She dropped her head back so he could continue the journey down her neck.

He lifted a brow. "I thought I was always romantic."

She kissed him again. "We neither one were very romantic toward the end and you know it."

He slid his arms around her and drew her closer. "Well, that was then and this is now. I guess it just proves that a couple of middle-aged folks can get to sparking if they want to."

She laughed and pulled away, swatting at him playfully. "You help me empty that kiddy pool and haul in the chairs and toys, and I'll fix you that supper Mary Beth talked about. I cooked too much, as usual, and there's plenty left."

"All right." He ducked in to give her another kiss. "I admit I only ate a quick sandwich on the road that Amelia packed for me."

Lydia sighed. "She's sweet like that." She fixed John with a stern look. "I'll expect you to tell me a lot more details about your visit while I'm fixing dinner, John Cunningham. And I'm still half-provoked with you because you drove down there and didn't take me."

His hand tightened on hers, his smile fading. "I needed to do this on my own, Lydia. You know that, and I have you to thank that I went, you and J. T. You both riled me up so that I got angry and finally confronted this issue." She saw his jaw clench. "I hate to admit it, but you were right that I needed to go to my sons and not the other way around."

Lydia laid a hand on his arm. "I'm glad you and the boys have made some peace."

He snorted. "Well, it's an uneasy one—and still a little volatile around the edges—but we're making progress. And that's something."

John dumped the pool, turned it on its side to dry out, and helped her carry the chairs and toys into the shed. They unloaded the truck next, hauling in the boxes and bags from Atlanta loaded in the back of John's truck. Then he followed her into the kitchen, sitting to watch her as she pulled out leftovers to heat up for their dinner.

"What's that?" he asked, eying a casserole she'd popped into the microwave to heat up.

"It's called Curly Casserole, a quick dinner casserole I used to make when the children were small. I thought Bucky and Billy Ray might like it, so I fixed it for them for lunch today. J. T. and the twins still love it." She sent a glance his way. "You used to."

John chuckled. "Is that the dish that had spiral-shaped noodles in it of different colors?"

"The same." She felt pleased he remembered it.

"I did like that one." He watched her pull another dish from the refrigerator to heat. "Green beans?"

"Yes." She nodded. "And watermelon. The boys loved that, plus I made apple dumplin's for dessert—a big hit with Cool Whip on the top."

"I think that apple dish is a new one," he said as he watched her pull the foil cover off the top of the Pyrex dish that had been sitting on the stovetop.

She turned to smile at him. "I couldn't resist trying it with the fresh apples coming in now."

He sniffed at it appreciatively. "Smells good, what's in it?"

"Chopped apples wrapped in Crescent Rolls, sprinkled with cinnamon, and then covered with sugar, butter, and orange juice sauce before baking. Wait 'til you smell it when I heat it up." She popped it into the oven to heat while she quickly warmed up the other dishes in the microwave.

He fell silent for a time as she put the dinner together. To help, he took out the garbage for her, set the table, and poured iced tea from the chilled pitcher in the refrigerator.

"Lydia," he said at last when she came to a stopping point in her work, "I told the boys I wanted to be married to you again and not separated, to live with you and care for you."

"Oh, John, I'm not sure it was time for that." She bit her lip with worry.

"The boys asked me straight-out my intentions. I had to be honest with them."

She twisted her hands. "How did they take it?"

"Better by Sunday than they would have Thursday night when I first came." He drummed his fingers on the table. "They realized by then I wasn't the wicked ogre they'd made me out to be—that I was only a man, trying to do the best I could with a hard situation in my life. Trying to honor my mother, a difficult woman, and honor my father's last wishes, trying to learn to run the farm alone after his death and struggling to get the place out of debt. Working too hard and too long, and too tired most of the time to be a good husband or a good father. Always hating discord and coveting peace. Expecting too much of everyone to keep harmony when my mother made life so difficult for you and for the boys."

He paused to collect his words. "I was so used to her ways, Lydia, that I didn't see how her issues affected your life and the boys' lives so adversely." He sighed. "I did better with Mary Beth when Mother tried to come down hard on her and the twins later on. Or at least some better. But Mother was never a rational sort of person to work with."

That was an understatement, she thought silently as she set the food out on the table for their dinner. But she decided to keep her thoughts to herself on this.

"Tell me how everyone is," she said instead, changing the subject, hungry to get firsthand news of the boys and their families.

John filled her in while they ate. "Marie found the perfect wedding dress. She passed pictures around, sent one for you to see." He grinned, dishing out another helping of casserole. "Jack has learned to ride a bicycle, one of those little bikes for kids, and he said he wished you could see him ride it. He's another 'watch me' exhibitionist like J. T. was."

"He was the first grandchild, and he does love attention." Lydia passed John the rolls. "What else, John?"

He scratched his head, trying to remember. "Amelia's online business is taking off, and she wants you to look at the new products on her Web site. And Parker is excited because they're negotiating with Chihuly, the glass artist, for another exhibition at the Botanical Garden. He wants you to come down for it."

"Oh, Chihuly is wonderful, John." She sighed. "If you haven't seen his glasswork, you need to go down with me. It's stunning in any exhibit, but even more so displayed in the ponds and landscape of the gardens."

He grew still, watching her. "Do you miss it, Lydia? Do you miss Atlanta and all the culture and things to do there? All the shops? The concerts? Moving in more educated and cultured circles?" He laid his fork down. "I went over to the college on Saturday, saw where you worked, walked around the campus, saw where the boys studied and went to classes. It's a very different world from Maggie Valley, North Carolina."

She smiled at him. "I know, but I love Maggie and western North Carolina and the mountains. I enjoyed the city and its culture, but you have to remember, I grew up in the mountains above Boone. It's a small town, too. I'm really a rural girl at heart, John."

Lydia watched him visibly relax.

"Atlanta also lacked one other important thing. I missed— you." She reached a hand across the table to catch his. "I missed you, John."

His eyes darkened. "If you keep sweet-talking me over dinner, I might not get around to tasting that fine dessert you made."

Lydia felt herself blush and dropped her eyes. She concentrated on finishing her supper.

As they came to the end of their meal, they took their dessert out on the porch. She'd made coffee for John and Earl Grey tea for herself. There John told her more small details about his trip with her questioning probes—what people ate, what they wore, things they said, how Martha acted, what words little Rachel could say now—the sort of information women generally needed to worm out of men. But Lydia wanted to hear every detail.

As the evening grew late, Lydia and John curled up together on the old swing to smooch, drifting quietly back and forth in the swing in the dark.

"John," Lydia said in a quiet moment. "I want you to know I can help you with finances for the farm if you need it. I have a little money put back, and the salary I've been offered at the college is a good one."

He shook his head and chuckled. "I figured Mary Beth or Rebecca would have told you by now there are no financial problems. They sort of made that up, knowing Hill House was vacant. Mary Beth wanted you to live close so she could rebuild her relationship with you and so the boys could get to know you better."

Lydia slanted him a sharp glance. "You mean you all lied to me? Let me think you might have to sell off part of the farm when that wasn't true?"

"Now, don't get whipped up about this." John shrugged, too casually to suit her. "Mary Beth and Rebecca cooked this up in love, and I didn't even know about it until a week or two before you moved in."

"Honestly, John." She leaned away from him and put her hands on her hips, provoked. "Surely you suspected I had some reason for deciding to move into Hill House. I doubt you thought I'd move into the house simply because it was empty. Didn't you ask Rebecca how I even knew it was for rent? I find it really hard to believe you couldn't figure out that Mary Beth was up to something, either. You know how transparent she is about her feelings."

"I admit I wondered and eventually got to asking some questions." He blew out a breath. "I guess this means you're not going to let me stay overnight."

Lydia felt a blush steal up her face. "I never intended that anyway." She stood up, feeling annoyed.

"You're a prickly woman, Lydia Ruth Cunningham." John stood, too. "And I'm too tired to take you on tonight after this long weekend and the battles with the boys. I think I'll head on home and talk to you some more tomorrow."

He started down the steps, then turned. "I'll always be grateful to you for helping to pull the farm out of debt after my father died. Things stood in a bad way then, and I wondered if I'd need to sell off a large portion of the farm to keep us afloat." He ran a hand through his hair. "I don't know if I ever thanked you for all you did then. I felt guilty about it, but I needed the help. I did get a lucrative offer for Hill House then and for this property. Mother urged me to sell, but I had sentimental feelings about the house and I didn't want to break up the farm, either. I'm glad I didn't have to sell."

She watched him. "You're sure Hill House is in no jeopardy now? That you're not simply trying to shield me from the truth?"

"No." He leaned against the porch post. "The farm is in better shape than it's ever been. The diversification moves we made to have rental cabins, the lodge, the tube run for the winter, and our expansions in opening the store and hosting more events during apple season have kept the farm from being in jeopardy even when a bad year occurs for the crops."

"I'm glad." Lydia knew she meant it. "But I'm still a little provoked you let me worry all this time that there was trouble here."

He gave her an easy smile. "Didn't you enjoy today, having Mary Beth here and watching the boys play in the pool?"

"Yes." She spoke softly, dropping her eyes.

He moved up a few steps to reach out and tilt her chin to raise her eyes to look at his. "Even though a little deception occurred, I'm glad you moved here close by. And I want you to know I'm putting all your rent money into a little savings account for you."

"What?"

"I'm not letting my own wife pay rent to me." He leaned over and kissed her. "And there's nothing indecent or immoral about you leading me into your bedroom here one night. We slept together until you left, you know. We made four children together. And we never divorced. In the sight of the law, and in God's eyes, too, we are still man and wife, Lydia Ruth."

She felt suddenly embarrassed. "I know, and I'm thinking about it."

"Good." He kissed her again. "You think about it in more detail while you're trying to fall asleep tonight. I surely will. Good night, Lydia."

CHAPTER 16

Later that evening, John sat outside on the back patio of Main House with Mary Beth, listening to the shrieks and shouts of the twins playing kick-the-can with Nevelyn and Charlie Sheppard's girls, Sara, eleven, Kristen, eight, and the two Crowe boys, Nalin and Davy, ten and six.

"How did Nalin and Davy get into this mix tonight?" John asked, seeing Nalin streak out from behind a shrub to race across the lawn. The boy kicked the can with a *thwack,* freeing the captives that Sara—currently "it" for the game—had tagged and captured earlier.

"I'll get you for that, Nalin Crowe!" Sara's fun-loving threat echoed through the night as the children raced from the base to hide out again. Plopping the can on the sidewalk, she turned her head to the wall, counted to twenty, then ran across the yard looking for where her friends hid. Spotting Davy behind a big tree, she called, "One, two, three on Davy. You're tagged!" while she raced back to put her foot on the tin can to secure her capture.

Mary Beth laughed, her answer to John's question interrupted by the children's shrieks and shouts. "I loved that game growing up." She turned a sunny smile to her father.

"I remember." He smiled back at her. "And about Nalin and Davy?"

"Oh." She shook her head, realizing she'd forgotten his question. "Manu and Ela offered to keep them tonight while the family drove over to the Long House Funeral Home in Cherokee. A distant relative died—one that the boys didn't know well—so Ela offered to feed the boys supper and let them play here tonight until the family returned."

"That was kind of her. I imagine those boys don't get many treats."

"They've known some hardships." Mary Beth looked out into the night, thinking. "Ela said they lost their house and a plot of land they owned near the reservation through some misunderstanding." She gave a small snort. "Manu said some crooks at a bank took advantage of them, encouraged a loan with terms they knew the family couldn't easily meet—then foreclosed at the first late payments."

"Is that true?"

"I'm not sure. You'd need to ask Manu or Alo Youngblood. Manu said Alo and his wife, Reena, owned a nice house on the land. Their daughter Nita, her husband, Falgun Crowe, and their children, Izabelle, Nalin, and Davy, lived in a trailer on their land, too. They lost it all. Now they're all sharing the rental on Silas Green's upper land. And recently Alo's widowed sister, Mala, moved in with them. It has to feel crowded, Dad, and I'm sure they miss their own place."

He watched Kristen dart from behind a bush to steal closer to the game base. "They can't be making enough money from farming that mountain land to make ends meet."

"No, although they have found things to grow and sell." Mary Beth shifted in her chair. "All the family are artisans, Dad. The women make exquisite baskets and detailed beaded jewelry, and the men create handmade weapons they decorate with natural fibers and feathers. They sell their work in several shops and galleries in Cherokee, which supplements their income. I carry some of their baskets and crafts in the store. The tourists love them." She paused. "Falgun started working in the casino on the reservation this year, too. It's good money and they're hoping to save to buy another place of their own again."

Sara's voice rang out in the middle of their conversation. "One, two, three on Kristen." Sara raced to put her foot on the can. "And Bucky, I see you squatted behind the well."

John frowned, thinking about Nalin and Davy's family situation. "I can't imagine Silas Green has made life any easier for that family. He's a mean-spirited man."

"I've always heard that." Mary Beth made a face. "He used to scream at J. T. and the twins and chase them off whenever they played too close to his property. They always fumed and grumbled about it."

John raised his eyes in surprise.

"We didn't tell you everything we did when we were kids." Mary Beth wiggled her eyebrows. "Kids don't, you know."

His jaw clenched. "I didn't notice J. T., Parker, or Will holding back much this weekend."

"Were they hard on you, Dad?" Mary Beth's face softened.

"No more than I expected, I guess. Lydia gave me warning they'd built up a stack of resentments." He scratched his neck. "I'd say they aired them all out right well."

"It was probably needed."

John watched Sara raise a fist in triumph after capturing the last of the children. Davy, caught first, would be "it" now. He hid his eyes against the toolshed and began to count out loud to twenty while the other children raced in every direction to hide.

"It's getting late for these kids to be outside." John glanced at his watch.

"Oh, Dad." Mary Beth waved a hand. "It's summer. There's no school tomorrow and children grow up so quickly. Let them play a little longer."

He glanced across at her, suddenly seeing her round face much younger—remembering back. "Have you heard any more from Sonny about when he might arrive in Maggie?"

Her smile faded. "No, and I really should have heard back from him if he's still coming."

"Perhaps he changed his mind."

"Maybe." She twisted her hands. "I'm uncomfortable about it, Dad. He wasn't happy when I refused to send money to him the last time he got in a bind. He claimed I owed him, since I let him change the boys' names back to Cunningham without him objecting."

John's shoulders stiffened. "Seems to me I recall we had to send a chunk of money to him, along with the paperwork, to get him to sign for that."

"Yes." She dropped her eyes. "He's changed so much from the boy I dated in high school. It's sad to think about it. I know it hurts his parents, too, that he ran off and keeps so little contact with them."

"Have you asked the Harpers if they've heard from him? Or if he wrote to tell them when he's coming through?" John kicked at a twig on the patio. "Sonny's usually broke, so he'll need somewhere to stay."

She shook her head. "I saw Wilma last week when I took the twins to her place to get their hair trimmed. She told me quietly, when the boys weren't listening, that she hadn't heard from Sonny in a year."

John mulled this over, watching the children play. "If Sonny comes, I want him to see the boys here at the farm with supervision."

"I agree." Mary Beth's eyes drifted toward the twins, both tagged and sitting captive on the wall by the toolshed. "Dad, do you think I should talk to Bucky and Billy Ray about their father? Let them know he might be visiting?"

He considered this. "I guess there'll be time enough if he contacts you again or shows up. I'd hate to see the boys expectant to see him and then be disappointed if he doesn't show."

"You may be right." She sighed. "But perhaps one of us ought to show them pictures, tell them a few stories about Sonny, so seeing him again won't be too much of a shock—if he does come. You know, they don't remember the last time they saw him. They were only three."

John bristled. "It's hardly their fault they have no memories of the man."

"Yes, but he *is* their father." She stood, seeing Ela step out on the front porch of her house. "There's Ela. She must have gotten a call from Davy and Nalin's parents that they're home now. Manu said he'd drive the boys home when they got back. I'd better help Ela round them up."

John thought of their earlier conversation later as he helped the boys into bed while Mary Beth worked on her online course work at the computer.

"Read us a story, Daddy John," Bucky begged as he climbed into his twin bed and pulled up the covers.

"Yeah, read a scary one." Billy Ray bared his teeth. "About wolves or dinosaurs or ghosts."

John picked up the stuffed dog Billy Ray liked to sleep with and tucked it under the covers with him. "There are no such things as ghosts. Remember what your mother said about that?"

"Yeah, she said that bad people probably just act like ghosts." He repeated the words with regret, his eyes lifting to John's.

Bucky sat forward, scowling. "Nalin says our daddy is a bad man to run off and leave us when we were only little. Is he bad, Daddy John?"

John sighed. He guessed the conversation he and Mary Beth discussed would be conducted sooner rather than later now. "I don't know that your daddy is a bad man, Son, but I reckon it's safe to say he's a mixed-up man."

He pulled up a chair to sit between the two beds, thinking about what he wanted to tell the boys. "I remember Sonny Harper as a good, fun-loving kid growing up. He liked baseball, music, and singing, had a fancy for motorcycles. Loved the motorcycle rallies at the fairgrounds here in Maggie. He collected those little Matchbox and Tonka motorcycles. I remember he still had a lot of them when he and Mary Beth got married."

Billy Ray interrupted. "Mama still has those in a metal suitcase. Sometimes she lets us get them out and play with them."

John nodded. "I liked hearing Sonny sing, too—enjoyed hearing him play the guitar. He had a God-given musical talent. Starred in a lot of high school events and shows around here. Performed onstage at a young age."

"He played and sang in a band. Mama has pictures of it."

Bucky sat up in the bed, punching the pillow behind him. "I think they were called Flat Ridgers."

"The Flat Ridge Boys," John corrected. "Three boys played in the band besides Sonny—Bailey Hanks from over near Jonathan Creek, Damon Bradley, and Rocky Sykes from Canton, and later, Ross Dodds managed them. At first they played mostly bluegrass, a little country, but gradually got into playing more country rock music."

"Grandma Harper says that's when Sonny started getting wild, when the band changed and they began to travel and play in honky-tonks." Bucky paused. "What's a honky-tonk?"

John rolled his eyes. Wilma Harper always did run her mouth too freely. "A honky-tonk is a bar that offers musical entertainment. Some offer dancing and are fairly nice places. Others are rough and often filled with drunks and trouble." He paused, crossing a foot over his knee. "What else did Grandma Harper tell you?"

Bucky wrinkled his nose. "She said our daddy was a sweet boy who got misguided and went astray. She told me we ought to pray for him to come back to the Lord and quit his wrongful ways."

John bit down on a smile.

"Grandma said he wasn't a bad person," Billy Ray added. "Just a good person gone bad for a while." He fiddled with the bedcovers. "Do you think he'll get changed?"

Bucky chimed in before John could form an answer. "Grandad Harper says Sonny needs to straighten up and fly right. Does that mean he flies planes now?"

"It means he needs to act right, and you boys have already gotten the gist of this story, from what I hear." He ran a hand through his hair. "Sonny started spending time with some bad company, took up a harmful lifestyle, and soon lost interest in the good things that really matter."

Billy Ray's voice dropped low. "Like us."

John reached over to tousle his head. "Yes, I'm sorry, Son, but that's the truth of it. Other things became more important to Sonny than his family—and that included his parents, his brother, Eric, and Eric's family, your mother, and you guys." He got up to kiss both of them on the forehead. "He sure is missing out on something special not knowing both of you, I'll tell you that. I'd say he'll come to regret it one day. Maybe come around wanting to make amends."

"I've seen pictures of him, but I don't really remember him." Bucky put a hand to his head, rubbing it through his brown hair, cut in a typical childish bowl cut. "Sonny had his hair all shaved off the last picture I saw and he had a little bit of a mustache and a beard, like he forgot to shave."

"Where did you see that?" John asked in surprise.

"Grandma Harper had it. Her friend, who's the mother of one of the other guys in the band, gave it to her."

"Bailey Hanks's mother?"

"I think." He shrugged his shoulders. "Grandma does the lady's hair and she brought the picture over to Grandma to keep. It's a shiny picture and shows all the band. Grandma put it on her beauty parlor mirror."

"I bet it's a promo picture—a picture bands use to promote themselves and give out to fans."

Billy Ray crossed his arms, pushing out his bottom lip. "I'd rather have Neal as a daddy than for Sonny to straighten out and come back. I like Neal, and I heard Ela tell Manu that Neal really likes Mama."

Bucky's eyes brightened. "Manu said Neal is smitten with her. That means he likes her a lot, doesn't it, Daddy John?"

John hesitated on this discussion. "I think whatever friendship that's between your mother and Neal Caldwell is their own private business until they tell anyone otherwise." He focused his gaze on the twins. "And you two had better keep those matchmaking ideas to yourself, you hear?"

"You do like Neal, though, don't you, Daddy John?" Billy Ray lifted big brown eyes to John's as he asked the question.

"I like Neal very much." He got up to pick out a book from the shelf nearby. "Neal practically grew up at our home and he was J. T.'s best friend. He's a fine man." He sat back down with the book. "Now, if you boys expect to still hear a story before bed, I'd better get to reading it."

He opened the pages of *Andrew Henry's Meadow,* one of the boys' favorite books, as well as one of his, and started to read.

A little later, he found Mary Beth at the computer. "The boys got to asking some questions, and I had that little talk with them about their daddy you and I discussed earlier."

She looked up at him. "How'd it go?"

"They know more than we thought." He leaned against the side of the desk where her computer sat. "Seems Grandma Harper filled them in on her view about things."

"I see." Amusement filled her eyes. "I guess we can't be sorry they know what folks think about their father."

"Those boys don't miss much." A half smile played over his lips. "They told me they thought Neal would make a good daddy."

His daughter blushed. "You didn't talk about that with the twins, did you?"

"Just told them they ought to keep their thoughts to themselves about that. That any relationship you and Neal might have was your own business."

She dropped her eyes and twisted a ring on her finger. "I don't know what to do about that relationship, Daddy."

He didn't reply at first. "I guess you'll figure it out. You're the only one who knows your heart in this. It's not for me to suggest what you should do, Bee. You're the one who has to wake up to him every day if you decide to marry. As you know, that's a serious decision."

"Yeah, I know." She sighed. "I didn't give enough time to that decision the first time. I don't want to make the same mistake again."

John watched her. "Sonny Harper and Neal Caldwell are two real different men, daughter. Don't judge one by the other."

Her eyes softened. "I won't." She turned off the computer and yawned. "And thanks for talking to the boys. I'll slip in and check on them before I head to bed."

John started for the door.

"Daddy." Her voice stopped him. "I'm glad it was you and not me who talked to the boys. It's hard for me to talk to them about Sonny."

He nodded as he left, thinking that it hadn't been easy for him, either. He hoped Sonny Harper would bypass Maggie Valley altogether as he traveled this way. The man had hurt people he loved too much for John to be eager to see him again—ever.

CHAPTER 17

Lydia let her mind wander over the events of the last week as she drove back from a meeting at Western. Her recent talks with the boys, Amelia, and Martha Howard filled her in on more of what had happened on the weekend John drove to Atlanta.

"I felt really proud of him. I admit it," Martha told her during one of their evening chats. "I thought it courageous of him to assemble all the boys together at once and let them go at him—three on one. Hardly good odds." She hesitated. "Blessedly, Laura noticed when the situation started to escalate into a free-for-all, took charge, and saw to it that they talked things out constructively." Her throaty laugh echoed over the phone line. "Laura Bridger Cunningham is a force to be reckoned with when she gears into her administrative mode."

Lydia smiled. "I've seen that a time or two."

"Well, I stand amazed that resolution evolved so readily once reasonable sharing began." She paused. "Most of that is to John's credit. Once they all started to talk and not sling accusations, his love shone through blindingly—for the boys and later for you. No one could doubt the sincerity and humility of his words. Even I came away with a new understanding of the man."

"I've heard some of the same from Parker and Will. Even from J. T., which surprised me."

"The boys still nourish some anger and bad memories, but they're coming around. You stressed so often to them that harboring resentment is destructive to the one who holds on to it—not the other way around."

A spear of conviction made her wince. "Too bad I didn't preach the same message to myself more."

Martha's voice softened. "You're coming around, too. Finding resolution and forgiveness isn't instant. It takes effort, risk, and bravery."

"Ela gave me similar counsel. She said, 'Cowardice can't step free of the past . . . only bravery can.' " Lydia paused. "Ela encouraged me to go through the rooms of Main House to make peace with my bad memories of Estelle."

"How did that work out?"

"Better than I expected." What Lydia didn't mention to Martha before they hung up was Ela's further suggestion to visit Estelle's grave.

Lydia hadn't done that yet. Frankly, she knew she'd found a multitude of reasons to postpone it. But now, as she followed Black Camp Gap Road toward the farm, she gathered her courage and turned her car up the winding drive to Fairview Methodist Church on the hill.

After parking under a shade tree, Lydia walked across the grass to let herself into the iron-fenced cemetery, scattered with monuments. Toward the back of the cemetery she found the Cunningham graves—the joint stone of Mary and John Cunningham, the granite angel of Stuart's grave, and the side-by-side monuments of John's parents. She'd attended Grandpa Will's funeral when he died, came to the gravesite service, but she'd avoided visiting Estelle's grave, even though she came to church here on Sundays.

She stopped to read the words across the marker: ESTELLE WHITMEYER CUNNINGHAM. They were cut into a striking pink granite marker, the dates of birth and death below her name. Holly had told her Estelle insisted on colored granite stone, wanting to distinguish her memorial stone from the others of traditional Georgia gray in the cemetery.

"Even in death you had to find a way to put yourself forward." She made an effort to bank the swamp of memories of the many times Estelle stressed how being a Cunningham or a Whitmeyer made her one step better than everyone else.

Lydia shook her head. "I need to forgive you here at the cemetery just as I did at Main House, Estelle, and I need to let all those bad memories and resentments go." She straightened her shoulders. "Ela reminded me that you're gone now and it's time for healing—time to move on." She sighed. "I wish I could forget all the times you tried to hurt and humiliate me, tried to hurt my children—worked to tear my family apart. You almost succeeded, Estelle, but—in the end—the love John and I held for each other proved stronger than your efforts to tear it apart. We're being restored as a family now. Healing and moving on."

She pushed away the rush of hurtful words and recollections that tried to invade her mind. "I'm purposing to think on the positive now, Estelle. To dwell on the good and not the bad things of the past. At Main House, I forgave you by faith and not by feelings. I'm doing the same here. I may have to repeat this again in the future when old hurts and memories try to creep back into my mind. But I'm purposed to succeed. To move on. To not let you hurt my life or my heart any longer."

Taking a deep breath, she added, "I'm sorry if I hurt you in any way I wasn't aware of. I realize you had problems I didn't understand. I know we were very different women with different ways of seeing things. I regret we never found peace and understanding before you died."

Lydia heard footsteps behind her and turned to see the pastor walking across the grass. "I saw you from the window." He pointed toward his office on the corner of the church. "I hope I'm not interrupting by coming out to say hello." He stopped beside her, looking down at Estelle's grave and then turning questioning eyes to hers.

"Making my peace," she said, deciding to be honest. "Ela said until I moved forward in bravery, the past would hold on to me, continue to hurt and control me, keep me from future happiness and freedom."

"Sounds like a wise woman."

"She is." Lydia put a hand out tentatively to touch Estelle's monument. "I can still hear Ela's words: 'You have to face your ghosts, your fears, and banish them.' "

"I wouldn't be a good pastor if I didn't remind you that you don't have to face your fears alone. God will help."

She nodded.

He tapped a foot on the ground, thinking. "With God's help we're empowered to break free of our fears. A scripture in Second Timothy reminds us where our fears come from, too—certainly not from God. Maybe you recall the words: 'For God hath not given us the spirit of fear; but of power, and of love, and of a sound mind.' "

"It actually feels empowering to make an effort to let all the fears and hurts go." Lydia drew back her hand, amazed it hadn't burned to touch the stone. "You got another helpful scripture, Reverend?"

"It's Oliver." He offered a slow smile. "How about Psalm twenty-seven: 'The Lord is my light and my salvation; whom shall I fear?' Or Hebrews thirteen: 'The Lord is my helper . . . I will not fear what man shall do unto me.' "

"Those are good." She released a long sigh.

"You know, Lydia, I think the truths you've learned since you came back, the fact that you sought for understanding and truth, and wanted to find a way to forgive and move on, really opened the door for freedom for you." He steepled his fingers. "Truth is a powerful thing. A verse in John eight says: 'And ye shall know the truth, and the truth shall set you free.' "

She considered this. "You may be right. The things I've learned since coming back did help me get to this place."

"Being in the Lord makes us more able to forgive and forget, too. It's hard to do that only in the natural man—or woman."

Lydia pushed a strand of hair behind her ear. "I know God has helped me in this journey, Oliver, from the day I decided to come back. I've felt His help in the sweet days of new discovery and in the hard days when I bumped up against obstacles."

"That's a nice testimony." His eyes moved across the Cunningham monuments. "Do you think you'll feel better after coming here today?"

"I already do."

Oliver's cell phone interrupted them. Lydia watched him frown as he listened to the caller.

He punched the phone off, distress crossing his face. "There's been a bad accident. Kristen Sheppard fell over the edge of a cliff above your farm. She's been taken to the closest hospital, Haywood Regional Medical Center in Clyde. I need to head that way. She's only eight."

"I'll follow you." Lydia picked up her pace to match his. "What happened? Do you know?"

He let out an agitated breath. "She and her sister, Sara, saw the ghost on Drop Off Ridge. Kristen was frightened and backed up too near the edge of the cliff and slipped and fell."

"Is it serious?"

"I don't know." He opened and shut the cemetery gate. "The family is at the hospital. Charlie called me from the waiting room. John's there, too. If you want to ride with me, you can drive back with John later."

Lydia ran to lock her car and get her purse, hurrying to join Reverend Wheaton as he started his SUV. He started praying out loud as they drove, and Lydia joined him mentally, hoping desperately Kristen wasn't badly injured. It hurt to think of the small, carefree child with the laughing brown eyes suffering—or worse, taken away from them.

$\mathcal{C}$HAPTER 18

John reached out to take Lydia's hand as soon as she and Oliver Wheaton entered the hospital waiting room. "They're still checking Kristen out." He filled them in. "She took a hard fall."

He watched Lydia go to Kristen's mother, Nevelyn, to give her a hug and then move around speaking to each of the Sheppards in the waiting room, offering her love and support. The minister also spoke to each and then he joined Sam and Charlie, where they stood leaning against the wall, waiting for word about Kristen.

John reached out to shake the minister's hand. "Thank you for coming, Oliver. Maybe you passed the sheriff coming in. He talked to Sara at length since Kristen is still unconscious as far as we know."

Sam clenched a fist, glancing at the pastor. "I told the sheriff he'd better take this ghost business seriously now, Reverend Wheaton. Both of my granddaughters could have been killed."

"We're still scared for Kristen," Charlie added. "And the waiting is difficult." His eyes shifted to where Sara sat huddled miserably in a chair by her mother. "My girls like to play house on the lodge porch. They walked down into the woods above the ridge to pick berries for a dinner for their dolls." He grimaced. "Dang ghost came out from the trees, waving its arms and hollering, scaring them out of their wits. Kristen—frightened—backed up, forgetting the edge of the ridge lay right behind her. She slipped and tumbled over. Sara scrambled down

after her and then ran to find us when she found Kristen unconscious."

Seeing her father's eyes on her, Sara got up and walked over
to lean against his side. He wrapped her in a warm hug.

She sniffled, trying not to cry. "We shouldn't have walked
down on the ridge. You told us not to, but we always go there to
pick berries and we forgot. I'm sorry, Daddy."

"It's all right." He petted on her, smoothing her sandy-blond
hair back from her face. "It was an accident. Don't fault yourself. The farm has always been your play yard, and none of us
understands why this crazy ghost is wandering around the area
scaring people."

Sara sighed. "He crept out from behind a tree, all white, waving his arms, with blood all over him—just like everyone said.
We both screamed, it startled us so."

The doctor came out—interrupting their discussion—and everyone moved toward him anxiously.

"How is she?" Nevelyn asked, holding a hand to her heart.

"She'll be okay. It's a good report." The doctor glanced down
at his chart. "Kristen's injuries are not life-threatening. She has a
concussion, bruises, scratches, cuts, a sprained ankle, and a frac-
ture of the forearm. The latter didn't break the skin so surgery
won't be needed. We aligned the ulna and casted the arm. We'd
like to keep her overnight for observation, but she can go home
tomorrow if all is well." He smiled. "She's lucky. Children are
resilient. She's awake now and asking for you."

"Can we go in to see her?" Tears of relief slid down Nevelyn's
face.

"Yes, of course." The doctor glanced around at the crowd in
the waiting area. "But limit the visits to immediate family for
now, if you would. Kristen needs to rest."

After a few more questions, Charlie, Nevelyn, and Sara followed the doctor to Kristen's room. Sam slumped into an empty
chair by his wife, Doris, in relief, patting her arm while she wept
with gratitude.

"I'd better call Eugene," he said after a moment. "He, Ozetta,
and Clyde will be worrying."

Doris pulled off her glasses to wipe at her eyes. "Call Chuck and Vera at the house, too, Eugene. They wanted to come over here with us, but I told them a hospital waiting room was no place for a three-year-old and a crawler."

"I'll call the prayer line at the church again," the minister added. "Let them know to get the word around that Kristen will be okay. Praise God."

As he walked over to speak to Sam and Doris, John put a hand on Lydia's back. "I'll drive you home with me, Lyddie. I left Ela, Manu, Mary Beth, and the kids at the house—concerned. I'll call them as we head home to let them know all's well."

Thirty minutes later, they arrived back at Main House to find the family gathering around the table for dinner. John noted Neal added to the family mix but Manu was missing. "Where's Manny?" he asked, pulling out a chair for Lydia after Ela insisted she stay to eat.

"I can't rightly say." Ela took off her apron to sit down at the table. "He had a theory about that ghost business he said he needed to follow up on."

John lifted a brow.

"Don't ask me," she complained. "The man simply took off to see about it in his own way like he does sometimes."

John bit down on a chuckle and reached for the platter of fried chicken.

"Is Kristen really going to be okay?" Bucky asked.

"Yes." John passed the platter of chicken on and took a bowl of butter beans coming his way. "She'll need to rest a few days, especially her ankle, and she'll wear a cast for a time while her arm heals."

Billy Ray reached for a roll. "Kristen could have got killed falling over that hill. I was scared when I heard how Sara found her all knocked out."

"She was unconscious," John explained. "That often happens temporarily when a person experiences an accident, an injury, or a fall like Kristen did. It's sometimes a symptom of a concussion, too—a jolting or shaking of the brain."

Mary Beth made a face. "Ugh. Let's don't get too graphic, Dad. We're eating." She glanced at Billy Ray, reaching for a second roll. "You eat your vegetables and chicken before getting another roll."

The subject, however, wasn't easily dismissed, and questions and comments continued throughout dinner. After they finished, Mary Beth suggested they go sit on the porch so the boys could play in the backyard. Manu had built them a big sandbox, and the boys loved driving a bevy of trucks and cars over the sand streets they'd constructed. They hardly noticed Manu striding across the yard toward the back patio.

"Have you eaten?" Ella asked, as he took off his hat and sat down on a metal lawn chair.

"No." He shook his head.

"I'll fix you a plate and bring it out." She rose and headed for the kitchen.

"Our riddle is solved." Manu turned toward John as she left.

"About the ghost?" Mary Beth leaned forward, her eyes eager for news.

He nodded, laying his straw hat on the chair beside him.

"Did the sheriff catch who is behind this?" Mary Beth asked.

Manu nodded.

Seeing her open her mouth with another question, John sent her a warning glance. "Quit asking questions and let Manny tell it, Bee."

She sat back in her chair with a sigh. "Oh, all right."

Manu grinned. "After you headed to the hospital, John, I kept going over and over the story Sara told us about the accident. A few peculiar facts kept standing out in my mind." He paused. "First, Sara stated that someone—not the ghost— hollered when Kristen fell over the ridge. Second, she described the ghost as short in stature, not much taller than herself, and she's only eleven."

Manu stopped to take the dinner plate from Ela and to eat a few bites before he continued. "I kept thinking on the fact that two people were there and one was short." He took a drink of iced tea. "Then I went back to explore the area after the sheriff left and found several things of interest."

"What did you find?" John asked the question, even after telling Mary Beth not to interrupt and to let Manny tell the story. She sent him a saucy look.

"I found several small footprints, too small for a man, and one set too small for a woman." He finished off a chicken leg. "Down at the bottom of the ridge, I noticed more footprints around the edge of a small cave under the ridge—you know, the one where the rocks hang over."

He hesitated, eating a few more bites of his dinner, before looking up to catch John's eye. "I found a body shoved back in that cave, buried under leaves and debris—"

"A body?" This time Neal interrupted, lurching forward and almost knocking a plant off the table. "Do you know whose it was?"

Manu reached out to push the plant back from the table edge. "I thought I did and now it's confirmed. Silas Green."

John felt his mouth drop open. "Silas Green? Did anyone even know the man was missing? I hadn't heard."

Manu shook his head. "His wife told the sheriff she thought he'd gone traveling with his company. She said half the time he never bothered to tell her when he planned to leave or when he might be back. Simply showed up again one day—sometimes a month or more later."

Ela jumped into the conversation. "Loretha told me she felt right glad every time Silas went out of town. She enjoys life more when he's gone and hates to see the day he comes back."

Manu glanced her way, frowning at Ela's words. "Well, Silas won't be coming home again this time at all."

Ela dropped her eyes, realizing she'd spoken insensitively.

"Do you know what happened? Was he murdered?" John wanted all the facts Manu knew now.

Manny picked up his hat to twist in his hands. "I meddled a bit in police business, John. Maybe I shouldn't have, but I did." He paused. "You see, when I moved some of the debris to see who lay under the rock cave, I noticed a piece of beaded turquoise jewelry clutched in Silas's hand. It looked like part of a necklace."

Mary Beth's breath caught. "Like the jewelry the Youngblood and Crowe women make?"

"Exactly." He nodded. "Because I saw that, I took a walk toward their house. As I followed the path, I saw more small footprints, like the ones on the ridge. And a clear print or two every so often. Then I found a scrap of white cloth stained with red on a bush."

Ela gasped.

"But why would any of that family play at being a ghost?" Neal voiced the question in everyone's mind now.

"I wondered the same." Manu scratched his head. "So I decided to pay a little social visit. Started tossing out a few comments—about Kristen, how she fell, what she heard, about what I found at the cave—like I was wondering out loud about it all. When I mentioned finding Silas Green's body, young Izabelle started weeping. Then the boys broke."

"Those children were involved in this?" Lydia put a hand to her mouth in shock. "Surely that's not possible."

Manu exhaled slowly. "Nalin stood up tall and straight like a man to explain, walked over to stand protectively by his sister. He said he and Davy heard Izabelle screaming—a muffled scream—while they played near Indian Creek. She'd gone to pick berries on Drop Off Ridge nearby, on their property side of the creek. They ran to find Silas Green on top of the girl, his pants dropped and half her clothing stripped off. It seemed evident what he planned. Nalin picked up a big rock and hit him on the back of the head. It saved Izabelle, but it killed Silas."

"Oh my heavens!" Ela exclaimed. "Those poor children."

"When they realized Silas lay dead, rather than only knocked out, the children got scared and dragged Silas across the creek onto our property to the cave under the ridge. They pulled him inside and covered him with tree limbs and debris. Nalin said they hoped anyone who found him later would think he'd fallen."

"So why the ghost act?" Neal asked.

"The boys feared someone might find Silas too soon, be able to tell he didn't fall." He shook his head. "Nalin came up with the ghost idea to scare people away from the area. To give Silas time to deteriorate, and to obliterate any evidence."

John felt stunned. "So, Nalin Crowe was the ghost?"

"He found the sheet, added blood for more authenticity. Then he and Davy spent their play days around the Drop Off area, watching for anyone who might come too close to the ridge or cave. At that point Davy kept an eye out while Nalin got into his costume, stashed in a sack in an old tree. Then Nalin waved his arms and moaned from the shadows."

"I can hardly believe this." Ela crossed her arms. "I admit to sympathy for Izabelle's sake, but those Crowe boys went too far with the ghost idea. Several people claimed the ghost waved a bloody knife—certainly extreme—and I think scaring small children for any reason is simply cruel."

"I saw the knife when I saw the ghost." Lydia's brows drew together. "I find it hard to hold sympathy for those boys, considering all the people they terrified—and with Kristen injured, too."

Manu leaned over to pet Cullie's head. The collie had come to sidle up against him. "The boys did wrong," he continued. "They know that and they felt horrified when Kristen fell over the ledge. Both were really frightened when that happened. They got careless running home after that and didn't brush out their tracks as usual." He scratched the collie's neck. "Nalin said they only meant to scare the girls a little. They never thought Kristen would fall."

John flexed his fingers. "Does the sheriff know?"

"Alo called him, asked him to come. He told the sheriff they had information about the ghost they wanted to share." Manu reached for a side dish of pie. "I got on the phone and encouraged the sheriff to come immediately."

"Merciful day." Ela lifted her eyes to John's. "Whatever will happen to those boys? And to Izabelle and the family?"

"I don't know." John scratched his chin. "The boys are minors. They acted to save their sister from rape. Silas's death wasn't intentional. However, the boys and Izabelle covered it up. And the boys' pranks at playing ghost caused frights and an injury. I'm sure there will be charges."

"How old is Izabelle?" Lydia asked.

Manu's eyes narrowed. "She just turned thirteen."

"Why, she is only a child!" Lydia's eyes widened. "What sort of man would attack a child that way?"

John reached a hand toward her in comfort. "That fact will weigh heavily in this situation, Lydia. I doubt the attorney general will indict, given the circumstances." He turned to Manu. "What did the sheriff say?"

"He gave Izabelle and the boys the what for. Let them know all the wrongful and illegal choices they made—voluntary manslaughter, even if accidental, and concealment afterward." He forked into the cherry pie. "The sheriff explained to the family, as John suggested, that the attorney general probably won't indict. He didn't take the children into custody, either, but he left them in the custody of their parents. He also cautioned them to stay in the area until this is resolved."

Mary Beth shivered. "Who told Loretha about Silas?"

"Alo and the sheriff and I went to tell her." He hesitated. "She showed little sorrow. She offered more sympathy and concern for Alo and for what Silas tried to do to Izabelle. She told Alo not to worry that she'd ask him to move. She said he could stay on the property renting as long as he liked."

While they sat there stunned, Manu added more. "Loretha told the sheriff she'd testify in the Crowe children's defense if asked. She said her husband went after his own girls in times past and that she regretted not doing more then. She feared his temper."

"Mercy." Lydia put a hand to her heart.

"I'm glad my boys didn't hear all of that story." Mary Beth reached over to take Lydia's hand in hers.

Manu frowned. "I wouldn't have told it in front of the boys. But they'll hear of this from others with less discretion. You'll need to talk to them tonight before the gossip starts. Little pitchers have big ears."

"I dread that." Mary Beth shook her head.

"I'll talk to them with you," Neal offered. "Children can bear truth better than you think."

"Thank you for that offer." Mary Beth turned grateful eyes to Neal. "They're fond of you. I think they'd like it if you helped to tell them about this."

He looked at his watch. "How about now, Bee? It's time for Bucky and Billy Ray to come in and settle down for the night anyway. I'll help you with their baths, and then we'll talk to them together."

As they rounded up the boys, Manu helped Ela gather dishes and glasses to take to the kitchen. Left alone for a moment with Lydia, John reached a hand across to take hers. She looked white with shock. "I'll drive you to pick up your car and then follow you home after if you're ready."

"Yes, I'm ready." She stood up. "Let me get my purse from inside and tell everyone good night."

Seeing her glance toward the Upper farm, where the ghost sightings took place, he added, "Maybe I'll sit with you for a time after we get back. This has been a hard day. You might like some company."

"I might." She smiled at him. "Thank you for suggesting it."

As Mary Beth headed toward the house with the boys, John called out to her, "I'm going to drive Lydia to pick up her car and then follow her home and stay with her for a while."

Mary Beth sent him a secret smile as the boys skipped toward the house with Neal. "It's nice for a woman to have a man around sometimes. I think Mother would like that." She wiggled her eyebrows. "Don't stay out too late, Dad."

He laughed as he headed toward the driveway for the truck.

CHAPTER 19

"Isn't it a relief to have that ghost issue finally resolved?" Rebecca asked two days later. She and Lydia sat by the window eating a late breakfast at Joey's Pancake House on the main highway in Maggie Valley.

"Yes, and Kristen is home from the hospital and doing well, from what I hear." Lydia stopped to cut a bite out of a stack of whole-wheat pancakes, smothered in cinnamon apples—one of Joey's house specialties. Rebecca loved Joey's, and always suggested they meet here for breakfast.

"I'm glad you could come this morning, Lydia. Lunch is harder for me to arrange. I get tied up in the office or in property showings." Rebecca reached across the table for syrup to pour over a mountain of blueberry pancakes. Both women had ordered pancakes with ham and cheese omelets today.

"You know I'm happy to get together whenever you can plan it for breakfast or lunch." Lydia dropped a tea bag into a cup of hot water, wishing for her home-steeped Earl Grey. "I won't have the luxury of all this time come fall when my work at Western begins."

Rebecca wiggled an eyebrow. "Getting spoiled?"

"A little," Lydia admitted.

"Will you give up your job when you and John get back together?"

"It's *if* we get back together, not when." Lydia frowned, emphasizing the word 'if'. "And the answer is no, Rebecca. I love my job. There are already days when I feel restless, miss working with the students, and yearn for the daily hum of the career services office."

"I'm like that about my real estate work, too." Rebecca stirred cream into her hot coffee. "I grumble about the workload, but I love it." Changing the subject she asked, "What are you doing today after we finish breakfast?"

"Shopping." Lydia grinned. "I need to buy some gifts—a present for Martha's birthday next week and one for Ozetta Sheppard's birthday the day after tomorrow. Ozetta sends me so many fresh vegetables and home-baked treats that I want to give her something nice to say thank you."

"Gracious, that woman bakes the best homemade breads and sweets. I've sampled some at your house. Isn't she the one who collects salt and pepper shakers and has a whole china cabinet full of them in the kitchen?"

"Yes, and that's a great gift idea."

Rebecca wrinkled her nose. "To be frank, a lot of those shaker sets she has are unbelievably tacky—Kewpie dolls, dancing pigs, smiling vegetables."

Lydia laughed. "It's what she likes. As Ozetta explained, she likes 'pretties,' having grown up poor with only the necessities."

"Isn't that a funny societal change?" Rebecca forked up a bite of her omelet. "The older generation loves and cherishes bric-a-brac and clutter while the new generation goes for a stark, un-cluttered look." She made a face. "I tell my older clients to hide or pack up everything if they want their houses to sell."

Lydia rolled her eyes. "I despise housing fads and people flocking after whatever is 'in' like a bunch of lemmings, whether they like the current fads and fashion or not."

"Most people don't possess the confidence to decorate simply according to their personal likes and dislikes. They only feel approved when they conform. People are like that about clothes, too—and everything else, you know. Always trying to keep up with the Joneses."

"Wasn't it Galbraith who said following convention protects

people from the painful job of thinking?" Lydia flashed Rebecca an arch smile.

"Oh, that's good." Rebecca's eyes brightened. "I know a better one—*one dog barks at something and a hundred bark at the bark.*"

Lydia punched at her. "You always think of something funny."

"Life's too short for overanalyzing." She waved a hand. "I say grab your happiness while you can and laugh often."

"I missed you in Atlanta, Becca." Lydia sent her a fond look.

"Back at you, kiddo. I'm glad you're home again. So is Tolley." She raised a brow. "And so is John. How is that going?"

"Good." Lydia hesitated. "But now I'm beginning to feel I'll disrupt the flow of Main House if John and I get back together. Ela and Mary Beth handle things so efficiently. A pattern and routine is already established."

"That's silly. I haven't noticed anything awkward when you're in the mix." She pushed back her plate. "Are you sure it's not you—reluctant to give up your single life and independence?"

"Maybe. I've lived on my own a long time now, Rebecca, except for my boys mixed into my life. Maybe the hesitation is mine."

Rebecca looked at her watch. "You know I hate to scoot, darling, but I need to meet a client at the office in ten minutes."

"You should have said so before." Lydia gathered up her purse and searched for the breakfast ticket on the table.

"My office is only down the road. Besides, I love these times when we share together, and I want every minute I can squeeze in."

They paid their tickets, hugged and blew air-kisses, and then Lydia set out to explore the shops in Maggie Valley to look for gifts. At the rustic and touristy Maggie Mountaineer Crafts shop she found the perfect collectible glass slipper she needed for Martha—Fenton Glass in a rich indigo blue. Martha had a lovely collection of china and glass shoes in a small case in her bedroom. Lydia also picked up a handmade rag doll to take to Kristen when she next visited, and she sampled the shop's homemade key lime fudge, a summertime specialty.

"Ummm." She licked her lips, leaning over the case. "I'll need a small box of that to take with me, too, and mix in some of that white chocolate fudge with it."

Plopping her packages into the car, she headed down the highway to the Market Square, a mini-mall in the heart of Maggie Valley across from the festival grounds. A row of blue-painted stores, with a covered boardwalk running in front of the shops, made the little mall distinctive. Lydia slipped into Aunt Bee's Blessing Shop for greeting cards, stopped by the Garden Deck Accessories to buy a wind chime, and ended with a visit to the Tarnished Swan to look for a salt and pepper shaker set for Ozetta.

"Can I help you?" asked the clerk.

"Maybe. I'm looking for a salt and pepper set for Ozetta Sheppard for her birthday."

"Oh, Ozetta has quite a collection." The older woman led her toward the back of the store, squatting to examine the salt and pepper sets on the shelf. "Here's my favorite." She lifted a black-and-white Dominicker chicken set from between a shaker set of green tractors and another of colorful cowboy boots.

Lydia studied them with a grin.

"Ozetta has chickens like this behind the barn at her farm. I think she'll love these." The clerk smiled as she stood back up. "I'm Mildred Hodge, by the way. I've known Ozetta since we played together as girls in the valley." She studied Lydia. "Aren't you John Cunningham's wife come home from Atlanta?"

"Yes, I am." Lydia reminded herself that a small town held no secrets.

"Well, everyone I've talked to is glad you're back." Mildred shifted the china shakers in her hand. "You want this set or do you want to look some more?"

"No, those will be fine. Thank you for your help."

Mildred nodded. "I can gift wrap them if you'd like." She reached under the cabinet to pull out a box. "I'll do it up nice, too, since it's for Ozetta."

"Thank you." Lydia followed Mildred to the register to pay

for the gift, browsing the shelves near the register while she wrapped.

Down the road a short time later, Lydia turned off at the Green Thumb Nursery to look around. The cute brown building sported wide windows, trimmed in green, with a variety of plants inside and out. Lydia found two pots of bright, carefree marigolds she thought would look great on the front porch of Hill House.

"These are called Golden Gates," the sales clerk told her. "They'll bloom until first frost and give you a lot of happy yellow color on your deck or porch."

She smiled at him. "That's exactly what I had in mind."

"These are healthy plants, too, but you keep a watch for spider mites in this hot weather." He glanced out the front window as he rang up the sale. "Want me to put these in the backseat of your car for you?"

"Yes, thank you. The back door's open. You can sit them on the floorboard." She glanced out into the yard. "I want to look around a little more before I leave, if it's all right."

"Go right ahead." He walked out the door with the plants, Lydia following. She turned to wander through the yard, wanting to check out the birdbaths and yard art. Her phone rang before she could walk far. Lydia pulled out her cell phone to answer. "Hello?"

Mary Beth's voice jumped onto the line, anxious. "Mom? Do you have the boys with you?"

"No. I haven't seen them all day. I met Rebecca for breakfast at Joey's. Is anything wrong?"

"Oh, probably not." She sighed. "Ela left them playing in the backyard while she went in to start lunch. Later when she went to look for them, she couldn't find them anywhere. She called and called but they didn't answer." Mary Beth paused. "Usually they come running when she calls."

"Have you checked around the farm?" Lydia asked. "Maybe they went up to Ridge House to see Kristen or over to watch Clyde work on a car. They love to do that."

"I've called everywhere. No one's seen them. That's why I called you. I hoped maybe they'd gone on an errand with you—maybe told you they got permission when they really never asked."

"Are you still at work?" Lydia walked toward her car now, waving a good-bye to the clerk in the store.

"No. Vera is there. I called her to come cover the store when Ela and Manu couldn't find the boys." Lydia heard the unease in her voice. "I hate it when they go off like this and worry everyone."

"I know." Lydia offered soothing words. "I'm at the Green Thumb Nursery down on the highway. It won't take me long to get to the farm. I'll come help you look. Children often start to play and then wander off and forget others will worry. We'll find them."

However, by dinner six hours later they had not found the boys. John, Sam, Charlie, and Neal joined the search in the afternoon, but as darkness fell, anxiety rose, and John called the sheriff's office.

Several men from the police department came to help with the search, but over the next three hours no trace of the boys was found. As night drifted in, Sheriff Sutton came to the house to talk to the weary family, gathered for coffee and counsel at Main House about what to do next.

"Do you think this is a prankster, imitating the ghost, who scared the boys into running to hide somewhere?" Neal asked the sheriff, sipping at a hot mug of coffee.

"I doubt it. Everyone in the valley knows the Crowe boys instigated the ghost sightings. I don't think there's any relation between that past issue and this." Sheriff Sutton pushed back his hat wearily, his eyes moving to Mary Beth. "Have you received any threatening notes or phone calls?"

She shook her head, hugging herself with the tension.

"What about e-mails?"

Her eyes grew large. "I didn't think to check that." She got up and ran down the hall to her computer, Neal following.

"I'm real sorry about this for your family, John. I know it's hard." The sheriff took a mug of coffee from Ela with gratitude.

"We've classified the boys as missing persons now. All the men we can round up are looking. I know you've been making calls around the valley from here, too."

A muffled scream sounded from down the hall.

Neal called out, "Sheriff Sutton, you need to look at this message on Mary Beth's computer. Sonny Harper, the boys' father, has them."

Lydia followed the sheriff and John to where Mary Beth stood weeping in Neal's arms beside the computer screen. Sheriff Sutton sat in the chair to read the e-mail message out loud:

> Hey, Bee. I've got the boys with me for a little fatherly visit. Long overdue, I'd say. They're both fine and staying with me overnight. I told them I got that worked out with you ahead of time. We're not staying nearby so don't start searching. It might rankle me. I'll bring the boys back tomorrow after you give me a little help money for the rest of my trip. A thousand would take care of things real nice. You can leave it under the steps of the vacant Rocky Mount Church over near Jonathan in one of Ela's round cookie tins. Be sure it's cash and not all in big bills.
>
> If you get anybody else involved, like the police or anything, I'll just take off—with the boys with me. I don't think you'd want that, so help me out, and let me borrow a little money, and I'll see to it that Billy Ray and Bucky get back safe and sound. I'll stop by the church tomorrow at eleven, in case you need to go to the bank in the morning. You check your e-mail after that, and I'll tell you where to pick up the boys.
>
> Bee, I wouldn't have done this if you'd been nice when I asked for a little financial help the first time. It's out of the way to come through Maggie to see family, and I think you owe me for letting you keep the boys and not making any

trouble for you about it. Unless you cause
problems, the boys will only think this a nice
little visit with their daddy like I told them and
not get scared or upset. So be cooperative and
everyone will be happy.

Thanks for the help. This is a real good gig the
band is going to. If things shape up like I expect,
I'll send the money back to you later. It's only a
loan so don't go making it into something it isn't.

Sorry I won't get to see you this visit . . .
Sonny

Lydia felt John's arm come around her as they heard the note read.

"He's kidnapped the boys." Lydia spoke the words no one else dared to speak yet. "Their own father."

The sheriff scratched his neck. "I never thought I'd see the day Sonny would act like this. He played on my Little League team as a boy. Good arm. Personable little kid." He stood up. "I'll get a message out to the men. Pull them in so we can talk about what to do."

"Don't do anything." Mary Beth grabbed his arm, her face white. "If he sees any police he'll take off with the boys. Please don't do anything, Sheriff. If I'd seen the e-mail earlier, I wouldn't even have called you."

"Now, that wouldn't have been wise, Mary Beth." He patted her arm. "I know you're panicked and scared, but we know what to do in cases like this."

John's face darkened. "Should we take the money to the church in the morning?"

"If we've not gotten a lead, it might be wise." Sheriff Sutton started down the hall. "We can post some men in that area discreetly to follow him from the church if we don't find the boys or get a lead on them sooner."

Back in the kitchen, he made some calls and then turned to the family again. "If we fail to get this straightened out quickly, I'll put out an Amber Alert on the boys. This is an illegal abduction, no matter how Sonny worded it. I don't think the boys are at risk, but we can't go on assumptions."

Mary Beth began to weep in Neal's arms, and Lydia found her own tears starting, in sympathy and fear for the twins.

The sheriff spoke again. "Can any of you tell me what kind of vehicle Sonny might be driving?"

John answered. "He used to drive a black Toyota truck, but that was a long time ago. He may have another vehicle now."

"Sonny owned a motorcycle, too." Mary Beth added. "He often towed it behind the truck."

Sheriff Sutton made notes of all these facts on a notepad, then looked at Mary Beth. "Now, don't let this frighten you, but I'd like to have a recent photo of the boys. To make copies of and pass around in case anyone's seen Sonny and the kids—eating at a restaurant, checking in to a motel, stopping for gas. We'll get police in surrounding areas working with us." He paused. "We could use a picture of Sonny, too, if you have one."

Mary Beth sniffed. "The picture I have of Sonny is old, but I'll get it for you—and one of the boys."

"I'll go with you." Neal, keeping his arm around her, walked with Mary Beth down the hall.

Lydia, her knees feeling weak, dropped into a kitchen chair. "This is a nightmare," she whispered, cold with fear.

John put a hand on her shoulder. "Sheriff, the boys told me they'd seen a recent photo of Sonny on the mirror over at Wilma's beauty salon. It might be more current than the one Mary Beth has. The boys said Sonny had shaved his head. That changes the appearance a lot."

The sheriff took a last swig of his coffee, before setting the mug on the table. "I'll go over to the Harpers and get the photo." He frowned. "I'll want to tell them myself what's going on with their boy. It will be hard on them to hear it, but they may know something that can help us. Places Sonny might hide out. Old haunts of his. Names of friends still in the area."

Neal and Mary Beth came back into the room. She handed pictures to the sheriff, her face streaming with tears. "Please find my boys, Sheriff. They're just six years old."

"We'll find them. I don't think Sonny Harper would intentionally harm two little boys—especially his own sons." The sheriff twisted his hat in his hand. "He's just gotten himself in trouble and needing money. I'm sorry for what's happened, but I've seen it before, even in good families."

Neal wrapped an arm around Mary Beth and led her over to the couch while the sheriff started for the door. The sheriff turned to John. "I have your number, and I'll call as soon as we know anything. I think, at this point, it would be best if you and the family stay here in case there's further contact from Sonny. This isn't a case of two little boys who got lost playing or forgot the time anymore."

CHAPTER 20

The night hours dragged as John and his family waited for word of the missing boys. Oliver Wheaton came by to pray and sit with the family for several hours, and Ray Harper, Sonny's father, came over to the house. He brought a check for the ransom fee, sorrowful and embarrassed that his own son would kidnap his children for money.

He sat, slump-shouldered in the back den, facing the family with reddened eyes. "We finally got in touch with Bailey, one of the boys in the band with Sonny—he's the other one who grew up nearby, family over at Jonathan Creek." He sighed. "He tells us Sonny's fallen into a serious drug problem. It's causing trouble with the band, too. Sonny's been beaten up a time or two, OD'd once and got hospitalized. Bailey says he's hit his friends and the band members up for loans so often that no one will give him money anymore. Bailey admits Sonny needs help real bad. The band manager, Ross Dodds, tried to get him to go into rehab."

Mr. Harper blew out a long breath. "So far Sonny's said no to that kind of help. Claims he's using less now, doesn't have a real problem. But he's lit pretty much of the time from what Bailey said, so the band knows things aren't good."

"I'm real sorry, Ray." John's heart went out to the man, obviously brokenhearted over his boy.

Ray raised distraught eyes to Mary Beth. "Bee, I never thought

Sonny would do anything like this. He must be real sick to act this way. Real desperate. Bailey says he owes money everywhere. Wilma and I—and his brother, Eric—told him a long time back we wouldn't give him any more loans. He never pays us back. I told Sonny to use his skills with upholstery or delivery if he needed money, to get a day job around playing with the band if he wasn't making enough with them to meet his needs. He's carried a big dream in his heart for a long time about his music, hoping for fame, but we didn't realize all this other trouble was going on."

"I didn't either, Ray." Mary Beth reached over to take his hand. "I don't think any of us knew enough about drug use or problems with drugs to realize what Sonny had gotten involved with."

Ray squeezed her hand. "The sheriff says drugs take over a body, makes them not care about anything or anyone but their habit. He says they'll do things they'd never do—steal, lie, and deceive to get what they need. Just to keep using." He shook his head. "It's grievous and heartbreaking to learn these things. We never raised our boy to act this way."

John's anger turned to sympathy listening to Ray. "It isn't your fault, Ray. Sonny made his own choices. Even the other boys in the band told you he slipped too far into experimenting and got addicted. He knew better."

Ray shook his head. "Wilma couldn't even bring herself to come over here with me tonight she's so humiliated and grieved over this." He stood slowly. "I need to get back to her now. She's taking all this even worse than I am. It's a terrible thing to face when your son would kidnap his own little boys for money. I wish I knew a way to make this better. I really do."

Reverend Wheaton passed a look to John. "I'll follow you over to the house, Ray. Sit with you and Wilma and the family for a while."

"I'd be grateful." Ray clasped Oliver's hand in his. "We could use some prayer and help from God to get through this, and we appreciate your kindness in reaching out to us." His eyes moved over the family, seated in the den at Main House. "I surely hope

Sonny gets the boys back in the morning and that no harm comes to them."

Lydia tried to comfort him. "I'm sure once Sonny gets the money that he'll tell Mary Beth where to pick up the boys. Even as desperate as he must be, I can't believe he would hurt Billy Ray and Bucky."

"I hope you're right. I sure do." He left with the pastor trailing behind him.

John looked at the clock. "Nearly midnight now. We need to try to get some sleep. Staying up all night won't help."

"You won't leave, will you, Neal?" Mary Beth reached out a hand to clutch at his shirt.

"No, Bee." He reached over to brush her hair back with a tender gesture. "I'll stay right here. But it would be good if you'd go lie down for a little while. The boys will need you tomorrow—need you to talk to them and comfort them. I don't think they're so stupid that they won't figure out something more is going on than what Sonny is telling them."

She leaned into him. "Will you come up and sit with me, Neal? Take turns resting with me . . . so someone can keep checking the computer? Sonny might e-mail or the boys might sneak to the computer. They know how to e-mail."

Neal turned toward John with a question in his eyes.

"Go ahead, Son." He glanced toward Lydia. "Ela has gone home to rest, and Manu is out with the search team. I'll get Lydia to lie down on the couch, and I'll rest here, too, near the phone—in case the sheriff calls or one of the men in the search team comes by."

Neal nodded and helped Mary Beth get up to lead her out of the room.

"Do you think she'll get any rest, John?" Lydia's eyes followed Mary Beth as she left. "Should I go sit with her?"

"No, I think it's Neal she wants and needs tonight. I think the doubts and confusion she's had in that area may be getting resolved through all of this." He walked over to sit beside Lydia and put his arm around her shoulder.

"Where do you think Sonny has taken those boys?"

"I don't know. They could be anywhere." He pushed a hand through his hair. "The sheriff's right, I know, that he and the search crew can more professionally continue the search through the night than we can, but it's hard to sit here and wait. I keep thinking I should be out helping. That I should somehow discern where to look."

"I know." She laid a hand on his thigh. "I feel the same way. It's horrible waiting like this."

"I'm glad you're here with me, Lyddie." John moved his mouth to kiss her softly. Then he adjusted some pillows on the sofa and settled back against them, propping his feet on the broad ottoman. "Lie down against me and rest." He patted a pillow he'd placed on his lap. "We both need to close our eyes and try to get a little sleep if we can. Who knows what tomorrow may bring, and I'll need to get out into the search again in the morning or to help pick up the boys once we know where Sonny has left them."

"I don't think I can sleep," Lydia said, tucking her head against him.

John stroked her hair softly, pleased even in this worst of times to have her with him again. "Well, even resting our eyes for a time will help."

Somehow sleep found them both and John woke with surprise as rays of light broke through the window to fall across him. He glanced at his watch, noting the time was a little after 8:00 a.m. It surprised him that he and Lydia had slept so long.

Usually Ela had rustled into the kitchen by now, starting breakfast, banging her pots, and humming, but John knew she'd gone to the lodge this morning to make coffee and food for the search team. Slipping Lydia's head to the sofa carefully, John stood up, stretching to get the stiffness out of his joints. He let himself out the back door, walking across the patio to look toward the mountain, wondering about the boys.

Propping his foot on a fence rail, John dropped his head in prayer for a moment. "Lord, have mercy on those little boys. Let them come home safely and well. Let no harm come to them." He sighed. "And, Lord, I pray that Sonny will see the light and get the help he needs to straighten out his life. To not keep living trapped in addiction, lost to any hope of a happy and productive life."

John prayed on quietly, looking up at last to see—like a mirage—two small boys heading down a well-worn path through the woods, waving at him madly. After blinking at the sight, John headed toward them in a run, soon catching up his grandsons in a fierce hug.

Squatting down beside the boys, he let his eyes roam quickly over their soiled but happy faces, glancing behind them up the pathway, wondering if trouble followed.

"We got away from him," Bucky announced, seeming to read his mind. "We escaped through the woods and hiked home."

Hearing shrieks behind him, John soon shared his joy with Lydia and Mary Beth streaking out from the house with Neal not far behind them.

"Are you all right? Are you all right?" Mary Beth kept asking them over and over.

Billy Ray pulled back from all the hugging, wrinkling his nose. "We're okay, just hungry, Mom." He looked toward the house. "Has Ela made breakfast?"

Neal tousled his head. "Ela went up to the farm lodge to cook for the search team that's been out looking for you guys all night."

"Wow!" Billy Ray's eyes widened.

"I'll cook for you." Lydia smiled, brushing back tears. "Tell me what you want."

"Pancakes and strawberry syrup." Billy Ray started toward the house, holding his mother's hand.

"And bacon and eggs," added Bucky, wiping at a scratch on his face.

At the house, John phoned the sheriff to call off the search for the boys while Lydia started breakfast. Mary Beth took the boys upstairs to clean them up, and by the time they returned, Manu and Ela had arrived with the sheriff. The boys chattered out their adventure while Ela and Lydia cooked.

"Sonny came yesterday when we were out back climbing in

Old Oak," Billy Ray stated. "He acted nice, hugged us and everything. He said Mom told him it was okay to take us to lunch with him."

"When we said we needed to tell Ela before we left, he said he'd already okayed it with her, too," Bucky put in. "He had his truck parked right down the road, not far away, so we thought it was all right to go with him." Bucky looked at John. "Daddy John, you said he might come sometime and be sorry he didn't know us better. He talked like that to us so we thought maybe he'd started to change."

Billy Ray plunked down the juice glass he'd been drinking from and then frowned. "He hasn't changed. He's still bad. He lied to us and then he wouldn't bring us back home. He started saying we needed more time together, to get to know each other, and that we had to spend the night with him in the cabin."

Bucky interrupted. "I told him we didn't have any clothes or toothbrushes or anything but he acted like it didn't matter." He crossed his arms in irritation. "Then he told us to stay in this room while he went out to run some errands and he locked the door on us."

"Oh, honey, I'm so sorry. Were you scared?" Mary Beth reached over to hug him.

"No, we were mad 'cause he was lying and stuff." Bucky pulled away from Mary Beth's embrace. "And because he wouldn't let us go home or call you, and he wouldn't even tell us where we were."

Billy Ray leaned forward with a smirk. "But me and Bucky knew where we were, 'cause he drove us up the same road you take when you're going to the Science Learning Center."

"Are you sure about the road?" the sheriff asked, pulling a notepad out of his pocket.

"Yeah." Billy Ray nodded. "It passed by the goat farm."

"How far up the road did you go?" asked the sheriff.

"Almost to the end of it, where you turn right to the science center, except Sonny turned the other way. He followed that road that leads to Cataloochee Ranch but then turned off and bumped us along a bunch of side roads me and Bucky didn't know until we came to this old cabin."

Bucky jumped into the conversation. "Sonny said the cabin belonged to his friend Bailey's uncle but that they never used it because it was getting run-down." He made a face. "It really was."

"Yeah, it was creepy." Billy Ray took the lead again. "All dusty and musty and the bathroom looked gross." He wrinkled his nose with disgust.

John suppressed a smirk.

The sheriff scribbled some notes on his pad. "Boys, did you see an old red barn with a big silo near where you turned to drive up to this cabin?"

Both nodded.

"Yeah, and Billy Ray and me started feeling creepy when Sonny drove us way up into the mountains instead of taking us to Maggie to eat lunch, like we thought he would." Bucky frowned. "He said we were going to picnic instead, but he started acting funny."

Sheriff Sutton looked up from his notes. "Where was Sonny when you left this morning? Was he still at the cabin? Did he try to follow you?"

Bucky crossed his arms in annoyance. "We were getting to that in our story."

John caught the boy's eyes. "Bucky, if Sonny is still at the cabin, the sheriff needs to know that right now so they can go find him. What he did was wrong, and they need to talk to him about it."

Bucky nodded. "Okay. We sneaked out in the night through the back window and left Sonny sleeping in the living room on the sofa. I don't know if he's still there, but he was there when we left."

"What time did you leave?"

"We sneaked out before light. I don't know what time it was, and then we walked across the mountain—"

John interrupted again. "Sonny might still be there."

The sheriff stood. "I'm going to radio one of my deputies nearest that area to take a team up there." He looked at his watch. "It's not much past eight thirty. We might get lucky and still find him at the cabin. If not, we'll put out an APB on Sonny's truck." He turned to the boys again. "What did his truck look like?"

"Old, black, and kind of beat-up," Bucky answered.

"It's probably the same Toyota he had before," Mary Beth added.

The sheriff put his hand on Bucky's shoulder and then Billy Ray's. "You've helped a lot, boys, and I'm glad both of you are safe. I'm going to make some calls and let you folks eat your breakfast now." He glanced toward Ela, heading to the table with a platter of eggs and bacon and another piled with pancakes. "I'll call later in the day when we know more."

John followed him to the door. "Should we still take the money to the church?"

The sheriff shook his head. "Sonny will run as soon as he realizes the boys are gone." He glanced at his watch. "If he was stoned or hung over, he might have slept in and we could get lucky and catch him at the cabin. But my guess is, he's on the road now. With descriptions of the truck—and photos of the driver—we might get lucky and catch him down the way."

John walked back to the table in the kitchen after letting the sheriff out. His appetite rose at the smells of breakfast food, and he pulled a platter toward him to fill his plate.

The boys chattered on while they ate.

"Did Sonny hurt either of you?" Mary Beth asked. "Or did he say anything hurtful to you?"

"No." Bucky answered around a bite of pancake. "He acted kind of nice until we started saying we wanted to go home. And when we tried to sneak out anyway, he locked us in the bedroom. He told us to take a nap, like we were still little babies."

John saw Lydia hide a smile, dropping her eyes to stir her tea.

"Tell us what happened when you got to the cabin," Neal said. "You were starting to tell us that before the sheriff needed to ask you more questions."

Billy Ray finished off a piece of bacon before answering. "Sonny had some bread and peanut butter and stuff at the cabin.

He made us a sandwich and we talked some. But he kept acting weird. Kept looking out of the window, checking messages on his cell phone. Walking around. You know, stuff like that."

Neal nodded.

"After lunch, when we said we wanted to go home, that's when he told us we were spending the night with him at the cabin."

"We didn't want to," Bucky added. "Sonny tried to act like it would be fun, that it would give us time together. When Billy Ray and I got mad and said we didn't want to spend the night, he got kind of mad. Said we ought to want to spend time with him because he was our daddy."

John saw Mary Beth put a fist to her mouth. Tears started at the corners of her eyes.

"Ah, Mom, don't start crying again." Bucky made a face. "He didn't hurt us or nothing. He just wasn't real nice then. When he caught us trying to sneak out while he was in the kitchen, he made us go back in the bedroom and that's when he locked the door. But we could hear him talking to someone on the phone about getting money soon, saying someone was giving him a lot of money in the morning. He made some other calls, but we couldn't always hear him. Sometimes he went out on the porch. He said he was having trouble with his reception."

Billy Ray looked at John with eyes too wise for a child. "Was he going to make you and Mom pay him money to get us back safe, Daddy John? That's kind of what we thought from what he said on the phone."

John nodded. There was no point in lying to the boys. "Sonny needed money and I think that's what he had in mind. I'm sorry it's so."

"Man, he must be really messed up to do that." Billy Ray shook his head.

Bucky frowned. "He had a lot of pills with him. I asked him if he was sick, but he laughed. Sonny drank a lot of beers, too, after he made us go to bed. At first he locked us in, but then he unlocked the door when it got real dark so we could go to the bathroom if we needed to. He listened to music for a long time and then he fell asleep on the couch."

"We knew where the cabin was by then, Daddy John," said Billy Ray. "We heard Sonny tell somebody the cabin stood almost at the park boundary near Double Gap and not far from the bald. Bucky and I knew Sonny was talking about Hemphill Bald. So we decided in the night that we could sneak out before light, walk through the woods behind the cabin, and then find the trail across the mountain."

Bucky grinned. "We remembered Daddy John telling us when we went hiking in Cataloochee how to get home across the mountain. That it wasn't real far. He said sometime he'd hike with us to the bald, and maybe to Cataloochee Ranch from our farm, and me and Billy Ray knew we were already closer to home than the ranch. Daddy John said it was only about four miles from Double Gap to where the path cut down Sheepback Knob to our farm."

"You have a good memory," Lydia said. "But wasn't it dark when you left? And how did you get out of the cabin?"

Billy Ray shrugged. "We opened the back window and climbed out. There wasn't even no screen on the window."

Bucky bounced in his seat. "I had one of those little flashlight key chains in my pocket. We used it to find our way behind the cabin, but we found a trail right off and it wound up and dead-ended into this bigger trail. We knew to turn left to start home and in a minute we saw a trail sign. It said how many miles to Polls Gap on Balsam Mountain, but Billy Ray and me knew we didn't have to walk half that far."

"There was a big moon and pretty soon the sky started lighting up." Billy Ray smiled. "We walked fast at first 'cause we were a little scared in case Sonny followed us and got mad or something. But Bucky said he thought Sonny would think we walked down the road to get away and that he wouldn't think we'd know how to walk home on the Hemphill Bald Trail."

"That was about a three- to four-mile hike to the ridges above the farm, boys," Neal put in. "And then farther down to the farm."

"We've walked it before with Daddy John." Billy Ray dismissed the distance easily. "We recognized stuff along the way as soon as we found the big trail on the mountain, and there were signs and stuff."

"Didn't you see people on the search team when you came by the lodge?" John asked.

He shook his head. "We cut over after the lodge and took the trail through Upper Woods down to the Upper Farm Road." Billy Ray reached for another pancake. "We thought it would be faster and we were getting tired."

"Hungry, too." Bucky grinned over a bite of scrambled eggs.

More discussion and questions continued over breakfast, and then Billy Ray turned serious eyes to John. "What will happen to Sonny? He did a really bad thing, didn't he? Lying and trying to get money and stuff."

"I don't know what will happen," John answered with honesty.

"Will he go to jail if they catch him?" Bucky's round eyes found John's as he forked up a last bite of pancake.

"I don't know that, either, Son. But Sonny needs help. He has some real problems."

Billy Ray, who'd gotten up to take his dishes over to the sink, stopped by Neal's chair to lean against him. "Do you think you could be our daddy now, Neal? We kind of got a bad one the first time and we could use a new one."

Bucky reached over to lay a hand on Neal's arm. "Yeah, could you? Billy Ray and me saw you kiss Mom upstairs when we were in the bathroom. It looked like the kind of kiss that means you really like Mom."

Neal grinned while Mary Beth blushed. "It was exactly that sort of kiss, and I've been asking your mom if we might form a new family. I'm glad to hear you guys approve."

Billy Ray's mouth dropped open. "You're going to marry our mom? That's neat!"

Mary Beth sat up straighter. "I haven't said yes yet, so you boys need to settle down about this."

"Well, why not?" Bucky made a face. "Neal's a great guy and everybody likes him. Don't you like him?"

She blushed. "I like Neal very much."

"Well?" Bucky crossed his arms. "If you don't say yes, someone else might come along and get him. Me and Billy Ray see stuff like that on TV all the time."

John watched Neal flash Mary Beth an arch smile.

She giggled. "Well, I wouldn't want that."

Neal got up to walk around the table, stopping to drop to one knee. "Mary Beth Cunningham, your boys and I would like it very much if you'd consent to be my wife. Do you think you might say yes?"

She smirked. "You mean, before someone else gets you?"

"You might notice I'm asking you first." He grinned back at her.

Mary Beth found John's eyes with a question in them. John smiled, knowing she was asking for his approval.

"Where's your ring?" Mary Beth turned her eyes back to Neal's.

Thinking quick, he answered. "I thought you'd like to drive into Asheville with me to pick it out. The boys can go with us. We can make a day of it and have dinner in the city."

"Oh boy!" Bucky and Billy Ray jumped up and down.

Neal kissed her as he stood, not seeming to mind an audience looking on. But John noticed tears in Lydia's eyes and a wistful look in Ela's.

The reverie ended quickly as the phone rang. John answered, learning from the sheriff that Sonny had escaped before anyone arrived at the cabin. And at this point, there'd been no sign of his truck on any of the highways leading out of Maggie Valley.

CHAPTER 21

July slipped to a close before Lydia realized it. The local gossip about the ghost sightings and the twins' abduction had finally become less prominent in everybody's talk and thoughts. She and John took the twins to the annual Folkmoot Parade in Waynesville, a celebration that kicked off the international Folkmoot Festival every year. They sat in lawn chairs in front of Holly's bookstore on Main Street where they could enjoy the colorful groups from different countries dancing and singing their way down the main avenue of town.

"I really enjoyed the parade in Waynesville last week," Lydia told Mary Beth as they sat on the porch at Hill House one day, watching the boys romp in the plastic wading pool again. "I think the group from Trinidad was my favorite, with those wonderful drums."

"The boys loved going with you and Dad. They talked about the groups for days and showed me pictures on the digital camera you bought them." She stroked the calico cat settled across her lap. "Buying them a camera really wowed them, Mom, but you didn't have to do that."

"It's a grandma's pleasure to give her grandchildren gifts occasionally. Don't fuss at me, Bee."

Mary Beth smiled, looking down at the cat. "The kittens are growing fast, Mom. And Trudi's fur is growing longer than Ava's."

Lydia's gaze shifted to Ava, curled up in a cushioned chair

nearby. "Trudi has more Persian blood than Ava, but both have pretty markings, don't you think?"

"Yes." Mary Beth's eyes moved to watch the boys, where they splashed in the pool in the sunshine. "You know, I worried the boys would be scarred after their encounter with Sonny, that it might hurt their confidence or self-esteem." She laughed a little. "Actually, the whole incident bothered me more than it did them. I'm the one who had nightmares and worries afterward."

"Has anyone heard from Sonny? You or his family?"

She shook her head. "No. It's sad. Bailey said Sonny had a run-in with their manager after he showed up in Florida. The police called making inquiries and Ross Dodds wasn't happy Sonny had gotten on the wrong side of the law. They argued, and Sonny disappeared afterward. I guess he feared Ross would turn him in or that the police might pick him up in Florida, knowing where he was."

Mary Beth dropped her eyes. "I couldn't bring myself to press kidnapping charges, not with Ray and Wilma Harper so torn up about all that happened, but the sheriff said child abduction with a ransom demand involved was a felony offense no matter what I did."

"Does Bailey know where Sonny is now?"

"No. He said he thought Sonny left the country. A friend had some sort of band at a resort in the Caribbean. Sonny bragged to Bailey that he had another job offer with them if he wanted it, even claiming that they'd pay his way to come down." She reached over to pick up a glass of iced tea beside her. "Sonny is very talented, despite his problems, Mom. He plays and sings well—and he writes incredible lyrics."

"Maybe he'll get help." Lydia crossed her legs. "Maybe this served as a wake-up call for him."

Mary Beth shrugged. "I don't know, but I hate that this situation hangs over Neal's and my head as we start our new life together. It seems unfair to Neal." She studied the engagement ring on her finger.

"I love the ring you and Neal picked out." Lydia changed the subject to happier thoughts. "Have you set a date?"

"We'd like to do something simple in the fall, after Parker and Marie's wedding in Atlanta in August—although it might be hard to get away during apple season for a honeymoon. You know how crazy it is on the farm and in the store at that time. We offer 'Pick Your Own' days, wagon rides, and tours of the farm, and the store simply buzzes with business while we have fresh apples, fritters, pies, cider, and apple butter to sell."

She shifted the cat onto the cushion beside her. "Neal and I are looking at a piece of property on the Caldwell Farm where we can build a house." She sighed. "I hate to leave our farm, but the Caldwell Farm is right next door. It won't be far. Neal's dad said we can live with him while we're building." Mary Beth paused, lifting her eyes to Lydia. "Or if you and Dad don't mind, we could live here at Hill House while we build."

Lydia's mouth dropped open.

"Don't look so surprised." Mary Beth grinned. "Surely you're about ready to move back in with Dad. He said he offered to do a renewal of your wedding vows if you'd like."

Lydia looked out across the yard, not sure what to say.

Mary Beth crossed her arms. "Mom, you can't simply go on living next door to Dad. It's not right. And he wants to be with you again, to be married again. Don't you love him? When I watch you together, it seems good between you. Am I wrong?"

"This is highly personal, Bee," Lydia hedged. "And frankly I assumed Neal would move in with you and the boys at Main House."

"That wouldn't be right. That's Daddy's house." She frowned. "He shared it with us these years. Took the boys and me in when Sonny deserted us. I'm grateful for that—but it certainly doesn't make Main House rightfully ours. It's your and Dad's house."

Ava jumped on Lydia's lap, kneading gently before she settled down, giving Lydia a minute to think how to answer. "I know your dad wants to be remarried, Mary Beth," she said at last.

"And?"

"*And* it feels funny to be discussing this situation with my daughter." Lydia stroked the cat until she purred with contentment.

"I didn't mean to pry." Mary Beth's voice sounded prickly now.

Lydia let out a long sigh. "I know. It's just that I still have a few old issues I'm working through. Sometimes I find myself glad to leave Main House after being there for a while. I still feel Estelle's presence there. I feel like she's watching me."

Mary Beth's mouth dropped open. "Mother, I had no idea you still worried over those old memories." She paused. "If anyone should feel haunted at Main House, it should be me. Grandmother came down hard on me after the boys and I moved back home. She didn't like the noise and aggravation of small children underfoot again. She didn't like the boys' toys scattered around the house, their crying that woke her at night, their messy table manners." She grinned. "I don't know what she expected of two-year-olds at the table, but Bucky and Billy Ray failed to fulfill it."

Bee propped her feet on a chair across from her. "Grandmother constantly told me I'd been her last hope of marrying an agriculturalist, a man to take over the farm someday. She layered my sins on me daily, reminding me of my mistakes." Mary Beth rolled her eyes. "I finally got sick of it one day and started retaliating. A lot of quarrels and disharmony ensued. I started wondering if I'd need to move out when Dad finally intervened and began to stand up for me."

Lydia knew she looked surprised.

"He told me he wouldn't allow his mother to run off any more of his family if he could help it." Mary Beth stroked a hand over the kitten beside her. "He had some talks with Grandmother, set some ground rules. Insisted on civility at meals. He made Grandmother stop trying to run my life or tell me how to raise my boys. Dad also insisted that I get a chance to open the store, like I wanted to. He told Grandmother I needed an enterprise of my own, and he insisted he'd pay Ela and Manu extra to watch after the boys the days I worked."

Mary Beth blew out a sigh. "It was my salvation, getting out of the house and away from Grandmother, finding work I enjoyed that was my own." She sent a loving gaze to Lydia. "I knew for the first time then how much it meant to you to work at Western, to find a job you loved that you could give yourself to. I didn't understand that before, Mother."

"I think I'd have gone crazy if I hadn't started the job at Western when I did."

Mary Beth nodded. "I know. Things got even worse when Estelle got sick. Cancer is a harsh disease, and people with warm, sweet natures tend to weather it sweetly, but people with harsh, critical natures often handle it with bitterness. You can imagine where Estelle fell on that scale."

"Rebecca said those two years were difficult for all of you."

Mary Beth laughed. "*Difficult* is a mild word for it. But we couldn't help feeling sorry for her near the end. She was so sick and frail."

The two women sat silently for a little while, watching the boys play.

"Mother, you need to stop blaming Daddy for all the bad things Grandmother did. It wasn't his fault, and even when he tried to stop her from being so critical and judgmental, it didn't help much. She just got mad at him, too. I don't think anyone could have changed Grandmother into a sweet, understanding, kind woman. It just wasn't in her."

Mary Beth ran a hand through her hair. "I know you and the boys think Daddy should have stood up to Grandmother more than he did back when you were at home, but, honestly, I doubt it would have changed a thing. Dad tried when I came back but it did little to help."

Lydia pursed her lips. "At least he tried with you."

"And Dad sees that now. He's told me he was wrong not to stand up for you and the boys when you lived at home. That's why he did try more with me when I came back with the twins. But I'm telling you truthfully that it didn't make much difference. So if you're still harboring the idea that his standing up for you would have changed everything—changed Grandmother in some miraculous way into a nicer person—then that's an illusion."

Mary Beth took a swig of her tea. "To be frank, Grandmother didn't like other women very much. Any other women. She felt competitive with them. Ela said she thought it was self-esteem issues leftover from her childhood." Bee shrugged. "I can't say. I only know, as I grew older, that I realized she had no real friends. Acquaintances, yes. Social contacts and church relationships, but no friends she met for lunch, talked and laughed with on the phone, let down her hair with. I felt sorry for her about that."

"I did, too, when I'd let myself," Lydia admitted.

Mary Beth smiled at her. "You're a fixer, Mom. That's what you do in your work, help direct and fix people, help steer them on the right track, counsel them, help them. I think it totally frustrated you when you couldn't do anything to fix Estelle."

Lydia considered that thought. "You may be right. I know I was always trying some new way to fix my relationship with her. Wishing things could be different."

"God rest her soul," Mary Beth said kindly. "I hope she found healing and a way to develop friendships in heaven."

"Me too," Lydia said and realized she really meant it.

Later that evening, Lydia kept thinking about her conversation with Mary Beth as she and John shared a quiet, elegant dinner at the Maggie Valley Country Club's Renaissance Room. John wore a suit coat tonight, not a look Lydia saw often, and he looked deliciously handsome. Lydia knew she looked nice, too, in a loose, flowing skirt and a silky, fussy blouse covered in tucks and embroidery.

"I'd forgotten how nice it is here." Lydia looked around at the plush dining room, with its white linen tablecloths and napkins shimmering in soft lighting. Out the window, the deepening shadows of the mountain ranges lay in the hazy twilight.

"A formal invitation for Parker and Marie's wedding arrived today." John pulled it out of a pocket to pass to Lydia. "It was addressed to the two of us. Bee got a separate one with a note inviting Neal to attend with her, since the two are engaged now."

Lydia studied the crisp invitation, decorated in twining

greenery—a nice touch, considering the fact that the wedding would be held at the Botanical Garden, where Parker worked.

"I made reservations for all of us, including Ela and Manu, at the hotel Parker recommended near the gardens. I thought there were too many of us to stay with Parker and Martha, but you can stay with one of them if you prefer."

"No." She toyed with a string of pearls around her neck. "I know Parker and Marie have started renovating the house to their own tastes. It wouldn't feel the same."

John reached a hand across the table to cover hers. "I hope that means you're beginning to feel more at home here than in Atlanta now, Lydia."

"I think so," she admitted, watching his eyes warm.

The waiter came and John ordered trout and Carolina rice for both of them, letting Lydia tell the waiter what salad dressing she wanted and consulting with her about a wine for their meal.

He toasted her a short time later, lifting his wineglass toward her. "To the most beautiful woman in the room."

She blushed. "You still know how to be graciously romantic, John. I always liked that about you."

"I can be even more romantic." She watched a muscle twitch in his cheek. "Dare I ask again if you'd consider being my wife once more, Lydia?"

She felt her heart kick up at the words. "I've been considering it."

His brows drew together. "Seems like everyone else—Parker and Marie, Neal and Mary Beth—is getting married except us." He grinned. "I guess I'm hoping it might be contagious."

Lydia took a shaky breath. "Mary Beth told me she and Neal plan to build a house next door on the Caldwell Farm." She watched a small frown cross his face. "That little frown lets me know you'd rather they stayed on at the farm."

"It's their happiness that matters most," he answered.

"I agree and I've been thinking about that." She gathered her courage. "Would you consider moving in with me at Hill House,

John, and giving Main House to Neal, Mary Beth, and the boys? There are four of them and only two of us, and I know from whispered talk I've heard that Bee and Neal want more children. They need a big place for their family and we don't."

He didn't reply at first, his eyes finding hers instead. "That's a very unselfish gesture, Lydia Ruth."

"Not really." She dropped her eyes. "All my happiest memories are at Hill House. We lived there when we were first married, and I brought my babies home to that house." She smiled at him. "I chose the paint colors and wallpaper at Hill House, decorated and furnished it as an excited young bride."

Lydia watched John's eyes, trying to read his thoughts. "We made love there the first time." Her voice dropped to a whisper now. "I have many warm memories of tender times in that house, of meals I made, of children's laughter, of so many joys." She felt tears smart her eyes.

John's soft voice touched across the table. "I have the same happy memories of that house, Lydia. And when I'm with you there, my blood races like a young man's again." He reached to catch her hand in his, leaning over to bring her fingers to his lips.

She felt her heart begin to trip a little faster. "You wouldn't be disappointed to move back to such a small place with me?"

He shook his head. "No, it's a wonderful idea. But you'd have to cook for me with Ela at Main House."

A faint smile played on her lips. "You know I do that now at Hill House whenever you come. I like to cook. You know that."

"Well, then." She felt his foot teasing up her leg under the tablecloth and realized he'd slipped off his loafer before sending his foot journeying up her leg.

"John!" Her eyes widened. "We're in a public restaurant."

"I'm feeling happy." He grinned at her.

She felt herself blush. "Well, try to feel a little *less* happy for now. We haven't even had dinner."

His eyes, darkening, caught hers. "Would you like to plan a little ceremony, say our vows again before others?"

She considered it. "Not really. We can say our vows to each other in our own way, don't you think?"

He nodded, reaching to cup her face gently with one hand. "I take thee, Lydia Ruth Cunningham, with great joy and respect to be my lawful, wedded wife again. I promise to be a faithful and true husband, before God and all His witnesses—in sickness and in health, in poverty or in wealth—as long as we both shall live."

Lydia caught his other hand with hers, bringing it to her lips to kiss. "I'm happy to start a new life with you again, too, John." She smiled at him, repeating his words. "To be a faithful and true wife to you—in sickness and in health, in poverty or in wealth—as long as we both shall live."

He leaned across the table to kiss her, drawing a few stares from diners nearby. "We'll be happy, Lydia."

"I think so, John." She fought tears that threatened, putting a hand over her heart.

"Well, whoopie-do!" Tolley Albright's voice boomed from the doorway as he and Rebecca headed across the room. "I hope from that fine kiss that Lydia finally said yes!"

Lydia's eyes widened in surprise.

"Oh, honey, don't be mad." Rebecca swooped over to hug her and then hugged John. "We invited ourselves to join you tonight, but John said he had something to ask you first and told us to give him some time alone with you before we came." She pulled out a seat, wiping tears from her eyes. "It wasn't hard to figure out what was going on from the doorway. In fact, I think you've misted up the whole room."

Lydia looked around and saw several couples raise a glass to them and smile.

Tolley signaled the waiter. "This is a happy day, I'll tell you that, and dinner is on Rebecca and me tonight. We're celebrating!"

John found Lydia's eyes. "I only planned to ask again tonight, but I didn't envision how everything would go—"

"Oh goodness," Rebecca interrupted. "If you two would rather be alone, Tolley and I can slip right out. You just say the word."

Lydia smiled then. "No. It's wonderful to have you both here. It is a time to celebrate."

A happy evening ensued between the old friends, but Lydia grew shy as John drove her home later. And as they started up the driveway to Hill House, Lydia heard herself gasp. There, across the porch rail, hung the banner that had greeted her the first day she'd arrived. The words "Welcome Back" stood out in black ink, but now underneath them in red was added the word "Forever."

"Do you like it?" John walked around the car to help her out with a smile.

A lump filled her throat. "How did it get here, John?"

His mouth quirked in an impish smile. "I called Mary Beth when I went out to the restroom and asked her to hunt it up and rehang it before I brought you back to the house. She and Neal must have decided to add 'forever.' " He kissed her fingers. "I like it."

As they drew closer to the porch, John swept Lydia into his arms, carrying her up the steps and pushing open the door with his foot to carry her over the threshold, just as he'd done the day he'd first brought her home to Hill House. Inside the doorway, he leaned over to kiss her with enough passion to sizzle her shoes off.

"We're going to have a happy life, Lydia Ruth—starting now." He kissed her again and then strode with purpose through the house toward the bedroom, his hands roaming as his mouth moved down her neck.

No longer shy, Lydia's fingers worked eagerly, unbuttoning his shirt. "Welcome home, John," she whispered in his ear, knowing with a surety that her future looked bright indeed.

EPILOGUE

In the midst of apple season in September, the whole Cunningham family gathered at the family farm for Mary Beth and Neal's wedding. Two giant white tents spread across the yard behind Main House, and Ela Youngblood and the Sheppard women had worked feverishly for weeks getting favors, decorations, and food ready for the big reception. In keeping with the season, the bridesmaids wore dresses of apple red and all the decorations for the reception echoed the chartreuse greens and warm reds of the apple varieties coming into full season on the farm.

"This is so exciting," Rebecca said to Holly, as they waited for the new bride and groom to drive over from the church.

"It makes me happy to see all of John's family reunited and back together here at the farm." Holly sighed. "I didn't know if I would ever see this day."

"Me, neither." Rebecca sneaked a treat off a table groaning with food. "It's certainly happier coming to this beautiful wedding today than to the funeral last month for Sonny Harper. I know everyone hoped he would get help. It nearly broke Wilma's heart to learn he'd died away from his family down in Providenciales."

"Where is that?" Holly asked.

"It's in the Turks and Ciacos Islands. I heard Sonny was playing and writing music with a reggae band there at one of the big resort clubs. But, sadly, he overdosed. It hurts my heart to see a talented young life like that snuffed out."

"Me too. I remember hearing Sonny sing and perform a long time ago. He was truly gifted. He might have become famous one day if it weren't for the drug problems."

Rebecca turned to Holly. "Speaking of local people who became famous, is it true W. T. Zachery is coming to your bookstore in Waynesville to do a signing? My grandson absolutely loves his books. I hope I can get signed copies for him."

Holly sipped on a glass of punch. "Believe it or not, Zachery has moved from New York back to Bryson City, where he grew up."

"Whew! That's a big culture change." Rebecca licked chocolate off her fingertips from the last pastry she'd popped in her mouth. "Maggie Valley is somewhat remote, but at least Waynesville and Asheville are nearby. Bryson City isn't near any major city for shopping or entertainment. Wonder what caused Zachery to move back home?"

"Your roots draw you back to where you started, I guess." Holly looked around her. "Even despite all my problems with my mother, I found it hard to move too far from the farm and the mountains. And Wade's roots formed here, too, being raised on the Barber Orchard."

"Do you think a woman drew him back—like Lydia coming home to see if she and John could get together again?"

"No, I don't think that's it." Holly shook her head. "I read that his wife got shot in a small market not far from where she and Zachery lived in New York."

"Oh, well then. Maybe he's running from the memories." Rebecca moved toward the punch bowl nearby. "I guess the big question is whether he'll stay long in a small town like Bryson City after life in the Big Apple." She stopped to point toward the doorway of the tent. "Oh, look, here come Neal and Mary Beth. Let's go get in the line to greet them and see all the family."

The women moved forward, amid gaily decorated tables, to greet the bride and groom. Beside them, John and Lydia stood, all smiles, their three sons lined up beside them.

Welcome Back

Lin Stepp

About This Guide

The suggested questions are included
to enhance your group's reading of
Lin Stepp's *Welcome Back*.

DISCUSSION QUESTIONS

1. In Chapter 1, Lydia Cunningham is leaving Atlanta to move back to North Carolina. Her sons—J. T., Billy Dale (Will), and Parker—are not happy about it. Why? What reasons does Lydia give them for going back? Why did she leave the farm before, and what work has she been doing in Atlanta?

2. Lydia calls her mother-in-law, Estelle Whitmeyer Cunningham, "a difficult woman." Do you think Lydia's statement was accurate? What things did you learn about Estelle, as the book unfolded, that show why Estelle might have been a difficult woman for many to get along with and understand? Have you ever known anyone like Estelle or had to deal with an "Estelle" in your own family?

3. How long has Lydia been gone from North Carolina and Cunningham Farm? When she returns she finds some things the same and some things changed. Discuss examples of each. How is her husband, John, different and the same?

4. What did you learn about Hill House and Main House as you followed Lydia's journey back to the farm? Study the map of Cunningham Farm in the front of the book to see where these houses and others in the book stand. Do you remember who lives in each? Have you ever been on a large farm where several families live in homes on the overall property? Which home does Lydia have the happiest memories of? How does Lydia later dispel some of her negative memories of Main House? Who gives her counsel in how to do this?

5. It is Lydia's grandsons, Billy Ray and Bucky, who made the "Welcome Back" banner that greets Lydia at Hill House. The boys soon call Lydia "Nana Lydia." Why do they call John "Daddy John"? Where is their natural father? What happened to break up Mary Beth and Sonny's relationship? What do you think has helped these boys to be so unaffected by their father's desertion? What did you enjoy about these six-year-old twins in the story?

6. Cunningham Farm is known for its "calicos and collies." What is the story behind this statement? What gifts are left for Lydia as soon as she arrives back at the farm? Have you ever owned collies or calicos?

7. In Chapter 4, Lydia tells John that she had expected arguments, awkwardness, quarreling, angry looks, stony silences, and recriminations to occur when they first met again. What happened instead? Why was this so unexpected? How do John and Lydia have different feelings about this?

8. Lydia tells John at one point that one of his problems is that he never wants to talk things through, that he always wants to deal with problems tomorrow or pretend they either aren't really there or aren't of importance. As the book progresses, what do you learn is behind this characteristic of John's? Does he see this trait as wrong? Do you know people who are reluctant to talk things out? Do you think this is a trait more characteristic of men than women? Why? How did John's sister, Holly, handle the same issues? How does she help Lydia understand John's childhood better?

9. Cunningham Farm is an old historic apple orchard—and a large one—which has been in the same family for generations. There are many apple orchards around the area in western North Carolina, busy with events in the

fall season. Have you ever been to one, attended an apple festival, or visited a large apple orchard? What did you learn about apple farming in this book? What is June drop? What is a Rattler apple? What are some other types of apples grown on Cunningham Farm?

10. There are two budding romances in this book—one between Lydia and John and the other between Neal Caldwell and Mary Beth. What is different about the two relationships? What obstacles exist that make it difficult for both couples to get together easily? What changes occur in the book helping each couple to realize they are right for each other and resolving the difficulties between them?

11. There is a ghost in this book. The twins see it and later Lydia sees it. How did the boys, and later Lydia, describe it and where did they see it? What were the two legends, about the Cherokee Indian Red Hawk and about Nance Dude, that people used to possibly explain the ghost? Who did you imagine the ghost might be as you read the book? Do you believe in ghosts? Why or why not? What do Mary Beth and John believe about ghosts—and what do they teach the twins about them? Who did you learn the "ghost" really was? Were you surprised by this revelation?

12. Many Cherokee live around the Maggie Valley area, as well as on the nearby Cherokee Indian reservation, and there were Cherokees in this book. What did you think of Manu and Ela Raintree? What were their best characteristics? Why had the Crowe and Youngblood families come to live on Silas Green's land? Did you think Nalin and Davy were justified in doing what they did to save their sister, Izabelle? What mistakes did they make afterward and why? What did you think of Silas and Loretha Green? Did Loretha throw the family off her land after

she learned what had happened to her husband? Why or why not?

13. Clogging is very popular around the Maggie Valley area, and many champion cloggers live there. Where did Lydia, John, Tolley, and Rebecca go clogging together? How does John talk Lydia into going? What did they wear? Have you ever seen pictures of the Cataloochee Ranch on the top of the mountain where the two couples went or been to the Stompin' Ground in Maggie Valley? Have you ever seen or tried clogging?

14. John has a broken relationship with his sons as well as his wife. What caused this? John tells Lydia he thinks his sons should have been the first to reestablish a relationship with him after their differences. What is Lydia's response to this? Why does she say it is John's responsibility more than the boys? How does he react? What does Lydia say that causes John to go to Atlanta later to talk with his sons? How does that turn out?

15. What did you think of Lydia's aunt Martha Howard? What part does she play in this book in being a help to Lydia, to her sons—and later also to John? What did you think about her frequent advice to Lydia to: "Get more information." How can that help to resolve problems? How did J. T.'s wife, Laura, use her "information" and understanding about conflict management and mediation to help John and the boys resolve their differences? Have you ever studied about—or participated in—any conflict management techniques or methods?

16. Lydia and John take the twins hiking in Cataloochee Valley on a lovely trail called the Caldwell Fork Trail. How does this day help to bind Lydia and John closer together? How does the information John shares with

the twins about "how far they are from Cunningham Farm" and "how far it would be to walk across the mountain to the farm on Hemphill Bald Trail" later help the boys to get home when they are kidnapped?

17. Why does Sonny Harper kidnap his own children? What does he hope to achieve in doing this? How do his actions affect his parents—and his sons? What does Sonny's father do when he learns what Sonny has done? How do the boys get away from Sonny? How is Neal a help to Mary Beth in this situation, and how does Neal's support make her feel more certain about her feelings for him? Who initiates the idea that Neal and Mary Beth should get married after the twins are found?

18. Oliver Wheaton, the pastor of the Fairview Methodist Church, ends up being a counsel and help to many members of the Cunningham family, including John and Lydia. How does he help John as they talk in the cemetery? How does he also later help Lydia in the same setting? What little weakness is revealed about Oliver, as he talks to John earlier in the book, showing that he is very human? What was the problem with the minister before Oliver? Have you met any ministers like Oliver who were a help to you in times past when you had a problem or concern?

19. Besides the main characters in this book, there were many interesting side characters throughout the story— the Sheppard family, Eugene and Ozetta, Sam and Doris, Charlie and Nevelyn, Chuck and Vera . . . Sheriff Sutton and his deputy . . . Lydia and John's friends Tolley and Rebecca Albright . . . Ela and Manu Raintree. Who was most memorable among these . . . or what other side characters in the book did you enjoy and why? What main character did you like the most in this story? Why?

If you enjoyed *Welcome Back,* be sure not to miss Lin Stepp's

SAVING LAUREL SPRINGS

In a heartwarming novel set amid the lush splendor of the Great Smoky Mountains, Lin Stepp reunites two kindred spirits in a charming story of first love and surprising second chances. . . .

See ya later—and love you forever, Rhea Dean. Those are the words Rhea's childhood sweetheart, Carter Layman, used to say whenever they parted. Not that she places much stock in words anymore. After all, Carter drove off to college in California, promising to make a fortune to help save their families' vacation resort. Instead he stayed there and married someone else. It fell to Rhea to keep Laurel Springs going and she's done just that, working long hours on the campgrounds, buoyed by the beauty of her Smokies home.

Now a widower with a young son, Carter has achieved huge success as a games developer. But he always planned to return to the spring-fed lake and the soaring mountains, to the covered bridge where he and Rhea made wishes and traded kisses. He's coming home to turn Laurel Springs into the place they planned to build together. And as he reveals the truth about his past, Rhea must decide whether to trust in the man—and the dreams—she's never forgotten.

Turn the page for a special look!

A Kensington trade paperback and e-book on sale now.

CHAPTER 1

"Ugh. Are we about finished, Rhea?" Jeannie asked, balancing a load of dirty sheets on her hip while she pushed open the screened door of one of the assembly grounds' picturesque cabins.

"Yes. Just about." Rhea looked up from sweeping the front walkway of Azalea House, a cute pink cottage with white gingerbread trim. She watched her best friend angle her way down the porch steps and, with a strength surprising for her petite size, heave her load of sheets into the back of a green pickup truck.

Rhea grinned, but felt her smile fade as she noticed some of the letters of *Laurel Springs Camp Assembly Grounds* flaking off the door of the truck.

Jeannie caught her gaze and waved a hand dismissively. "No sense in wasting worry over a little paint picking off, Rhea. Nearly everything shows a well-worn look around the assembly grounds these days."

Sighing, Rhea sat down on one of the front steps of the house. "Yeah, and I hate to see things getting so run down."

"I know." Jeannie gave her shoulder an affectionate pat before settling down on the step below her. She leaned back against the porch rail and blew out a long breath. "Whew, it sure feels good to sit down. We've been busy today."

"Don't be regretful for that, Jeannie Ledford." Rhea shoved her playfully with a foot. "We need the money, and it's always a blessing to rent more than half our cabins on the weekend." She pushed a stray strand of honey-brown hair off her face.

Jeannie gave her an impish smile. "Wouldn't it be great to win the lottery and get a big pile of money, Rhea? What would you do if you won a half million dollars or something?"

Rhea leaned back against the porch rail to think. "I'd fix up all the rental cottages, repave the roads and the campsite pull-in spaces, and put a strong roof on the covered bridge coming over the creek."

She leaned toward Jeannie, warming to the subject. "I'd buy a dozen rental bikes and nice washers and dryers for the coin laundry, a new cash register for the store, and updated computers for the administrative offices. I'd paint the assembly church and fix that broken stained-glass window near the front door. I'd hire someone to resurface the swimming raft and put fresh rails on the gazebo by the lake, and I'd buy a few new canoes." She paused. "I think I'd reseed the meeting grounds where the grass has worn away to dirt, too, and buy a popcorn machine for the market. I think we could make some extra money if we popped corn and sold it every day."

"Stop! I wish I hadn't asked." Jeannie laughed. "I should have known you'd spend it all on Laurel Springs." She leaned back and sighed. "As for me, my mind veered more toward how nice it would be to take one of those luxury cruises in the Caribbean about now. That would be sweet."

Rhea studied her. "Would you really like to do that?"

"Absolutely." She closed her eyes dreamily. "I'd leave little Beau with my mother, and Billy Wade and I could have a second honeymoon on one of those big ocean liners—sitting on the deck in the tropical sun and sipping little pineapple drinks with umbrellas in them."

"You think Billy Wade would like that?" Rhea smirked at the idea, trying to picture it.

"I'd be sure Billy Wade had a *good* time, if you know what I mean." She giggled. "Besides, he works too hard. I'd like to see him enjoy a real vacation—and if not a cruise, then something else."

Rhea sighed. "Seems like we often talk about wishes and what-ifs."

"Oh, don't be getting all serious and down-in-the-dumps on me 'cause I was doing a little dreaming at the end of a busy day." Jeannie punched Rhea's arm playfully. "It's not like cleaning tourist cottages is a real glamour job, you know. It would be fun to use some of that lottery money to hire cleaning help for this place. I remember when a lot more staff worked at Laurel Springs."

"So do I." Rhea sighed again and checked her watch. "You'd better take the truck and the laundry on back. You'll have time to throw a couple of loads in the washers before you need to pick up Billy Wade and drive him to Newport to get his truck at the shop. Nana Dean said she'd keep Beau until you got back, but I don't want her to get too worn out."

"Your grandmother is a peach to keep Beau for me so often. I know at six he's a handful."

Rhea stood up and stretched. "Nana enjoys him. She says Beau helps to keep her young."

"I feel just the opposite." Jeannie laughed and headed toward the truck. "By the end of some days, that child makes me feel old!"

She paused at the truck door, turning to give Rhea one of her crinkly grins. "You going to ride up to the front of the camp with me?"

Rhea looked across the road toward a brown cottage, called the Dancing Bear, tucked under a group of pine trees. "No. I still need to sweep off the porch at the Bear. I'll clean and check inside, too. A family from Indiana is coming tomorrow to stay there for a week. I want to be sure everything looks good. I'll walk back when I finish."

"Okay." Jeannie bounded into the truck with her usual enthusiasm and then turned to wave two fingers cheerily in good-bye.

Rhea envied her carefree disposition. "You always bounce around all cute, cheerful, and bubbly like the proverbial cheerleader."

Jeannie wrinkled her nose. "So? You know I coach the cheering squad at the high school. It makes me feel young and carefree—reminds me of my own cheerleader days, too." She sent a sunny smile Rhea's way. "Besides, you cheered, too, when we went to Cosby High."

"I know." Rhea grinned at the memory. "You coached me so I could make the squad even though I was too tall and not very good."

"You did fine." Jeannie shut the truck door and laughed. "We had some great times in high school on all those game weekends, too—you, me, Billy Wade, and Carter."

Rhea smiled thinking of Jeannie's husband, Billy Wade. "Everybody still calls Billy Wade the best wide receiver Cosby ever had."

"And Carter made a good kicker before he injured his knee." Jeannie giggled. "After he got sidelined, I remember Carter took pictures at every game during senior year and wrote up great articles for the newspaper."

"Well, that was a long time ago. Nine years." Rhea frowned and picked up her broom and started toward the cottage across the street.

Jeannie's voice, in a softer tone, followed her. "I wasn't going to tell you, Rhea, but Carter is coming in for a vacation soon."

Rhea kept her eyes toward the Dancing Bear cottage and didn't look back at Jeannie. "So? Why should you not want to tell me that? Carter's family lives on part of the grounds; they co-own the Laurel Springs Camp Assembly Grounds. It figures he'd wander in sometime. He is Wes and Mary Jane's only son, after all."

"Yes, but, like you said, he hasn't been home in nine years, Rhea, not since he went away to college and then got married. It's been a long time." She paused. "Mary Jane said he's bringing his little boy to visit. His wife's been gone a whole year now."

"What's your point, Jeannie?" Rhea turned to glare at her friend. She knew her voice snapped more sharply than she intended it to.

Jeannie twiddled with her watchband. "Well, you and Carter were special to each other before he went away."

Rhea gripped the broom handle with clenched hands. She didn't like the direction this conversation was heading. "Yes, and then Carter went away, got married, started a family, and made a new life. I went to college here and made my own life, too. Time has marched forward a long time since high school, Jeannie Ledford. There's no sentimental, yearning spot left in my heart for Carter Layman. So don't start playing around with that idea in your mind."

"All right." Jeannie shrugged. "But I hope maybe you and Carter can be friends again when he comes back. It would be fun for the four of us to get together while he's here. Like old times."

"I wouldn't count on it." Rhea turned and started toward the Dancing Bear. "And it wouldn't be like old times. Ever. Those times are gone."

In the background she heard Jeannie blow out a breath, start the truck, and drive away. Only when the sound of the truck's engine faded into the distance did Rhea turn to look after it. When she did, there were tears dripping down her cheeks she hadn't wanted Jeannie to see.

She kicked at a pinecone on the cottage's walkway as she headed toward the porch steps. *If it wasn't summer and the height of tourist season, I'd take off on a trip somewhere to avoid even laying eyes on that traitor again.* Rhea started sweeping the Dancing Bear's porch with a vengeance, furious she'd spared even a tear for the memory of Carter Layman. She shouldn't feel even a twinge of pain anymore after all this time.

"I hate him for what he did to me and how he hurt me. I really do." She spat the words out, needing to give vent to her thoughts as she whacked the broom against a porch rail, her anger kicking up. "Jeannie must be crazy to think I'd want to buddy up to Carter Layman and be chummy friends again. No, sir. I'm going to stay as far away from him as possible while he's here for his little visit."

Checking inside the cottage later, Rhea's thoughts drifted to Carter again, despite her intention not to think about him. They'd grown up together, she and Carter, been best friends through childhood and sweethearts later on.

It was hard to sweep away a lifetime of memories, even if you tried. She heaved a sigh. And she certainly had tried.

Walking into the boys' bunkroom in the Dancing Bear, Rhea

encountered still more unwanted reminders of Carter Layman. Old prints of classic cars from the sixties and seventies marched in a somewhat crooked row across the wall. Rhea straightened them with reluctance—hating to even touch them in her present mood. Carter had chosen and framed these car prints one summer when they painted and fixed up the cabin's bunkroom.

Rhea ran a finger across the faded photo of a red convertible. She didn't know the make of the car, but Carter would know right away. He loved vintage cars. Especially that old red Pontiac Firebird convertible he'd fixed up and driven through junior and senior year of high school.

She pressed down the sweet memories trying to creep into her thoughts as she looked at the photo. *Oh, no you don't. Don't you dare go soft thinking about Carter Layman even for one minute. He's a snake. He didn't prove true to you—or even to his own professed dreams.*

Turning away and encountering her own troubled face in the dresser mirror, she shook a finger at herself. "You keep in mind that Carter Layman drove off to California to college in his Pontiac convertible. Drove off to study computer gaming so he could make a lot of money to help save Laurel Springs. Or so he *said*." She snorted. "Remember all that big talk? All those big plans? And then he became a hotshot computer game developer, married some rich man's daughter—and never came back. You keep that firmly in mind, Rhea Dean, and you remember just how much you can trust Carter Layman. Not one inch."

She stomped out of the room and pushed open the door to the back porch, where she began to sweep the leaves and debris away with a fury.

An hour later, Rhea's long strides took her back along the East Cabin Road, following the dusty tracks left by the assembly truck, and then up the paved North Assembly Road toward the main entrance of the camp on Highway 32. She'd vented out her frustrations and anger in work and felt calmer now. As she approached the historic covered bridge over Little Cascades Creek, she could see a car parked inside in the deep shadows.

Rhea frowned as she started toward the bridge. It could be

dangerous to stop on the bridge. What were those people thinking? The road through the bridge was a narrow two-lane one, long and dark inside; traffic could hardly see a stopped vehicle from either direction.

With annoyance, she moved closer to the entrance of the bridge and called out a warning to the driver. "You need to pull your car out of the covered bridge. It's dangerous to stop in there."

Hearing the vehicle start up now, Rhea stepped back off the road, leaning against the fence rail out of the way.

As the car nosed out of the shadows of the bridge, a familiar voice floated out before it. "I see you're still as bossy as ever, Rhea Dean."

Rhea gripped the rail behind her to steady herself as her heartbeat escalated. She'd know that voice anywhere—even after a hundred years.

Into the summer sunshine drove Carter Layman, his familiar black hair a little too long, his dark eyes still mischievous and sleepy, his mouth tweaked in that old sardonic, know-it-all smile. He pulled the white convertible to a stop beside her, draping an arm over the door to study her slowly from head to toe.

She could have died right then. She wore a soiled white T-shirt, a shabby jeans romper with a faded overall top, and battered canvas shoes. Terrific. Her hair straggled down her back and stuck out from under the barrette she'd tried to pin it back with. Any semblance of makeup had faded over the day, and dirt streaks undoubtedly decorated her face from sweeping and cleaning. She still carried her dilapidated work broom, too.

It was definitely not how she'd wanted to look when she saw Carter Layman again for the first time, but, of course, she'd never let him know that. Lifting her chin, she studied him back, giving him the same once-over he'd given her, steeling her face not to give away a shred of discomfort.

She let her eyes sweep over him casually. Dastardly man. He looked heartbreakingly the same—and yet different somehow. She'd seen occasional pictures of him through the years, so she shouldn't be shocked at how he'd matured, filled out, and become more sophisticated. He seemed tan and fit, easy with himself, his dark coffee eyes watching her with amusement, his even white teeth flashing in a typical Carter grin. Despite the casual clothes he wore, he reeked of money, too. A big diamond ring winked on a middle finger of his hand, and she stood close enough to see the word *Cartier* on the watch on his arm.

And the car. Good heavens. Her eyes swept slowly over that now. A classic white Mercedes convertible—certainly a cut above the old junker he'd left Laurel Springs in years ago.

He caught her glance assessing the car. "Nice convertible, huh? It's a 1970 280SE Benz classic, fully restored."

Rhea tossed her head. "You always did like old cars," she said in an unimpressed voice.

He chuckled and let his eyes drift leisurely over her again, more intimately than she'd have liked. She crossed her arms defensively and glared at him. "I heard through the grapevine that you finally planned to visit your parents. You sure they'll still allow you home after all the years of neglect?"

A slow grin spread over his face. "My mom said she made me a blackberry cobbler and my dad's cooking ribs. That sounds like a promising welcome."

"Maybe." Rhea leaned back against the fence, making an effort to assume a relaxed pose. "Wes and Mary Jane always have been hospitable. Even to strangers." She stressed the last word.

Carter laughed. "Guess that witch's broom you're carrying sort of fits your mood today, Rhea Dean."

A small voice piped in. "Are you *really* Rhea Dean?" A dark-haired boy leaned around Carter to study Rhea with wide brown eyes. "Dad said you were his best friend *ever* when you were kids."

Rhea gripped the fence rail behind her for added support as she realized this was Carter's child. A pain ripped through her heart at the sight of him. He was the spitting image of Carter at the same age. Well, almost. She looked more closely. The child possessed a sweetness and vulnerability she didn't ever remember seeing in Carter. Carter had always been a rogue.

She struggled to find her voice. "Your father and I were friends once in the past," Rhea said to the child.

Her eyes shifted to Carter's. "But that was a long time ago." She emphasized the word *long*. "We don't know each other anymore."

"That could change." Carter's voice softened as his eyes met hers.

"No. Actually, it couldn't." She said each word slowly and emphatically, not dropping her eyes from his.

Rhea thought she saw a wince of pain pass over Carter's face before his old smile returned. "Rhea, this is my son, Taylor Layman. Taylor turned six in January and I thought it was about time he got a chance to see Laurel Springs."

"Well, summer is a good time for it." Rhea picked up the broom she'd leaned against the fence rail and started around the car, wanting to put an end to this conversation.

A large brindled mutt of a dog—maybe an Airedale terrier mix—lifted a sleepy head to eye Rhea curiously from a backseat carrier. He didn't bark; he just watched her walk by.

Nearing the covered bridge, Rhea paused and looked back. "Why did you stop on the bridge?" she asked impulsively.

Taylor answered before Carter could. "To listen to the water," he told her with solemn eyes. "It sounds like magic to hear the creek rushing under the covered bridge, and Dad said it was good luck to drop a penny through the bridge cracks into the water below."

The child leaned over the backseat to pet the big dog's head through the crate. "I dropped in *two* pennies for double luck." His bright eyes met Rhea's, and then he gave her a concerned look. "Do you think that's all right, to put in two instead of one?"

"Sure. I'd say so. However many you want." Rhea tried to keep her voice nonchalant. She and Carter used to drop pennies through the bridge rails—making wishes, planning dreams, whispering and talking in the dark shadows of the covered bridge. Touching, kissing when they grew older. Rhea stopped her thoughts from moving on.

She saw Carter's eyes probing hers, watching.

Offering a practiced smile, Rhea turned to start up the road again. "I need to get back to work."

Carter's voice followed her on a soft note. "See ya later—and love you forever, Rhea Dean."

She bit her lip not to react to the old greeting they'd always called out to each other through their lifetime, willing away the memories the words tried to conjure up. Increasing her pace, Rhea marched into the covered bridge, leaving Carter Layman and the pain he'd brought her quickly behind.